HELLYER'S COUP

HELLYER'S COUP

AN ESPIONAGE NOVEL

Philip Prowse

Kernel Books

First published in Great Britain in 2021 by Kernel Books.

Kernel Books
7 Camaret Drive
St Ives
Cornwall
TR26 2BE

kernelbooks.com

Typeset by Design for Writers in Adobe Garamond Pro.

A CIP catalogue record for this book is available from the British Library.

The author is grateful to João Abel Manta for permission to reproduce the poster: MFA, POVO POVO, MFA (page vii).

ISBN 978 1 5272 3312 6

For Rhiannon

O MFA está com o povo e o povo está com o MFA

The MFA is with the people and the people are with the MFA

– Slogan of the Armed Forces Movement:
Movimento das Forças Armadas (MFA),
25 April 1974

PROLOGUE

Tete, Mozambique, 20 August 1972

'MINES!' SHRIEKS THE BLACK sapper crouching on the front mudguard of the lead Berliet truck. He raises his arm, and the convoy of heavy vehicles laden with construction equipment concertinas to a halt in a fog of dust.

The soldier clambers down, and with three other sappers works his way forward on the dirt track. Using long wooden steel-tipped probes, they check any freshly disturbed soil, until they uncover two large Russian anti-tank TM-46s, each capable of destroying an articulated lorry. Cautiously circling their discoveries, they unearth a further six homemade anti-personnel mines planted to kill anyone attempting to disarm the TM-46s. In the oppressive heat, legs dangle out of open cab doors as the drivers wait for the sappers to detonate the mines in controlled explosions.

The convoy moves on through three-metre-high elephant grass and past a rusting red Ferguson tractor in the yard of a burnt-out roofless farmhouse.

In the heart of the Portuguese army column, Nick Hellyer shares a Panhard armoured personnel carrier with eleven conscripts clutching their Heckler & Koch G-3 assault rifles. Sodden with sweat, he longs to escape from this airless travelling inferno. Soon there's another halt to clear land-mines, and the vehicles crawl around a deep crater in which the shattered remains of an identical Panhard lie. Nick peers out at a slew of bloodstained dressings and abandoned boots lying in and around the blast hole.

Finally, the convoy lumbers into a camp ringed by high double barbed-wire fences and wooden machine-gun towers. The drivers abandon their vehicles in favour of rickety wooden stools around a makeshift beer stall in the shade of a tree.

Exhausted, legs stiff, Nick wanders towards an improvised football pitch. A shot goes wide. He stretches, fills his lungs and trots across the sand to the ball.

Two sightless eyes stare back at him from a hacked-off teenage black head, the neck ringed with congealed blood.

CHAPTER 1

Levada do Norte, Boa Morte, Madeira, 17 July 1968

THE SEMI-CIRCLE OF EARLY-MORNING light at the end of the kilometre-long tunnel grew mesmerizingly ever larger. Nick lengthened his stride and the dark waters of the levada, the narrow irrigation channel beside him, began to glisten. His neck muscles relaxed as the repetitive thump of his feet brought an inner calm.

In his jogger's trance, he skidded on a pool of drips from the tunnel roof, failed to keep his balance and crashed to the ground. A rush of self-doubt flooded back, almost washing away his hard-fought-for physical and mental confidence. No, that might have been how he'd have reacted then, but this was now. He climbed back to his feet, stepped over the old Nick and abandoned him on the path. The new Nick gathered up all his negativity, cast it into the channel and strode towards the light – he had come through.

Pupils narrowing as he emerged into brilliant sunshine, he caught fast approaching steps from behind and paused where the path widened slightly, so that the runner behind could sweep past. At this point, the levada corkscrewed along the hillside above a vertiginous drop to the village of Boa Morte in the valley below.

Nick let him through, and the runner came to a sudden halt, blocking the path. A black ski cap and wrap-around sunglasses obscured his features. An electric shock of terror juddered Nick's spine as the man grabbed his shoulders.

'Jump now,' the runner hissed, trying to twist him over the edge.

The two men danced a slow, tantalising waltz of death and Nick's head began to spin: the drop, the tunnel, the water, the path, the drop … So easy to surrender. A year ago he would have, but not now. He dug his heels in, turned his back on the precipice.

A thrust to his chest sent him over the low concrete wall and into the irrigation channel. He lay motionless on his back under the water, eyes open, lungs burning, calculating odds, all fear gone.

His assailant leaned over the wall, face crimped through the water. Nick erupted out of the levada and grasped the man's right leg, pulled it towards him, then thrust hard away. His attacker lost his balance and tumbled to the edge of the path, halfway over the drop. He scrambled to right himself but slipped and swung by his arms over the chasm. His fingers turned red and then blue as the nails slowly and inexorably scraped across the ground, tracing ten lines of bloody agony.

Nick squatted beside him, transfixed by the plea in the man's eyes. If he put out a hand to help, he too would be dragged down.

The man's grip failed and he fell, the valley echoing with a high-pitched dying scream.

Nick peered over the edge but was unable to make out the body. He ran his forefinger across the lines on the path. Odourless. He washed the blood off his hands in the channel, and, torn by a sudden paroxysm in his gut, threw up into the water gliding past.

Slumped by the side of the path at the tunnel entrance, Nick dangled his shoes in the levada, catching his breath and slowing his heart rate. This had not been a training exercise. So who had wanted to kill him and why?

The would-be assassin had chosen his spot well. Boa Morte. Nick felt his way through the tunnel, his sodden running shoes squelching. He paused halfway and leant against the wall, dizziness overwhelming him. Would it always be like this? Choices to be made over his and other's lives and deaths? Slow deep breaths calmed him, and the truth stared him in the face: Life as a spy had been thrust upon him; now he had to embrace it.

João would be waiting. Head up, he set off, heading once again for the light.

***

Funchal, Madeira, 12 July 1967

'I AM YOUR DANCING master.'

The crisp confident voice interrupted Nick's dark morning reflections and brought him back to the sunny wisteria-clad terrace of the department's villa in São Martinho.

He had just received a call from his superior. Major Patrick Quinlevan had informed him that he would be parked on the island for twelve months.

'Time to recover from your ordeal, build up your strength, immerse yourself in the language. You deserve it after what you've been through. And you will, I'm sure, be more than pleased to learn that we have great plans for you thereafter.'

That crisp voice again. 'I am your dancing master.'

Nick stared up at the smiling face of a shaven-headed, immaculately suited man in his thirties. Nothing at all to dislike there. But who the hell was he? And how had he got in?

'I have a key to the gate, you understand. But accompany me now. We must commence. My name's João, but London finds it easier to call me Joe. I work for Q. I've been briefed on who you are, where you've come from and the reasons for your stay here.'

'Give me a clue.'

'Alexandria.'

Nick followed his new mentor out to a green-and-black taxi. João opened the rear door for him.

'This morning we ride, but in the future you'll walk down. Excellent for your rehabilitation.'

The taxi navigated the corrugated hairpin curves from the heights of São Martinho to the city centre, and deposited them in Rua da Carreira. João led the way up an alley to a black-and-white cobbled courtyard and waved him through a faded-green door with a dull brass plate embossed in English: DANCE STUDIO FIRST FLOOR.

The studio's wall of floor-to-ceiling mirrors and unforgiving neon lights cruelly emphasised Nick's bent neck and sagging shoulders. He scarcely recognised his own battered face.

João pointed. 'The changing room's over there.'

Nick returned barefoot in faded cotton shorts, and followed the Madeiran as he padded across the polished wooden floor. João swung a mirror open and they stepped through into a windowless fully equipped gym.

Heck of a dance studio. Rather, a serious professional physio and workout setup.

His dancing master, now in a faded red Liverpool T-shirt and shorts, closed the door and inclined his head towards the treatment table. Nick lay on his back and stared at the shadows reflected on the ceiling. Felt like he was an operating table. Instead of a scalpel, expert fingers worked their way down his torso and arms. João instructed him to raise his legs, hold them in mid-air, and slowly lower them.

'Turn over.'

João ran his fingertips over the lacerations from the Egyptian jail beatings. '*O meu amigo*, what did you do to deserve this?'

Alert and unwilling to give a direct answer, Nick sat up on the edge of the treatment table, legs swinging loose, eyes fixed on his dancing master.

'You gave me to understand that you'd been briefed by London.'

'Only the bare bones. Spying in the docks. Missiles. Betrayal. Jail. Israel. Enough? And I'm so sorry for what happened to you.'

Nick lay back. 'Thank you for your sympathy, but I don't need it, however well meant it is. I messed up there, big time.'

João ignored him. 'The process is going to take time, certainly. Your wounds are healing, will heal. But you're seriously out of condition. We'll start with physiotherapy and exercises today and continue each morning at ten.' The first brief smile crossed João's severe face. 'Except on Sundays, of course. I've been tasked to make you fully combat ready. Forgive me, but you appear somewhat surprised – didn't Q fill you in?'

A part of Nick flinched – so much was being withheld from him. João's tone morphed into that of his controlling father, who while succeeding in manipulating him as a child had singularly failed to do so once he'd reached his teens.

Another part of him slackened and relaxed, like dough awaiting proving and kneading, an hour of pummelling, stretching, bending, oiling and massaging.

On João's recommendation – 'Water only, no wine' – Nick enjoyed a light sandwich and salad in the Restaurante Londres around the corner, then returned to the studio.

João was no longer alone. A tall woman stood in front of the mirrors, scraping back heavy black hair with purple fingernails and trapping it in a tight band. He caught a flash from sharp blue eyes as she turned and extended her left hand.

'May I present Patricia, who will be your dancing partner and, much more importantly, your Portuguese mistress. She'll help me with physio in the mornings and conduct your language tuition in the villa in the afternoons.'

Nick held out his hands, palms up, towards João. 'I'd concluded that "I am your dancing master" was an identification code that Q hadn't shared with me. But dancing lessons? For real? Come on.'

'Balance, rhythm and co-ordination are fundamental to unarmed combat. These are the skills you'll acquire with us. Now, bearing in mind the condition of your back, we'll commence with the samba.'

While João introduced Nick to the movements, Patricia wordlessly tracked his steps. In the stifling humid air of the studio, Nick fixated on the tiny pearls of sweat forming on the barely perceptible hairs above her upper lip.

'Enough. You did really well. A natural.' João brought the session to a halt.

'*Até amanhã.*' Patricia met Nick's eyes as she left. 'See you tomorrow.'

'Who the hell is she? I honestly don't buy your theory, but I love the dancing.'

'My sister.'

'Wow. So you both work for the department? How immensely convenient.'

'You've no right to question me, as you are well aware. Nor to be sarcastic. But I'll give you the courtesy of an answer anyway because I'm sure we'll become like brothers over the coming year. I once, largely unwittingly, did Q a huge favour, and he repaid me by funding the rehabilitation operation here.'

'What about your sister? Did she also do Q a "favour"?'

'Careful there, Nick. No jokes about Patricia. And keep your hands off her. She's well able to take care of herself, but if you overstep the mark you'll also have me to deal with.'

'Got things wrong there. I do apologise. And of course I will, won't – you get what I mean.'

João smiled. 'I can see we understand each other. See you tomorrow.' He made to clap Nick on the back, withdrew his palm just in time and shook his hand warmly.

***

NICK'S BACK HAD BEGUN to heal and, true to his word, João led him like a brother through strength-building circuit training to unarmed combat exercises. He accompanied each routine with a mantra: 'Control, not kill.' 'Roll with the blows.' 'Chop and stop.' 'Fight with your mind.' 'Surprise and win.' 'Wait and wait, and then.' 'Two hands, two feet.' 'Slippery twists.' 'Fingers and thumbs.'

So much of it grated with his previous academic life, and yet he found satisfaction in the words whirring in his head as he carried out the actions. Poetry in motion. A zone he could enter, and trigger phrases that guided him. Just not the kind of verse he had been used to.

João responded to Nick's congratulations on his mantra technique with a beam. 'Better than "Float like a butterfly, sting like a bee." Worked for Ali in the ring, but not for us in real life.'

At his first language lesson, Patricia instructed him: 'Repeat after me. *Bom dia, Senhor Coelho. Com está?* The meaning is: Good morning, Mr Rabbit. How are you?'

Nick tried and failed. To his ears, the stream of sounds she wanted him to mimic might as well have been Russian.

Embarrassed, he resorted to facetiousness. 'Forgive me, but I don't plan on chatting up too many rabbits just yet.'

His Portuguese mistress rounded the long mahogany table and towered over him. Nick shifted in his chair.

'Dr Hellyer, Q has given me the more or less impossible objective of getting you to native-speaker fluency in under a year. I'm not here as your dancing partner or because João is my brother. I'm here because I'm by far the best language teacher you're ever likely to have.'

He'd got it all wrong again. Story of his life: too eager to please at first, then too flippant. He shook his sinking head.

Patricia lifted his chin with her forefinger and looked into his eyes. The storm abated and a warm smile crossed her lips.

'Enough. I trust we understand each other. Let us continue. *Bom dia, Senhor Coelho. Com está?*'

Nick came to discover two Patricias.

In the morning dance classes, he was ever aware of her physicality – her hair whipping across his face, breasts brushing against him during the tango. She held his arm around her waist, their bodies in harmony until she turned and span away. Arousing him again and again.

'Halt!' João shouted on one occasion. 'Nick, what planet are you on? You've lost rhythm completely. Stop daydreaming.'

In her one-to-one language lessons, Nick was confronted by her formidable intellect and rational analysis of his performance.

'Convincing, but most certainly not convincing enough,' she said. 'You sound like an Englishman speaking Portuguese. I plan to create an Englishman who sounds like a Portuguese, thinks like a Portuguese and behaves like a Portuguese.'

'So would you have dinner with such a man?' He couldn't say where the words had sprung from, and regretted them instantly.

She stilled, paused and offered a gentle smile. 'I would love to.'

At table in the upmarket restaurant in Reid's Hotel, and finally sitting head to head with Patricia now that they were released from the work context, Nick found himself tongue-tied. He desired her deeply, and with the slightest hint of encouragement would have tried to move things forward. But there was a slight coldness to her, and she kept a respectful distance. So he maintained his. She kept her private life shrouded, just as her neck was tonight, hidden in a gauzy grey scarf.

On the back of an awkward silence, he grasped the initiative.

'We've got to know each other so well in some ways, but not at all in others. Could you please provide me with just a few hints about the real you? After all, I suspect that there's very little about me you haven't been briefed on.'

'Fair enough. The headlines – what I've been told on a need-to-know basis. Cambridge college lecturer compromised in drug scandal. Recruited by military intelligence and sent to Egypt. Espionage trajectory concluded with his comet falling to Earth in Madeira.'

'Rather tabloid.' He gave a half-smile and let out a slow breath of relief.

'But this information gives me no lead at all about the kind of person you really are, Nick.'

He dropped the cream linen napkin he'd been twisting around his right forefinger and looked up. 'Who am I? Self-critical, I suppose. Full of internal voices telling me how inadequate I am, which to some extent balances the outward show. A feeling that I can never get things right, that I find it more difficult than others to achieve goals. Tonight though, for once, I have achieved something – I'm here with you. But now it's your turn to reveal all.'

Although she grinned back at him, her left shoulder drooped. 'Where to start? I'm an island girl at heart and going to university on the mainland nearly broke me. Most of the other students in Coimbra came from grand Lisbon or Oporto families. They looked down on me, patronised me as a provincial.' She raised her voice slightly. 'And they did patronise me, and I was excluded.'

'From their social circle?'

'Not only that, which I could bear easily enough. It was their attitude, which convinced others that I didn't fit in. In the end, I got a better class of degree than any of them and made one really good friend who helped me struggle through. Through her I got in contact with others who shared our beliefs about what's askew with Portuguese society. Not revolutionaries, but serious women who had issues with the status quo. She and I are still in touch actually, although I haven't seen her for a while. She's employed at the university and her husband's an army officer. Kind of a shock that they got married because she'd always been a bit of a radical – like me.'

'So how does a radical island girl end up working for British military intelligence?'

'Not going to tell you. Quite enough for you to know that João recruited me when he set up this operation, and that Q has vetted me thoroughly. You're not the first who's been through my hands, and I hope you won't be the last.'

'Talking of hands.' He stretched his over the white tablecloth.

'No, Nick, please. Not so fast or so crude. I hope we can be closer but let's see, shall we? You have a couple of tests to pass first.'

'So I'm a medieval knight who has to prove himself to win his maiden's heart.'

Patricia chuckled. 'In a way, but what are you going to do for shining armour?'

His first test turned out to be a practical one.

'Very simple,' Patricia said. 'Prove to me that your command of the language is good enough to hook you up with a Madeiran girl. Every Saturday, Funchal hosts an early-evening dance club – locals only, no tourists. You pass if you score without her suspecting your true origins.'

***

KITTED OUT IN 'SHINING armour' – the sharpest chalk-blue suit and tie that Funchal could provide – Nick shoved open the heavy door of a nineteenth-century church hall with some trepidation. He peered through a red velvet curtain into a brightly lit, smoke-filled room. Platoons of beer and soft-drink bottles stood to attention on the metal tables lining the walls, and empties littered the floor beneath them. A green-waistcoated band of middle-aged men sat and played an erratic waltz while serious-faced couples circulated as if rock and roll had never been invented. Around the walls, young women had gathered in groups, some with mothers in attendance, while a wolf pack of smartly dressed youths prowled.

Following Patricia's guidance on etiquette, he approached the nearest seated group of women, bowed and requested the honour of the next dance with one of them. A short-skirted redhead accepted and they were soon spinning around the room. His partner turned out to be a shop assistant named Conceição who, as waltz succeeded waltz, danced ever closer to him.

The band took a break and Nick lounged against the wall outside the ladies WC, caught in a fifties dance-hall time warp. Nothing might yet come of Conceição's mild flirtatiousness, conducted as it had been under neon lights in front of her mother. But he still cherished hopes of passing Patricia's test.

His self-congratulatory bubble soon burst. Two stocky youths split from the pack, swaggered up to him and grabbed his arms.

'Come with us, stranger.'

His reluctant feet were dragged over the greasy cobbles as they frogmarched him through a side door and into a covered yard. The youths thrust his head hard against the wall, and a trickle of brick dust ran down his neck and inside his shirt collar.

The taller one held Nick's head back with one hand tight around his throat.

'I'm Conceição's brother, and he's her long-term boyfriend. Stay away from her if you know what's good for you.'

'And if I won't?'

'Then we're going to have to teach you a lesson in island manners.'

His head hummed from the blow and his neck throbbed from the throat grip. No fear, only a squirm of excitement at the thought of putting what he'd been taught into practice.

The brother released his hold and swung his arm wildly. Nick twisted to the side, and the fist smashed into the wall. He grabbed the attacker's outstretched arm and spun him around, using him as a shield as the other youth charged. The boyfriend's head rammed into the brother's abdomen, and both crashed to the cobbles and into a pool of vomit. Wide-eyed, they started to crawl to their feet.

'Don't even think about getting up,' Nick said, panting. But he half hoped they would.

The boyfriend obliged with a drooling grin. It vanished as Nick caught his neck with a sideways chop that sent him reeling.

Chop and stop.

He turned to the other. 'How about you? Want to make something of it?'

The brother wisely stayed down.

Nick dusted himself off and, skirting the vomit, returned to the dance hall. There he offered sincere apologies to Conceição for his abrupt departure, and prudently left before the two youths could gather reinforcements.

***

PATRICIA TILTED HER HEAD to one side. 'How did it go on Saturday?'

It was the start of Monday's language lesson.

'I'm rather afraid I failed your test, although I may have got within a whisker. By far the most diverting part of the evening turned out to be an impromptu samba with two blokes in the yard.'

His subsequent account failed to conceal more than a little pride.

Patricia shook her mass of black hair and frowned. 'João would certainly be proud of your actions. And I am too in a way because they must have taken you for a Portuguese visitor from the mainland, not a foreigner. But people here don't forget easily. Memories are cherished. You can only make enemies with that kind of violence.'

'Did I pass?'

'Perhaps. All depends on how you acquit yourself at the next hurdle.'

***

NICK HAD MADE REPEATED efforts to finish a scholarly article on Henry James, but his heart no longer belonged to the literary research that only eighteen months earlier had been the centre of his Cambridge life. He tried putting his emotions into verse, but all he produced were trite rhymes rather than the free-flowing poetry he'd once written and had published in student literary magazines.

He was adrift, sloughing off one skin and waiting for the next to grow. As the weather improved, João started him on endurance-building runs on paths next to irrigation channels high in the mountains. These runs took him through remote and dramatically beautiful areas where he rarely met anyone but for the occasional tourist and the levadeiros, the canal workers who kept the water flowing and released it at agreed times into the fields and vineyards.

His second test came all too soon: the Diplomatic Service Advanced Level Portuguese exams. He sat them in the consulate in early July.

Patricia broke the results to him.

'I was always convinced you'd succeed – nothing at all to do with my tuition, of course,' She walked around the mahogany table and stood over him, her hands kneading his shoulders from behind. 'You also achieved a rare distinction in the written paper. Should be a pay rise for you in it at least.'

Nick grinned up at her as she continued to work his shoulder muscles. 'Any other kind of rise?'

'Cheeky!'

She pulled him to his feet, smiled broadly and opened her arms. Nick sank into her perfume and the firm contours of her body. He stroked her cheeks and brushed her lips with his. She pulled him closer; her kiss was open-mouthed. He took her hand and nodded towards the bedroom.

'Not here. Not now. Why don't we go downtown and celebrate with some sparkling wine? Then I promise to give you a very personal guided tour of my apartment.'

It was the first time he'd been invited there.

'But what about João? He warned me off you in the strictest terms.'

Patricia pushed him away and threw her head back. Her laugh was deep and throaty. 'For someone so clever, sometimes you can be astonishingly literal. You need to toughen up, darling. João and I aren't siblings. And would it have mattered anyway? Given your amatory track record in your last posting, London strongly suggested this subterfuge. It's to your credit, and admittedly my regret, that we went along with it for as long as we did. But our professional relationship is now at an end.'

***

Two glasses of espumoso later, they climbed the three floors of the downtown nineteenth-century building and entered Patricia's flat.

'The Mansarda das Aranhas, the Spider's Attic.'

'So you're at the centre of the web and I'm to be your prey.'

'Exactly. The spider and the fly – you recognise the song? Jump right ahead and you're dead. Rolling Stones.'

They lay naked, side by side on the sunset-lit bed. Nick's body ached, and his legs twitched as he surfaced from their lovemaking. Patricia's black curls half-covered his chest. Nick played with them, winding them around his forefinger.

'You pass with flying colours in oral skills, my dear Nick.'

He closed his eyes, ran his tongue over his lips, tasted her juices. Became aroused once more.

She gave him a playful slap. 'Down boy! Enough is enough!'

He grinned and stared at a striking charcoal sketch that hung over the bed – Patricia's face in profile.

'Glad you like that. By Al, one of your predecessors – still keeps in touch.' She rummaged in the bedside-table drawer and threw him a small bundle of postcards held together by a fraying red rubber band. 'No secrets between us now, you see.'

The cards were adorned with colourful stamps and had been sent from far-flung parts of the world, most recently Penang. Each one had a sketch of a person or place, and the signature 'Al' – nothing more. Nick and his predecessor might work in the same line of business, but this man could only be characterised as appallingly insecure – the postmarks betraying the destinations of his missions.

'Must have been a hell of a guy. Faithful, too, over a long period.'

'You could say so. But I wouldn't necessarily agree.'

'What does that mean?'

'None of your business, my lover. Now put them away and I'll make coffee.'

Nick returned the postcards to the drawer. A page torn from a notebook caught his eye. The handwriting matched the signature on the postcards.

Miss De Meaner
If you have urges, I can unfold them
If you have surges, I can control them
Al

Patricia returned and Nick rolled towards her, so that they were lying face to face. He kissed her eyes and stroked her cheeks.

'Thank you for sharing. We'll get closer and closer, I'm so sure of it. Going to have to go now though – João's picking me up first thing and taking me to the Levada do Norte.'

'I'll find you tomorrow. Don't go too far.'

But he already had.

***

JOÃO WAS WAITING AT the tunnel exit. 'Good workout then?'

His dancing master's speed around the mountain curves steadily crept up as Nick described the attack in detail.

'Difficult in that situation I agree,' João said, 'but don't ever let an assailant get so close again, my friend. Foolish in the extreme. Nevertheless, I have to admit, you did get away with it.'

'He fell. I didn't kill him.'

'So you say.' João's tone deepened. 'I do hope those who sent him view it the same way. They've got their claws into you now, whoever they are, and I very much doubt they'll let go easily.'

Nick stared at the blur of vegetation as the car navigated the steep curves of the descent to Funchal. His right hand trembled slightly, and he folded it into his left.

João broke the silence. 'London tasked me with your rehabilitation and security for a year. Clearly, you're in grave danger at this moment, meaning I've failed in that second obligation. I've come to understand more about you, and I hope we've become closer friends during this period. But now the dream's over. I strongly suggest we go straight to the consulate and contact London. Best if you wait outside.'

***

'Q's ORDERS ARE FOR you to return to the UK immediately. Your villa's unsafe,' João said. 'If the assassin was able to follow you to the levada, his masters must surely also know your address.'

João accelerated, undertaking two taxis and finally halting in Rua da Carreira with a Hollywood-style screech of tyres.

They went into his office, and he opened a wooden panel behind his desk, revealing a small combination lock safe from which he extracted a buff folder. He pulled a telex out of his pocket and stuffed it into the file.

'I'll get Patricia to book you on the first available flight. Stay here while I obliterate traces of your occupancy of the villa and get your stuff. Passport?'

'Bedside table. Top drawer.'

João sighed and shook his head. 'So much for your tradecraft.' He tossed the folder into the safe, but didn't close the door. 'I trust you not to interfere with the paperwork. Back soon.'

Nick didn't need a second hint. The folder bore his name and opened with the telex from Quinlevan dated that morning.

For your eyes only, Joe. Arrange immediate exfiltration. Mossad code of honour to eliminate target only and avoid collateral damage. Egyptians may have fewer scruples.

Nick slid the folder back into the safe and wriggled in the uncomfortable office chair, awaiting João's return. His back started to niggle so he moved to the gym and lay on the treatment table. Full circle. Back to where he'd begun a year ago. He drifted off.

***

WARM LIPS ON HIS forehead woke him, and he looked up into Patricia's moist eyes. 'I'm so relieved you got away with it.' She laid her head on his chest for a moment, gathered herself and formally handed over the plane ticket.

'Yes, cos I didn't jump right ahead. Good advice, my spider. Prescient almost.'

'How can you say that?' She pulled back. 'Now go. João's waiting outside.'

'I'll send you a postcard.'

She gave him a firm thwack on the backside as he swung off the table.

***

NICK GOT INTO THE front passenger seat and slid his arm around his mentor's shoulders. 'If it hadn't been for your training, João, I'd surely have been killed this morning.'

'Yes, I agree. That's more than probable.'

CHAPTER 2

London, 17 July 1968

THE TAP SUD AVIATION Caravelle broke through low cloud over bleak, wind-rippled reservoirs on its final approach to Heathrow. A strong gust raised the right wingtip on the crosswind landing, and the consequent double bounce, fierce braking and reverse thrust forced Nick forward, hard against his seatbelt. He relaxed his grip on the armrests. A harbinger of tomorrow's meeting?

The next morning, a greying security guard checked his list of expected visitors and admitted him to the offices of military intelligence squirrelled away in a mews behind King Charles Street. The brown-overalled receptionist brought him a chipped mug of sweet tea and digestive biscuits and gave him a nod of recognition. Nick acknowledged it gratefully and slumped on an ancient oak bench that offered comforting rolling hollows for his buttocks. The smooth touch of the wood carried him back to a student hitchhike to Barcelona. Overcome by the heat in Parc Güell, he'd sought respite on Gaudi's rippling semi-circle of seats and their panoramic view of the city. Later, he'd learnt that the architect had created these most natural and comfortable of all curved seats by instructing his workmen to lower their breeches and rest their buttocks on the moist concrete until it set, thus christening each seat with a unique outline.

'He'll see you now, sir. You remember your way?'

Nick jerked his thoughts away from Catalonia and hoped that this appointment wouldn't require a similar submission to authority.

***

MAJOR PATRICK QUINLEVAN LEAPT to his feet. 'Nick, what can I say? Safe and sound, that's the main thing.'

For a moment, Nick feared the major's firm handshake would convert itself into a hug. Then, at the last moment, his boss's left arm fell back.

'Take a pew, my boy,' the major said, indicating a dilapidated captain's chair.

The room appeared little changed since Nick's previous visit. Low ceilings, narrow windows and furnished with standard MoD-issue green filing cabinets and cupboards. The institutional ambience was leavened by the occupant's purchases at country-house auctions. Hunting prints lined the wall behind the large antique red-leather topped desk, which sported three telephones, one displaying an impressive row of colour-coded buttons across the top.

The man who'd recruited him sat down behind the desk, face shining with enthusiasm, expression tinged with concern. Oiled-down, wiry black hair still threatened to spring up at any moment. His guileless blue eyes fastened on Nick.

'Well, my boy, take your time and recount yesterday's event to me in full detail. Only got the bare bones from Joe.'

João's parting words hung in Nick's mind as he reported the details of the attack and subsequent struggle.

Quinlevan gazed unblinkingly at him throughout. 'Now, you must have some inkling of who the would-be assassin is.'

'I did have a run in with a couple of local lads at a dance a while back, but they were only interested in putting on the frighteners to scare me away from a girlfriend. I dealt with them severely and very much doubt they'd have come back for more.'

'I agree. Most unlikely – the whole ambush sounds far too professional for local amateurs. Almost certainly fallout from your exploits in Alexandria last year. Could be the Egyptians or the Israeli intelligence outfit. That's my best guess – Mossad – judging by the modus operandi. The Israelis are tenacious and patient, reconnoitre thoroughly, and typically choose an opportunity where their operation is deniable. In this case, if you'd gone over, your death would have been written off by the authorities as a regrettable accident. But you must concede that neither country will accept your version of events, given the death of one of their operatives.'

Great. His boss had summoned him back to London only to inform him that he'd henceforth be living under sentence of death. Thank you very much, sir.

'So I can't return to Madeira. Number one on someone's kill list. Pariah. Light years away from what I'd imagined it would be like.'

'That's as may be, but we have to deal with the situation we face now, I'm afraid. For the moment at least, you need to disappear – really only means bringing our plans for you forward somewhat.'

Quinlevan spoke as if he were discussing the replacement of a faulty piece of domestic electrical wiring.

'The time is ripe for you to be reborn, dear boy.'

'So once I've become a born-again Christian, confessed my sins and been absolved, I'll be a suitable sacrificial lamb. An offering to your enemies, or would-be allies.'

'You can stuff your cheap sarcasm, Hellyer. I really do have your best interests at heart, you know.' Quinlevan leaned back, steepled his forearms and folded his hands in to each other. 'I'm afraid the market for English literature lecturers who do a little off-hand spying for us on the side has dried up. Moving with the times, a decision has been taken to re-imagine you as an expert in ESP.'

'What? Ghost hunting? Table rapping? Water divining?'

'Very droll, but way off the mark. This is deadly serious stuff. ESP: English for Specific Purposes. Specialised language for specialised uses. No point at all in studying Dickens if what you need is English to build a nuclear weapon. So, EAP: English for Atomic Purposes; EGP: English for Guerrilla Purposes, and so on.'

'And no doubt ETP: English for Torture Purposes.'

'You're much closer to the truth than you could conceivably have guessed. So that's the direction in which we're pointing you. The go-to guy for ESP for the BC, ODA, UN, NATO, SEATO – choose your organisational acronym. This move will allow you to infiltrate sensitive situations that we've hitherto been unable to access.'

The major's circumlocutions infuriated Nick. 'I'm not entirely sure what you mean by sensitive, sir.'

'Would perilous be a more accurate adjective, then?'

Nick focused on Quinlevan's well-trimmed pink fingernails – an uncomfortable reminder of those he'd so recently studied at the edge of the levada.

'Hang on a minute, Major. So at a stroke, all my university experience and qualifications count for nothing?'

'Quite so. You've got it in one. However, you've proved to our great satisfaction what an adept learner you can be, and how you can adapt to and react in fresh situations. Your other great achievement is the discovery of your true vocation. Admit it. You adore not appearing to be who you really are, and your time in Alex was life-changing.'

'Life-threatening more like.'

'A regrettable downside, I agree. But once we've completed your re-education – your reimagining – that kind of thing will be much less likely to happen because you won't get caught so easily. We're lining up small-arms and sabotage training in addition to an applied linguistics course. Have faith in me, my boy. I'm confident you're going to love every minute of it.' Quinlevan's enthusiastic, persuasive gaze fastened on Nick. 'And you'll be quartered somewhere no intelligence agency on earth will be able to track you down to. Ever been to Essex?'

'Only trips to the coast from Cambridge with a girlfriend.' Nick smiled. 'Holding hands and kicking pebbles on the beach at West Mersea, that kind of thing. Strong winds and smoked oysters.'

'Conceivably less pleasurable this time, I'm afraid. Your fate is to be a guest of the MCTC, the Military Corrective Training Centre in Colchester. The Glasshouse is the UK's only military prison and by far the safest place for you. Ostensibly, you'll be treated in the same way as all the other inmates but, unlike them, you'll be able to come and go in the daytime within reason. Either to Roman Barracks for your weapons training or to the university. You have an appointment at 2 p.m. on Monday in the Linguistics Department with Professor Whiteside. All clear now?'

'How long am I going to be banged up for, sir?'

'Spare me the pathos, Hellyer, and drop that hangdog expression. If you pushed me, I'd think four months would be time enough for the dust to settle and for you to acquire your new skills. Take the weekend to reflect and catch up with London life. The office Humber will pick you up from the B&B at nine ack emma on Monday. Anything else?'

'No, sir. Most grateful of course, but that's a heck of a lot to take in if I may say so.'

***

HE WANDERED DOWN KING Charles Street, past Gilbert Scott's massive late-nineteenth-century Foreign Office building, now the FCO, head full of puzzles. Coming out of the tunnel again. Into the bright light of a brave new world? Or a sea of darkness?

Saturday night, he exulted in the vibrant exuberance of *Hair* at the Shaftesbury Theatre. Much of Sunday afternoon he spent on his back, lolling on the grass in a cloud of dope at a free Fleetwood Mac concert in Hyde Park.

Monday morning, he was ready to rock and roll.

***

Colchester, Essex, UK, 21 July 1968

'MOST IRREGULAR, ALL OF this – I'm running a military prison, not keeping a damned boarding house.' Regimental

Sergeant Major Crispin's ruddy cheeks shone. 'Don't bother telling me porkies about who you are. I can easily enough sniff out *what* you are. Say what you like about the squaddies sent here, but by the time I've finished with them they're as smartly drilled and turned out as anyone in uniform. Shame I'm not allowed to do the same for you.'

'Sir?'

'Don't you "sir" me, sonny,' the RSM said. 'You're not under my command, more's the pity.'

A military policeman escorted Nick from the guardroom to his cell where a much-washed faded army uniform awaited him.

Back in captivity, but at least a relatively more luxurious cell than his previous dank Egyptian one. And on the bright side, he'd been allowed to hang on to his own clothes for his daily outside excursions.

He dozed for hours, falling captive to dreams of Patricia's swaying freckled breasts and of missed trains and opportunities.

After a fifteen-minute bus ride the next day, he straddled a bench outside the Rose and Crown on the quayside in Wivenhoe, near the university. A pint of Abbot balanced precariously on the old wood while he relished every mouthful of his first ploughman's lunch in over eighteen months. He gazed through the clanging halyards of yachts resting on their sides in the mud of the Colne River at half tide, and across to the open marshes beyond.

Nothing wrong with this, was there? Certainly beat dreaming up abstruse points of literary criticism to cast in front of polite, but deeply bored undergraduates. His accommodation could be cushier for sure, but security-wise, it was safe. Allegedly.

Yet he shivered in the sunshine, all too aware of the illusorily peaceful scene. He could no more scramble through the mud to the far riverbank and stride out across the marshes than he could check out of the Glasshouse. His free will had once more been taken away; he'd become a mere chassis, fresh bodywork to be fitted on the espionage assembly line.

Nothing for it. Buckle down and swallow reality.

He tackled the long haul uphill and crossed the green campus park from which the grey brutalist concrete platform supporting the towers of the University of Essex rose.

***

'CALL ME PETER.'

Professor Whiteside's studied informality lifted Nick's mood immediately.

The man was tall, grey-suited, his face deeply tanned and etched with extensive vertical smile lines that became more evident as he pulled a telex out of his top desk drawer. He nudged his fringe from his eyes with the tips of two fingers.

'Really great to hear from Quinlevan again. Patrick and I go way back – West Africa and South America in the day. We got on blazingly well, although I must confess I never knew exactly where I had him or what he might be up to, if you follow me. Bit of a transformation artist. Now he's expecting me to do the same prestidigitation with you and convert a literature lecturer into a state-of-the-art ESP expert in two ticks. Impossible, of course. But Patrick's brief specifies that you're to be sufficiently equipped so as to give a convincing impression of an ESP specialist, without necessarily being the complete item.'

So, smoke and mirrors. Another acting job. Slated to tread the world stage as an academic fake.

'A counterfeit then.'

Peter smiled. 'Exactly thus. You'll be an occasional student here, auditing applied linguistics postgraduate seminars. I'm also assigning you to the Colchester Associates Language School. There, you'll follow a three-month course leading to a Certificate in Teaching English for Specific Purposes.'

'But I have no background whatsoever in English grammar, let alone linguistics.'

'Typical product of fifties secondary education. Eminently sortable. You're far from the first of that generation, so we have bags of experience in filling in your lacunae. Must dash now. Really good to meet you – brings back memories, I can tell you. Greetings to Patrick.'

A handshake later, Nick found himself in the corridor. His path wouldn't cross the professor's again until his final day.

***

THE GLASSHOUSE'S NICKNAME WAS a consequence of the ground-to-ceiling glazing at the end of each Nissen hut that enabled the guards to observe every movement within.

Nick kept to himself, fending off initial questions from curious fellow inmates, changing out of uniform and into civvies once they'd gone on parade, and back again before their return. The squaddies lost interest in the odd outsider once it had become clear he wasn't a plant.

Similarly, at the university he swam in a goldfish bowl among the multicoloured shoal of his fellow students, his movements as an occasional student unobserved. Applied linguistics seminars always provoked and challenged him, sometimes soared above his head. He attempted to master the terminology and kept up with the assigned reading.

'Noam Chomsky is God, and *Syntactic Structures* the Bible,' a fellow student explained.

So he hadn't been too far off the mark in his quip about being reborn.

More intriguing were the sessions at the language school where he observed, and then taught, classes for groups of Italian customs officials, Iraqi diplomats and members of the Royal Omani Police.

'How you say in English? Sockets? Yes, socks. Obvious he's a drug smuggler, because always have thick socks.'

'Large naval target? That is what we are calling oil tanker?'

'Empty pocket and kneel. Eyes down. Mouth shut.'

He could see his own reimagining reflected in the overseas students' struggle to gain another identity in a second language.

It was here that he also acquired the arcane art of needs analysis.

Barbara, whose classes he'd been observing, initiated him.

'Think of yourself as a medical consultant diagnosing a patient,' she said. 'You observe. You evaluate through questionnaires, tests and interviews. And you come to an analysis of what kind and level of language an individual requires to perform a task or carry out a function.'

'And then?'

'Devise a teaching programme. Now let's work out what situations these particular questionnaires were designed for.'

She pushed a pile of papers across the table to him. Much more like it. The direct connection with the new world he was about to inhabit was obvious.

At the Roman Barracks, in his ill-fitting desert camouflage uniform, his classroom introductions to the Walther PP semi-automatic pistol and Semtex plastic explosives preceded visits to the firing range and controlled detonations in sandpits.

'Here, sonny, stop jerking off that pistol – it's not your cock. Think of it as a woman and stroke her gently.'

Nick obeyed the sergeant instructor, and round after round hit the bullseye. He also mastered the swivelling ankle holster, enabling him to fire from the ground.

The instructor tossed the block of Semtex at the trainees standing in front of him.

'Catch!'

The throw was deliberately short. Nick awaited the seemingly inevitable outcome, as none dived quickly enough to catch the explosive.

Nothing. A dull thud on the hard-packed earth surface.

The sergeant marched up, stamped and twisted his boot on the explosive.

'Well behaved, see. Wish I could say the same about you lot, Hellyer excepted of course.'

The other trainees groaned.

'Now pay attention. The grunts in Vietnam break off bits of this stuff to heat their tea billycans. It'll do anything if you treat it right, just like your dream girlfriend.'

A visit to the assault course with its daunting death slide concluded each session. On the sergeant's shout of 'Go, go, Hellyer!' he dived forward, adrenaline pumping, grin fixed as the speed brought tears to his eyes. That challenge never rattled him. A final event at the university did.

***

CURLED UP IN THE university library, endeavouring and failing to grasp the central argument of Kuhn's *The Structure of Scientific Revolutions* in preparation for his final seminar, Nick caught the paternoster in his peripheral vision. He'd become accustomed to this design oddity: a doorless lift on an endless loop that moved slowly enough for its occupants to step on and off at each floor. Travel over the top or bottom, meaning you'd have to crouch low, was strictly forbidden, although the graffiti scribbled on the walls at each end told a different tale.

A blue-suited man was ignoring the strictures on riding around and passed by repeatedly. Nick waited by the lift and joined the platform when he came around again.

'Couldn't help noticing you're doing the whole circuit. On for a bet or something?'

'Not exactly,' the man answered in a wavering mid-Atlantic accent. 'I can quite understand your perplexity. It's far from being a wager though. I'm from the elevator company – checking out some safety issues.'

He hopped off at the next floor.

Nick got off the paternoster at the entrance lobby, more concerned with his own safety than the lift's.

With Kuhn tucked ostentatiously under his arm, he headed for the professor's office and his farewell appointment.

***

PETER BRUSHED STRANDS OF greying hair away from his eyes and sat quite still behind his desk for a moment. He put Nick in mind of a chameleon about to unleash its tongue.

The professor looked up at him. 'You've achieved a great deal, Hellyer. Well done. Only excellent reports.' His smile was unexpectedly broad. 'Just one thing, hardly worth bothering you with, but I've already reported it to Patrick. Yesterday, a persistent fellow turned up in the department enquiring about you. Wouldn't take no for an answer, and eventually got referred to me. Looked like an earnest Jehovah's Witness what with the blue suit, but sounded more like someone from the Middle East pretending to be an American. Of course, I could be totally wrong.'

Most unlikely, given Peter's international reputation as a phonetician.

'Said he wanted to deliver an urgent message. Naturally, I gave him short shrift. That's it. Now I do hope you've enjoyed your time here and wish you all the very best for your future missions, whatever or wherever they turn out to be.'

***

NICK RECEIVED NO SUCH fond farewell from the RSM on his departure from the Glasshouse.

'Granted you've not been any trouble, that's fair to say. But good riddance to bad rubbish is my opinion.'

So: reborn, re-imagined, re-engineered. For what purpose? It was a quandary, one that filled Nick's mind as he sat bolt upright in the captain's chair opposite Quinlevan the next day.

'Delighted to see military discipline has been good for your posture,' the major said. 'By the way, we can forget all about Peter's alert re the blue-suited man. Becoming a bit of an old woman between you and me. Mere coincidence,

I'm sure. First of all, many congrats on passing on all fronts so successfully.'

'Thank you, sir. And my little "local difficulty" on Madeira?'

'Sorted, dear chap. We've had lengthy words with both suspected parties through various channels, and it's all been put down to a slight misunderstanding between good friends. Forgive and forget, that's the watchword. All tickety-boo. From here on in, you'll be London-based. Your first assignment will be a training one, and once you've gained the necessary operational experience from that, the game's on. We've lined up a very straightforward mission for you in the Azores. I take it you're familiar with the location.'

'Archipelago off the west coast of Africa.'

'Top of the class. The Americans started flying from Lajes Field, a Portuguese airbase on Terceira Island, during the Second World War. They've now offered to fund the lengthening of the runway and other works.'

'Why on earth would they put money into that? I imagine they're paying through the nose for the use of the facilities in the first place.'

'Yes, they are – you've put your finger on it. The workforce is Azorean and, for all general purposes, the Yanks can get by in a mixture of Portuguese and English. But for one particular highly-classified element of the project, accuracy is paramount, and they've become jittery about communication problems. So, via NATO, we've proposed you to smooth over their minor linguistic difficulties. Basically, you'll be giving eight officers enough specialised Portuguese to manage the classified bit. Your aim is simple – find out what they're constructing.'

'But aren't we meant to be allies? Special relationship and all that? Why not request the information?'

Quinlevan's smile became even more reptilian. 'We're very much junior partners in that transatlantic relationship, and always have been, despite the politicians' claims. However, this request has presented us with a unique opportunity to get in under their radar and find out what it is they're actually up to.'

***

Azores, 24 March 1969

NICK HAD BEEN A guest of the USAF on Terceira Island in the mid-Atlantic for eight weeks. Having conducted a needs analysis, he'd delivered an intensive six-week course in Portuguese for military-construction purposes. The small group of officers in his class were assiduous and endlessly polite. But although they were hospitable hosts in the mess, he could establish no meaningful rapport with them.

Towards the end of the course, he warned the bronzed base commander, whose white uniform jacket displayed two rows of medal strips, that he'd need access to detailed drawings of a particular aspect of the project.

'No way, son – highly classified, top secret. Those babies ain't going nowhere near you. Anything else you want to raise? I trust the boys are treating you well.'

'Indeed they are, sir, but you must understand that it would be impossible for me to fulfil my mission without the necessary tools. In this case, those particular drawings. Do feel free to cross-check my security clearance with your superiors. You might well be in for a surprise.'

Nick got his hands on the plans and microfilmed them.

Dynamite. Not literally, but certainly explosive in the right hands.

He considered contacting London from the British consulate in the Azores and made his one and only trip to the capital, Ponta Delgada on São Miguel Island, expressly for this purpose. Unfortunately, the preoccupied part-time consul inspired little confidence and Nick backed out on security grounds.

Instead, he held his secret tight to his chest until the end of his mission.

Fierce blasts of scorching sand-laden wind drove him to seek refuge in the shade of a hangar while waiting for his flight to Lisbon. From there, he observed a Portuguese Air Force Nord NorAtlas 2501 land. Eight pairs of white-clothed medics climbed on board and returned down the steps with loaded stretchers.

'Who are the wounded?' he asked the officer standing beside him.

'Casualties from Mozambique. They receive an initial assessment and treatment here. Then they're flown on to Lisbon.'

***

NICK FLIPPED THE MICROFILM cassette across Quinlevan's desk. 'The Americans are constructing an underground nuclear weapons storage facility with lifts eleven stories deep. The runway's being extended so it can take B-52s. The facility's ostensibly intended for maritime tactical weapons – nuclear depth charges – and there are indeed submarine hunters there: US Navy P-3 Orions. But the reality is that from the Azores,

B-52 nuclear bombers would be capable of obliterating any city in Africa or South America, let alone Europe.'

'Excellent work, Nick. We'd construed that might be the case, but it's essential to have corroboration. Many thanks indeed. With your training mission successfully accomplished, you're now fully operational, so stand by for orders.'

'Thank you, sir. Just one point. I do realise that I'm compromised in Madeira, but what about contact with João and Patricia? They've become close friends.'

'One considerably closer than the other, as I understand it. Quite out of the question. Your relationship with them is and was purely professional – or ought to have been.'

Nick languished in the tiny brown-toned half-furnished flat he'd rented in Balham in the south of London, awaiting a summons from the office and haunted by memories of Patricia and what might have been,

***

'GOT TO MAKE BEST use of you while your Portuguese is still fresh, eh? Your first proper mission and, by golly, it's a juicy one – Angola. You'll love it. Attached to the embassy for six months, full diplomatic cover.' The major grinned. 'Think of all the perks. Oil's going boom-boom, really taking off. Official request for analysis of linguistic needs of offshore oil exploration workers. I'm sure you'll speedily develop good sea legs.'

'And the real purpose?' Nick said.

'Evaluation of the Portuguese response to the guerrilla campaigns of the independence movements: the communist MPLA and the CIA-backed FNLA. Problem is that official foreigners can't move around the country unhindered, while your role requires you to do just that. Embassy communications are secure, so report weekly. Our resident there will facilitate.'

Halfway through the mission, overwhelmed by the heat, helpful smiling duplicitous faces, repeated salty tender trips to distant rigs, dusty dirt-track jungle-jeep forays, and an aching inner tenderness, he made an unofficial communication. A postcard addressed to the Mansarda das Aranhas through the local mail, not the diplomatic bag. He'd drawn a lone coconut palm on a deserted beach and signed it 'Not Al'.

His final official top-secret telex began: *Can confirm prediction of Portuguese defeat if they lose control and an MPLA–FNLA civil war breaks out.*

***

London, 11 August 1972

'You're off to Mozambique next.'

Three years had passed but time had stood still in Quinlevan's office.

'Your presence is at the request of the Portuguese authorities themselves. They're building a dam across a gorge on the Zambezi River that will generate electricity primarily for sale to South Africa. Claimed to be second in size in Africa only to Egypt's Soviet-designed Aswan Dam. However, the German, British and South African construction companies have communication problems. Not with each other, but with the 3,000-strong workforce who mostly speak only local languages. You're to carry out a needs analysis on the potential value of training the workers in workplace English so they're able to understand directions from all parties. FRELIMO, the Mozambican independence movement, is dead set against the dam – the huge lake would disrupt guerrilla infiltration from Zambia. FRELIMO's backers are the Soviets and the Chinese. Now, if you subscribe to domino theory, first Mozambique goes, then Rhodesia falls and the commies ride into South Africa.'

Nick had come to enjoy the ritual call and response of his briefings and sang his part.

'And the actual?'

'The usual, dear boy. Find out what's really happening on the ground. Bugger the dam. We need a current assessment of the guerrilla war's development and possible outcomes.'

***

Tete, Mozambique, 20 August 1972

THE YELLOWING BLOOD-SHOT EYES of the decapitated teenage guerrilla glared up at Nick, who stood transfixed in the burning sunlight and suffocating heat.

A gentle touch on the shoulder made him turn.

'*Calma, paciência,* my friend. This situation is not at all easy for an outsider to comprehend.'

Captain Mario Mendes. The contrast between the softness of his civilised voice and the horror at Nick's feet didn't stop his shoulders from drooping, but he unclenched his fists.

'Allow me to give you a broader picture. Captured *terroristas* get a choice: change sides or die. They can lead us to FRELIMO camps and infiltration trails and prove they're not a plant. Then they can become one of the *Flechas*, the DGS special forces. If they don't, we hand them over to our fellow soldiers whose comrades they murdered or mutilated with mines, machine guns and machetes.'

Nick squatted, elbows on thighs, palms on his forehead and threw up the meagre contents of his stomach over his purple desert boots. Why had he accepted this mission?

He'd arrived in the capital, Lourenço Marques, over one thousand kilometres south of the war. His peaceful breakfast on the extensive terrace of the Hotel Polana overlooking the Indian Ocean had been fractured by a loud group of vacationing Afrikaners waving tankards of lager. As they passed, one had tripped and spilled beer on Nick's table, laughed and waved an apology. Nick had stood to remonstrate but a hand had grabbed his arm, gently, not forcibly.

'No, sir, not a good idea.'

He'd learnt from his smiling, restraining waiter that he'd be dealing with Boers building Dutch courage in anticipation of something forbidden at home: sex with black women.

'Best leave them alone, sir. Only trouble.'

'Contact the embassy on arrival and make your number. They'll take care of all necessary arrangements,' Quinlevan had told him.

He'd done so, but his number clearly hovered just above zero and his spirits had flattened.

'No real idea why you're here, something to do with trade I gather,' the harassed second secretary had told him, handing over a plane ticket to Beira. 'The consulate will provide transport from there.'

'Pretty hairy up in Tete.' The British consul in Beira had traced concentric rings in the condensation on his ice-cold beer glass as they sat on the hotel terrace by the lighthouse. The rusting wreck of a coaster on the beach beneath them glowed in the deep-red low rays of the sunset. 'Tete's a good two days' drive, so our Land Rover will pick you up bright and early in the morning. Seven okay?'

'Thank you, that's great.'

'Rather you than me, to be honest, but I do admire the spirit of you commercial wallahs. Of course, HMG has a keen interest in the progress of the dam – if it ever gets built, that is. One other thing I perhaps ought to mention. South African fellow called du Plessis came into the consulate yesterday and enquired about your whereabouts. Described himself as an engineer working at Caborra Bassa – apparently a colleague sighted you in the Polana and tipped him off. I'm afraid I got a strong whiff of commercial espionage – we've been in competition with the Afrikaners over the dam contracts – so I denied all knowledge. The right thing to do, I hope.'

'Absolutely.'

Once he'd finished his drink, the consul had departed with the abruptness of the sudden Southern African sunset. In the gathering humid darkness, Nick had strolled across the beach barefoot, havering between excitement and trepidation. He'd have bet on the consul's visitor being neither South African nor called du Plessis.

Back in the hotel, he'd put his feelings into verse, shamelessly stealing the title of the poem from Virginia Woolf.

TO THE LIGHTHOUSE

Lighthouse beams and moon gleams
A ship shape wrecked by the quay

Which too had headed for the light
Danger unseen
Sand under keel
Sand under heel

Two days later, the consulate Land Rover had deposited him in Tete, a sun-beaten, dust-filled settlement on the banks of the third biggest river in Africa. The Wild West transported to Southern Africa, dominated by the two thousand soldiers of the 17th Battalion of the Portuguese Army.

Desire for a hasty pre-dinner drink had led him to the deserted drab Zambezi Hotel bar, enlivened only by the brightly coloured short skirts of three Mozambican women swinging their legs to and fro on high stools. No sign of a barman or business for them. Initial welcoming smiles and greetings had vanished when he'd made it clear he wasn't a seaman in search of a good time, just a beer.

It was in the run-down dining room that he'd made contact with plump, confident Captain Mario Mendes, who'd commanded the convoy from Beira to the dam. Nick had immediately warmed to his frankness. As they'd waited for service, the officer had waved away a proffered stained menu.

'All they ever have is goat curry. We'll feed you far better in our mess on arrival. And just so you know, I'll also be your liaison officer for the week at Caborra Bassa.'

Nick had stolidly chewed his way through the only dish on offer, pushing away thoughts of the cracked windowpanes in his room and the intermittent plumbing. In the heat and humidity, he'd at least persuaded the well-intentioned receptionist to provide him with a much-darned mosquito net.

The convoy had left Barracks Square at dawn the next day and, following a two-day drive, edged through the sprawling construction camp's heavily guarded perimeter fence.

***

MARIO MENDES AND NICK spent much of the week in each other's company, interviewing sweat-laden, out-of-their-depth white contractors and, via interpreters, bemused native manual workers. No one could recall du Plessis, the 'engineer' who'd called in at the consulate.

On his last night, Nick put to Mario the question that had been gnawing at his guts all week, the essential contradiction being the absurdity of the way the conflict had developed.

'Your countrymen claim they brought civilisation to Africa. So how can you justify your fellow soldiers using a dead man's head as a football? I just don't get it.'

'I do not justify, but I can clarify. Let's go someplace where we can exchange opinions more easily.'

He took Nick past lines of tents and into a smoky corrugated iron-roofed hall jammed with a camouflage-uniformed crowd, all shouting and jostling.

'Most here are conscripts, and none have any love for the war.' Mario gestured towards the bar. 'Our official line is that we're colour-blind – same rights for all citizens.'

'The right to education?'

'You have been doing your homework. Few soldiers from the mainland have gone far in secondary education, and virtually none of the locals. I'm a regular officer and studied engineering at Lisbon University. I'm also closing in on the end of my third tour of duty in the overseas provinces. The previous two took me to Angola.'

'*Filho da puta!*'

The loud cry came from an adjacent table of disputative young officers. One leapt up and swept glasses of red wine onto the dirt floor.

'Enough is enough' the young officer bellowed. 'Let's go outside and sort it out man to man.'

Mario turned away, unmoved. 'Milicianos. Boys. Ignore them. Sometimes I convince myself that only we Portuguese could have dug such an elephant trap for ourselves. University anti-war protests have resulted in many students losing their military service deferment. And because of our class system, they've been drafted as temporary officers, termed milicianos.'

'So neither the conscripts nor the milicianos want the fighting to go on?'

'Would you? The milicianos were demonstrating against the conflicts and the government in the first place. But because of a gap in officer supply, our prime minister has enabled them to leapfrog regulars like me who've taken the brunt of the fighting.'

'So why are you still doing tours of duty? Why not just quit?'

'Far too much blood and spirit invested. Come and I'll clarify.'

Mario led Nick across the hall to a corner where six table-football games were in play. Sweating soldiers clustered around the tables, whooping encouragement at the players.

'We call the toy footballers *bonecas* – dolls. And there's only thing to drink while you play: *Totobola* – red wine and chilled lemonade. Blood and ice.'

Nick had bagged a battered game table by the time Mario returned with the drinks. The captain spun the rusting iron rods, forcing the small, cracked white wooden ball towards Nick's goal. He paused and looked up.

'I've had the chance to observe you closely these last few days, and I'm of the belief that you're considerably more than a mere language expert. A different kind of animal entirely.'

Nick glanced at the moustachioed captain, who promptly scored.

'*Gol!*' Mario raised his fist in the air. 'Don't worry – no one else has voiced the slightest doubt about you. To them, you're just a linguistic technician, but I can smell something different. We can't easily be overheard here, so get stuck into the game and pay attention. My fellow regular officers and I are not dissatisfied – we're active. We're going to end this futile war.'

Head down, Nick concentrated on driving the ball towards Mario's goal. He shot. With a cry of delight, the captain slid his goalkeeper across and slipped the ball down the side to Nick's end.

'This struggle's never going to be winnable, however many conscripts we bring in. And even that's starting to prove problematic. More and more teenagers are melting away over the Spanish border and heading for France to avoid conscription. They say Paris is now Portugal's second city.'

Mario fell silent for a moment and concentrated on the game, then glanced around, leaned forward and continued in a low growl, 'The FRELIMO guerrillas are well organised, trained and equipped, using the same tactics as the Vietcong. They mine the roads, make a swift attack, melt away and ambush us if we choose to pursue. They're motivated for the struggle in a way that our men aren't and can never be. Sure, the guerrilla supply lines from Tanzania are long, but the local population, willingly or unwillingly, assist them. We Portuguese have been here for almost five centuries, but from the natives' point of view, what have we done for them? *Nada*. No education to speak of, and all the semi-skilled jobs are taken by unemployed whites from the mainland.'

Nick blocked the captain's next attack and sent the ball ricocheting back.

Mario continued. 'Guess what Caborra Bassa means in Nyungwe, the majority local language? "Finish the job." And that is exactly what we captains intend to do on our return to Portugal.'

'*Gol!*' Nick had taken advantage of Mario's absorption to score. But inevitably the tide had turned back in the officer's favour by the time they relinquished the table.

***

EARLY THE NEXT MORNING, Mario waved him off on a return convoy for Tete and then Beira.

'I hope we meet again, my friend,' he called out. 'And do take our comradely chat over the *bonecas* to heart.'

Flights via the capital took him to London and Quinlevan. Nick repeated the captain's views verbatim, adding observations from his own experience in the convoys and camps.

'My evaluation is that of the three African wars that Portugal's fighting, this one will prove the hardest for them to prevail in. And the disaffection of the regular officers is key.'

'Most useful info indeed. We'll need to keep an eye on the situation as it develops. But for the moment anyway, none of our business. And the result of your cover mission, for what it's worth?'

'I can hardly see the point in attempting to teach the workforce English when the vast majority are unable to communicate effectively in Portuguese. A quick fix would be to equip enough of the locals and foreign contractors with the national language.'

'Don't see that coming to pass somehow, and your conclusion is most definitely not the outcome HMG desired and expected. But be that as it may, go home, write up your report and stand by for transport to RAF Northolt at six ack emma tomorrow. One day crash course in poison gas.' He pushed a folder across the desk. 'No need to concern yourself about the classification. Highest. Briefing document for you to memorise and abandon on the plane.'

***

Cornwall, UK, 10 September 1972

THE RAF DOMINIE TWINJET communications aircraft banked over Portreath on the north Cornish coast. The turquoise and black-blue patterns of the sea, the cream of the breakers and the orange slashes of mineral residues in the cliffs gave way to a substantial fenced-off clifftop industrial complex with four short criss-crossing runways. A flare of startlingly deep yellow smoke from a tall chimney belched a greeting as the plane made its final approach.

'Welcome to Chemical Defence Establishment, Nancekuke.'

The acting base commander wore a white laboratory coat with a flurry of brown flecks down one sleeve over uniform shirt and trousers. A large yellowing white moustache hung above his upper lip. Nick struggled to reconcile the man with his office, which was furnished Scandinavian style – glass-topped desk on stainless-steel legs and elegantly curved low-set chairs upholstered in primary colours. A large window gave striking panoramic views past the runways to the sea. The whole setup contrasted starkly with the dilapidated fifties buildings along whose corridors Nick had been brought upon landing.

The commander beamed at him over his shiny paper-free desk. 'Not often that we get a day visitor. But you must be starving. Can I get you coffee and a roll from the mess?'

'Very kind, sir, but I had breakfast on the plane.'

'Of course. Now I've no intention of requesting you to divulge what your line of work might be, Dr Hellyer, although I can make an educated guess. Highly unusually, the Ministry of Defence has ordered me to offer you every facility. Can I take it then that you're not a biochemist?'

'Correct.'

'Let me give you a bit of background. As you may be aware, at the end of the Second World War, the allies seized large stocks of G-series nerve gas from the Nazis. Based on the German technology, we've developed our own version, the VX-series.'

'I'm given to understand that the Russians have done something similar.'

'So you *are* up to speed. Yes, intelligence suggests that the Soviet Union are currently producing a similar derivative, which they call N-series, or novichok.'

'Not so far up to speed as to understand why this nerve-gas research is being conducted here and not at Porton Down, I'm afraid.'

'Ponder it for a moment. While we take every conceivable precaution, our main chemical-weapons research establishment lies far too close to the 35,000 souls living in Salisbury. What if, in a nightmare scenario, an accidental leak or spillage occurred? Disaster. Hundreds, possibly thousands of deaths. However, what does the population of this part of Cornwall consist of? Pigs, sheep, cattle, horses, chickens and a few farmers' families. And we even provide them with gas masks if they're working within the perimeter fence. The farmers, that is.'

Nick's eyes widened.

'I can see what you're thinking, but don't be at all surprised at these precautions, Dr Hellyer. You've landed in one of Britain's most secure secret bases; we're dealing with deadly substances, and cannot take the remotest risk. We've even mined a waste-disposal tunnel through the rock; it discharges directly into the sea beyond the base of the cliffs. Cornwall used to have the finest hard-rock miners in the world. Neither the local residents nor the hordes of tourists by the harbour have the faintest idea what's going on up here on Tolticken Hill. And that's the way we intend to keep it.'

'And your workforce?'

'Good question.' The commander leaned back awkwardly in his swivel chair, as if testing how far it would recline. 'Mainly service personnel, some outside scientific specialists and local workmen. All bound by the Official Secrets Act. No leaks there, if you'll forgive the pun. Now, let's have an orientation walk before we initiate you into our world via your participation in a routine nerve-gas experiment.'

'You're taking me around yourself? Most obliged and flattered.'

'Delighted to show off the old girl. Now pop this coat on and we'll be off.'

***

THE GIRL WAS CERTAINLY ageing. The walls bulged, ceilings were cracked, paintwork was blotched. Nick peered through inset door windows at teams of masked and gowned laboratory workers, walked through a giant hall full of intricate pipework and high-pressure tanks, and ended up in a much more up-to-date area. The floors, walls and ceilings were covered in shining white plastic tiles, and air-conditioning shushed in the soundproofed corridor. However, his peeks through door windows revealed unlit, deserted laboratories. He turned to his guide and tilted his head.

'Mothballed. Perhaps more about the reason why later. Time for your experiment now.'

Nick donned protective clothing and, on a technician's instruction, ventured alone, like an astronaut stepping onto the moon, into the gas test chamber. The airlock hissed shut behind him. His only companions turned out to be a dozen piglets, two of whom were taking a lively interest in his bright-yellow boots. He kicked one away but others soon took its place, nuzzling and licking. He backed into a corner, eyes frozen behind his sealed mask.

Get on with it, for Christ's sake. Don't want to be eaten alive by piglets.

A siren sounded and a red light started to flash.

Thirty minutes later, he was the only living creature left in the chamber.

Red turned to green as the powerful evacuation fans completed their work and Nick stepped over the carcasses, through the air lock and into the decontamination area. On his way to the showers, he removed his protective suit, transparent plastic helmet and gloves, and deposited them in the chute to the incinerator.

Glowing from an extremely thorough post-experiment strip-down, shower and scrub, he reported to the commander's office.

'Well, what did you make of it?'

'Fascinating and scary in equal measures.'

'Yes, to be expected. We had a visitor pass out once. Great shame because we had to redo the experiment, just in case.' The commander smiled. 'Come on, can't have been that bad. I'm sure you've experienced far worse.'

'But, if I may ask, why pigs?'

'I'm sure you recall the apocryphal story of Pacific Island cannibals describing the missionaries they ate as "long pigs". We test nerve gas on pigs on the grounds of neurological similarity, but also because human volunteers from the armed services nowadays are far scarcer than they used to be. Once upon a time, National Service conscripts, in the belief that we were trialling a cure for the common cold, used to jump at the opportunity of a day off, a cup of tea and a couple of digestive biscuits. Of course, we couldn't take things as far with them as we can with the pigs nowadays.'

'Have I just experienced VX in action?'

'No. You observed a different nerve gas at work. Sarin. Another bequest from Adolf H., although no one's been able to work out quite why he never deployed it. My best guess is that the collateral effect it might have had on his own troops deterred him. We manufactured over twenty tonnes of our own version here under direct orders from Churchill in the 1950s. Totally in breach of the 1925 Geneva Gas Protocol, mind you. But you must have heard what Winnie was like, and orders were orders. In a way, you could say he made a good judgement call because sarin has provided a base for some of our work today.'

Nick waited, like a cat freezing as it closes in on a mouse, confident that more would emerge.

'Officially, we've destroyed all the sarin. But the truth of the matter is that we had to retain a certain amount, just as we did with the VX gas. Purely for research purposes, of course. Until recently, we'd been working on a vaccine. Atropine's only partially successful as an antidote and, crucially, has to be administered within twenty minutes of exposure. My predecessor received shedloads of secret Whitehall funding for this research, which enabled him to bring in an oddball top-level scientist with his whole team. The grants also sub-sidised the spanking new facilities you've seen.'

Nick gestured with an arm around the room.

'The mothballed corridor, yes. And in fact this office – my predecessor had been on NATO secondment to Copenha-gen and caught the Danish design virus. Not my cup of tea, at all. But then I'm only acting up until a replacement's appointed. You see, the politicos got wind of the funding for the research programme last year. Massive concerns about breaching international treaties, as well as not having been requested to authorise it in the first place. Big shoot-out in Westminster: commander posted to a scientific station in the Antarctic and the newly-built research team disbanded. Catastrophic timing, they claimed, because they believed they were just this far from the breakthrough.' He held up his thumb and forefinger, a millimetre gap between them.

Nick maintained a respectful silence.

'Didn't worry me particularly one way or the other, to be honest. Always been excluded from the ultra-hush-hush stuff. Old school. Fuddy-duddy. That's how they saw me. Sooner they appoint a new commander the better as far as I'm concerned, and then I'll be able to get back to my lab.'

'May I ask why?'

'Because I've had something much more lucrative going on for a long time.'

The commander's nicotine-yellowed moustache moved closer to Nick's ear, and a waft of tobacco on the man's breath assailed Nick's nostrils.

'Forget daffodils and new potatoes. My little baby is Cornwall's major unknown export. Riot-control CS gas. Been snapped up all around the world, as far away as South Africa. Remember the Paris Spring of 1968? We supplied huge quantities. And, of course, it's currently deployed extensively in Northern Ireland. I don't mind telling you that CS has proved a very nice earner indeed, and the income from our tear-gas production subsidises most of the rest of the show here.'

A Q&A session with a panel of five scientists and two technicians followed. Nick flew back in the evening, trying and failing to fully process the flow of information and possible disinformation.

**

'Learn anything useful down west?' Quinlevan greeted him the next morning with a backward jerk of his head.

'Not as much as I'd have liked to, I'm afraid, sir. But enough. The point is that they could show me as much or as little as they wanted. While the acting commander appeared very forthcoming about their "research", I really had no way of sussing out how far he was shooting me a line. I did participate in an experiment where they gassed—'

'Spare me the gruesome details if you don't mind. You got acquainted with the theory from the file on the plane; now you've seen the practice. Vitally important that you've mastered the nerve-gas lingo and got to grips with the background because this is the world you're about to inhabit. Thing is, one of Nancekuke's top boffins has gone AWOL. Whole issue is all rather delicate as he happened to be the chief researcher into the sarin vaccine. He recently surfaced at the University of Coimbra in central Portugal. Our idea is to get you alongside him long term. Fortunately, Professor Laidlaw speaks no Portuguese and his biochemical research team little English. The university have officially requested the British Council to assist in providing someone to mediate linguistically between the professor and his assistants.'

'And my brief?' Nick failed to sing.

'To find out what the hell he's working on there – could be a long game indeed. My masters are seriously concerned that UK-developed nerve-gas technology could be transferred to the Portuguese and subsequently used in their guerrilla wars in Africa. Conceivably also sold on elsewhere. Has to be prevented.'

'Received loud and clear, sir, although it does constitute rather a tall order. Communicate through the embassy as usual?'

'Most certainly not. The British Council office in Coimbra, the Casa da Inglaterra, has been there since before the Second World War, but you'll be employed directly by the university. No harm at all, of course, in socialising with the Casa people – be odd if you didn't, in fact. But your orders are to stay strictly at arm's length from the embassy. Shall we say that, as regards nerve gas, two schools of thought co-exist within the MoD. One is Churchillian – all's fair and so on. My own masters hold a conflicting view.'

'So how will I keep in contact?'

'You won't. Basically, we intend to lose you there. The phones are totally insecure, the post's leaky, and the DGS – the secret police – permeate every institution. Portugal's the closest Western Europe has to totalitarianism, not excepting its neighbour, Franco's Spain. You'll have a code word and a London number to arrange a crash meeting with me if and when. But only me. Understand?'

Nick's eyes drifted over the fading hunting prints on the grey walls, empathising with the fox. So he'd have to go to ground as well.

CHAPTER 3

Coimbra, Portugal, 20 September 1972

'DR HELLYER? I'M AUGUSTA Mendes from the university's Foreign Relations department. Pleasant journey?'
Nick shook hands with an austere woman whose wide
trousers and tightly buttoned knitted top were silhouetted
in the light pouring over the River Mondego and into the
foyer of the thirties-style Hotel Astoria.

As Nick related the difficulties he'd encountered the previous night Augusta's features softened. He explained that he'd
confused the main line Coimbra B station, some distance out
of town with the city-centre branch-line terminus, Coimbra A.

'At least the hundred-metre walk from Coimbra A to your
hotel shouldn't have tired you too much.' Her brief smile
made the irony bearable.

He peered out of the revolving door and up at the ancient
university buildings, precariously balanced high over the river.
'Bit of a long trek up to work though.'

Augusta's face relaxed a little more. 'Our university's been
here since 1537, but I'm sure you'll be delighted to learn that
trams arrived in 1911. Let's ride up in one.'

Augusta grasped his arm proprietorially as she escorted him
up the long staircase to the rector's office for the ceremony.

The first occasion on which Nick had knelt in front of a porcine man intoning Latin while laying hands on his shoulders had been at his doctoral ceremony at Cambridge University's Senate House. On his knees again in front of *O Magnifico*, the rector of the University of Coimbra, Nick had just sworn an oath to seek out and destroy Communism and Socialism in whatsoever form they might present themselves.

Afterwards came a tour with Augusta of the eighteenth-century baroque library in all its gilded splendour and, in contrast with its dramatic gloom, a climb to the top of the tower where they stood in the blinding sunshine and took in the cascade of tiled roofs running down to the river.

'Incredible. Imagine working here.'

Augusta ran a hand over her wiry close-cropped hair. 'Please don't build your hopes up too much, Dr Hellyer. I'm giving you a tour of the historic university – the part the tourists come to see. However, I'm afraid the laboratory where you'll be working occupies a modern building on the outskirts, some distance beyond the stadium. Quite out of the way really. Hardly any housing near it.'

The remoteness of the research facility failed to surprise him.

As they strode together through the eighteenth-century botanical gardens towards the laboratory, Augusta emphasised the manner in which the range of plants and trees reflected Portugal's long overseas history.

'Coimbra's always been a halfway house. Midway between Lisbon and Oporto, equidistant to the sea and the mountains, marooned between the medieval and modern worlds. We have contradictions aplenty – a strong radical tradition and suffocating conformism.'

'And how do you fit into this mélange, may I ask?'

She paused on the gravel path. 'No, you may not – at least not just yet. You've landed yourself in a place of secrets, many of which are better left unrevealed. Perhaps, if and when I get to know you better, I can share some of those with you.'

'I sincerely hope so. And where is Professor Laidlaw situated in this secretive academic and political landscape?'

'I wish I could tell you more about him. The professor and I have only met a couple of times. At his appointment, he came across as very dynamic, and he certainly must have very considerable resources behind him. The laboratory's been substantially adapted to his own very particular specifications, at great speed. And he operates completely independently of the Faculty of Sciences.'

'These external resources – have you any idea what they are?'

'I'll give you an indirect answer to your very direct question. In our corporate state, the military and the industrial blend. So, for example, generals can and do hold directorships in large enterprises. There, that's more than enough background for the moment.'

Augusta led them at a good walking pace a considerable distance in a peaceful silence. They left behind an area of apartment blocks and arrived at an anonymous three-storey building standing on its own, surrounded by a fenced-in newly surfaced car park.

'Shall we go in?'

She pushed open frosted glass doors and ushered him into reception with a pat on the back. 'I can't accompany you any further than the foyer, I'm afraid. No clearance. I'll wait for you here.'

An uncommunicative security guard searched him carefully, and wordlessly issued a pass. Another guard escorted him to the lift. He glanced back at Augusta, who gave him a best-of-luck wave. The guard unlocked double doors to a long corridor and halted outside an office door signed *Diretor*. Nick knocked and entered.

'Splendid – how fulfilling to meet you at last, Dr Hellyer. Do meet my group – we're planning to do great things together.'

Professor James Laidlaw swung his ham-sized arms along the row of nervous researchers seated around a long wooden seminar table. In his energetic welcome, the short-sleeved professor almost succeeded in knocking over a large rubber tree plant.

'Whoops! Saved it. To be serious, we have an exceptional, a once-in-a-lifetime, opportunity to contribute to scientific advance here. Clara, please translate for the team.'

On the back wall of the minimally furnished room hung a chalkboard covered in equations and crossings-out in equal measure.

A lanky, athletic-looking researcher in her thirties stood, adjusted her glasses, and cleared her throat.

'Won't be necessary,' Nick said with a smile.

He translated the professor's words, introduced himself and shook hands with each member of the group – the last being Clara, who briefly held onto his hand.

'I'm so grateful you're here, Dr Hellyer. You must understand that I'm a scientist, not a linguist. So my recent role as translator hasn't always been an easy ride, trust me.'

Nick glanced at Laidlaw.

'Don't worry. He doesn't understand what we're saying. Nothing against the professor himself of course, but it'll be great to be able to get back to my real work. I can already see you'll be *liquidamente superior* in the role of intermediary.'

The researchers excused themselves, and Nick worked his way around the table. The heavily built professor shifted his weight from one foot to another and sat. Nick took a seat opposite.

Laidlaw's eyes fastened on Nick. Disconcertingly blue; long blonde lashes some would have died for.

'Good start. I can see you're most adept at making yourself at home. My question to you is simple: are you up for the task you've been set? To help me achieve something those dullards in the UK refused to countenance. I agreed to your appointment and have been informed of your academic background. But what of your commitment – to me personally and to total confidentiality?'

'I regret that's a question I struggle to answer, as I have so little inkling of what the project involves. You can hardly fail to agree with that premise.'

'But how can I reveal more until I've come to an assessment of your trustworthiness?'

'Professor, I'm here on a two-year contract that you've approved so judge me as you find me.'

'Fair enough. Didn't mean to get off on the wrong foot. Apologies. We'll become better acquainted with each other, and I'm sure it'll all go swimmingly.'

Great. He was in. But what had Clara meant by 'not an easy ride'?

***

AUGUSTA ESCORTED HIM BACK into town. 'How did it go?'

'Interesting person, as you indicated. To be honest, I've never met anyone quite like him before. Looks like he's put together some extremely sharp young people for his team though. I'm pretty sure I'll be able to fit in.'

'I do so love an optimist. Best of luck!'

She led him to the university flat he'd been allocated in Rua Dr Henriques Seco. The apartment was set in an older quarter near the top of a hill and nearer the centre of the city.

'Lucky you! You're next door to a *República*.'

Unsure of what she meant and unwilling to enquire, Nick thanked her for being such an excellent shepherdess and hoped they might meet again.

'Yes, I do too. Coimbra's a small town so I expect we'll run into each other sooner or later.' She patted him on the arm. 'But do make sure you take care of yourself.'

Her directness and increasing warmth was welcome after the initial austereness but he wasn't too sure what to make of her advice. Take it at face value in the context of daily living? Or had a warning lain behind it?

The second-floor flat, originally servant's quarters, offered wide views over the city, and the hole-in-the-wall grocery opposite provided basic supplies, including a five-litre *garrafão* of excellent Cantanhede red.

***

IN THE FOLLOWING MONTHS, his life was one of contrasts marked by occasional interactions with the ancient university and the hyperactivity of the laboratory. Initially, the bulk of Nick's role consisted of translating Laidlaw-speak for the team.

'Well, get on with it, then. No time to hang about.'

'Not finished yet? What's the matter with you?'

'Didn't mean to. Spill the coffee, I mean. Nick, wipe it up, will you?'

'That's ridiculous. Why hasn't it been delivered yet? All paid for.'

'Sorry, didn't see you coming. Can I help you up?'

'All gone quiet in here, hasn't it? Something the matter?'

The professor, a driven, intensely shy man, largely oblivious to the sensitivities of his colleagues, had inculcated a culture of secrecy. Nick had so far been unable to make any real progress in his mission. His attempts to find out more from Clara had been firmly rebuffed in a regretful, friendly manner: Not for your ears.

The invitation from the professor came out of the blue a month later.

'Would love to invite you around to my place for dinner.'

Maybe Laidlaw was about to open up.

'But to be honest, the flat's still a bit of a pigsty – but do let's have a meal out one night soon.'

Or maybe not.

The researchers' intellectual abilities and determination impressed Nick, and he resolved to capitalise on his rapport with them. Perhaps that might shed more light on the laboratory's work.

On a Friday in January, he invited them to a surprise post-class birthday party in honour of Laidlaw.

Eight researchers and a restless professor found themselves looking out over the Mondego River from the terrace of the Cervejaria da Fabrica. Nick picked at *tremoços* – yellow salty beans – and observed the interaction. Bags of goodwill from the Portuguese, but Laidlaw was clearly finding it hard to relate to them in an out-of-work context.

'Very smart idea this, Nick. Good team building. Never been here. Like it.' He emptied his beer glass, ran his fingertips around the top and waved for a refill.

Clara moved with a slight limp to the front of the group and addressed them in English. 'Professor, I've been deputed on behalf of the team' – she glanced down through black-framed spectacles at a menu covered with hastily scribbled notes – 'to express our gratitude for the opportunity to work with you. And to wish you a most happy birthday!'

Laidlaw frowned, blushed and abruptly patted her hand. 'That's very sweet of you, Clara. Not used to compliments like that. Not at all. You're a knockout team. Far the best I've ever worked with.'

Nick tapped his glass and rose. Confessed to his ruse of a mythical birthday to get them all there together. Laughter, clapping and toasts followed, until the applause forced Laidlaw to respond.

'While I'm far past marking the passage of time, I'm most grateful for your celebration of my phantom birthday.'

That evening, Nick and the professor had their oft-postponed dinner in the Pinto D'Ouro restaurant on the opposite bank of the Mondego.

'What the fuck was that all about?' Laidlaw pushed his half-eaten plate of steak, fried egg and chips away. 'My understanding is that you were hired as an interpreter, not a manipulator.'

'I'm your conduit and your facilitator. Just keeping my part of the bargain. But I'm completely hampered because I still have only the vaguest idea about the work you and your group are engaged in. I can't provide them with the specialised language they need without more information from you about what the project entails.'

The professor pondered his response. Nick watched the black-aproned waiter hold up glasses against the lighted mirror at the rear of the empty restaurant and give them a final polish.

'I'll forgive you your little subterfuge tonight – although I will admit it served its purpose.' Laidlaw's tone switched. 'But now shut up and listen. Be assured that if you repeat this to anyone, I will secure your much more permanent silence.'

Nick sat straight up but relaxed inwardly. This was the moment he'd come for.

A fold of Laidlaw's substantial belly flopped onto the table-cloth as he leaned forward.

'Sarin and the holy grail of the vaccine – I'd come so extremely close to a solution at Nancekuke until the MoD pulled the plug overnight. A purely political decision – nothing to do with the quality of my research, you understand. All change at the top and the pen pushers got dramatically cold feet. In some mysterious way, the word leaked out from the MoD and I immediately received feelers from the Portuguese that I couldn't possibly ignore.'

Laidlaw emptied his wineglass and lowered his voice. Nick leaned forward over the table.

'Were the Portuguese to use sarin in the theatre in Africa, the soldiers who followed up would need to wear full protective suits and breathe through respirators. You can imagine the impossibility of that in the temperatures down there. Yet vaccinated soldiers would need none of the protective gear, so the army could utilise the nerve gas freely. This action would dramatically shorten the insurrections. Now that the laboratory's up and running, we can start with small-scale trials on animals.'

Had there been, or would there be, trials on humans? It was a good question but Nick's response focused on gas production; he didn't want to raise any doubts in the professor's mind by rash questioning. He received his just reward.

'We're making what sarin we need for the moment in the laboratory and building a much larger plant in a more remote location for use once the experimental stage has passed.'

On their return, they crossed over the Mondego on the Santa Clara Bridge in apparent harmony, side by side. Then Nick caught the tram up to the Praça da República, and the professor walked home along the river.

***

THE FOLLOWING THURSDAY, NICK called in at the British Council. Senhor José, the Casa da Inglaterra's immaculate general factotum, greeted him with a warm smile and an inclination of the head.

Nick made his way over to a man whose pink flares evinced a fashion style firmly set in the late sixties – Tom Price, the Casa's director. Price also lectured at the university Germânicas department, which, as its name implied, taught both English and German. In an attempt to counterbalance the Teutonic influence, Price had organised weekly play readings of contemporary English drama for the younger lecturers, and he'd invited Nick to join. Hard for him to resist.

'I'm not actually up to speed with Professor Laidlaw's scientific work, but I'm sure you'll be a great support to him.

By the way, at some stage you'll need to go down to Lisbon and sign the book at the embassy.'

'For what reason?'

'Just so they have a register of how many Brits to evacuate in an emergency – not likely of course, as we have a very stable regime. Still that's the form and doing it will get you an invite to the QBP – Queen's birthday party – in June. Highpoint of the Lisbon diplomatic social calendar. Not exactly my kind of thing, though I may not be the embassy's either, come to that. I'm pretty well left alone to do what I want up here, which suits me fine.'

Nick milled around the director's crowded office, and as Price closed the door firmly to draw the group's attention, a familiar face jumped out at him.

'Evening all,' Price said. 'I'd like to welcome a new member – Augusta Mendes from the Foreign Relations department.'

What Nick soon looked forward to every Thursday wasn't the readings themselves, although he participated enthusiastically, but chatting to Augusta afterwards. They fell into a habit of going on to the outdoor café in the Praça da República. The gravel surface made the white metal tables unstable, and they often struggled good-humouredly to balance their cups of coffee.

'So you've made a long voyage from student radicalism and teaching literature in Cambridge to language training for scientists in Coimbra.' She stretched her long legs out under the table. 'In a very different way, my husband and I have also made a journey. He'll be returning from Mozambique in the early summer, and I'd very much like you to meet him. It might interest you that neither of us are exactly enamoured with the current regime.'

Nick felt unsure how to respond. Quinlevan's briefing had been clear about the ubiquity of informers. On the other hand, how could he learn if he didn't listen?

'On the surface, for me as a foreigner, life comes across as calm and ordered, albeit somewhat old-fashioned.'

'Exactly, because you're living under the *Estado Novo*, and our government controls every aspect of our lives. Jokes are one way for us to cope with these incongruities. Our parliament meets in the Palácio de São Bento in Lisbon, which boasts a mightily impressive façade. On entering the neoclassical semi-circular Assembly Room, the splendour is overwhelming. You'd love it.'

'A step up from our Houses of Parliament then?'

'A huge one. At the front of the Assembly Room sits an ancient mahogany chest carved with the shields of the navigators who made Portugal great. Inside the chest, an exquisite mother-of-pearl box rests on a plush velvet cushion and, within that box, resides a smaller engraved silver casket.' She paused. 'Open the casket and all you'll find is a well-used purple rubber stamp.'

***

NICK REGULARLY ACCOMPANIED LAIDLAW, Clara and the team in a minibus to a secluded farm in a valley not far from the northern outskirts of Coimbra. In a sealed tent within a barn, the professor replicated his Nancekuke experiments. Pigs, half of which had been injected with the vaccine, were gassed with sarin. Half survived.

Back in his flat Nick, would have a long, hot, soapy shower, well aware of the risk of contamination. Not from sarin, but by his complicity and acquiescence in the inevitable next step. Human trials.

Obtaining information was one thing, but the thought of participating in pre-meditated murder made his stomach cramp.

A further event reinforced his apprehension. It wasn't the fierce blast of air-conditioning in the Faculty of Sciences basement home of the Ferranti mainframe computer.

Not the stacks of thick circular hard drives he'd just glimpsed over Harry Crane's shoulder

Nor the vertical beige coffins of the computer itself.

What had made Nick shiver was the heading at the top of a pile of dot-matrix printouts with two columns of figures headed: M rate: + sv% – sv%

M rate? sv? Memories of his briefing at Nancekuke had come shooting back to him.

Price had put them in touch. Harry was a fellow Brit and he'd invited Nick to inspect the triumph of his virtually single-handed mainframe computer installation.

Despite the chill, his pink face brimmed with enthusiasm.

'Bit of a first for this university, and she's humming. Needed some assistance in assembly from the local lads, of course. And, luckily, I've also had considerable help with the bedding-in phase from your professor. I've given him full access at night to run his own programs. Means we get to test the kit over longer periods. He insisted on confidentiality, obviously. But as you can see, the printouts are just streams of numbers from his previous research. Now that we've met, you must come around and meet Harriet. Dig up a partner and we could play doubles.'

Nick guessed it wasn't a double entendre and politely declined. He had much more on his mind than tennis.

The printouts could be construed as evidence that Laidlaw had already tested sarin vaccine on humans and measured the mortality rates. Nick's pulling out wouldn't stop the professor doing it again, but the longer he stayed, the deeper he'd be dragged in. And the more culpable he'd become.

***

NICK HAD RECEIVED AN embossed invitation card from the British embassy for the Queen's birthday party on June 16th and accepted, despite Quinlevan's admonition to stay away. Deep cover might be all very well in the short term, but he'd already been stuck in the Beiras for nine months with very little to show for it. A night out in the capital appealed; surely the very least he deserved.

He glanced up at the blue and white azulejo tiles above the entrance to the embassy and made his way to the packed rear garden. A hesitant tapping on a microphone indicated an impending speech, and he wriggled through the dated outfits and wide shoulders of the British community. Underneath an ancient olive tree, bathed in TV lights, stood an impressively large figure in kilt and tartan waistcoat.

'Good evening, ladies and gentlemen,' the ambassador began. 'By a remarkable coincidence, tonight marks the 600th anniversary of the signature of the treaty of "perpetual friendship" between England and Portugal – the oldest such treaty in the world. Like the olive tree behind me, for some years it was allowed to lie dormant, but now we can all see vivid green shoots of recovery. So I give you … the Anglo–Portuguese alliance!'

'Tosh,' Nick muttered.

A hoarse whisper came from behind.

'Is that you, Nick? I swear I'd recognise your voice anywhere.'

Aisha – whom he'd last seen in Beirut seven years earlier at the end of their shipboard affair. Aisha – who'd lodged herself in his heart. Aisha – whom he'd long given up hope of ever seeing again.

He leant forward to kiss her cheek and her deep-green eyes searched his face. As the applause for the ambassador died, she led him away from the party to a triangular grey summerhouse deep in the garden. They sat half-facing each other. The hairs on his bare forearms stood up despite the warmth of the evening. He caught a tremor in his hands.

She took both in hers, stilling them. 'I can't credit it. Mertens assured me categorically that you were dead. Executed in the naval prison in Alexandria.'

'As you can see, not the case at all. Very much alive and kicking.'

His flippancy drew a frown.

He went on more seriously. 'No thanks to your husband that I'm here, though. He visited me in jail, refused point blank to help get me released, and assaulted me in front of the guards. The only conclusion I could draw was that he'd found out about us.'

'I'm so sorry, Nick. I couldn't deny our fling when he confronted me in Beirut. He never harmed me physically, but he shut me out emotionally. It was cold, spiteful. As if I had no worth.' She lifted her hands to her chin and rested her head on them, avoiding his gaze. 'And once we moved to Portugal, matters only got worse. He distrusted me on every level and insisted on being informed in the minutest detail of what I'd done, who I'd met and where.' She looked up and she gave him a brief smile. 'Then I met Proudfoot at a dinner party. He was able to sense Mertens's mental abuse at once and moved to protect me.'

Nick, half-inebriated by her proximity, stared. 'You've just lost me completely. Mertens's behaviour doesn't surprise me in the slightest. But who on earth is Pussyfoot?'

'Proudfoot. My new husband.'

'Bit of a shocker that, Aisha. You've divorced and remarried?'

'Colonel Paul Proudfoot happens to be the military attaché at this embassy. After the divorce, Mertens got himself posted to Vietnam and has cut off all contact with me.'

Nick sighed. 'So you swapped a Belgian military attaché for a British one. No signs of learning there, my darling. I do hope he treats you better than the first one.'

Aisha drew her index finger down his forearm. 'Paul rescued me, you must understand. But I admit there may be some similarities between the two men in terms of controlling behaviour. You can make your own mind up about him when you meet in a minute or two.'

He couldn't resist. Ran his hand up inside the long wide sleeve of her bright art deco print dress.

She caught it. 'Enough, Nick. But I just can't get over meeting you again. Our brief time was very special to me.'

He gave her an abbreviated, highly edited account of his life since they'd last seen each other. Hypocrite. Someone who criticised state censorship while exercising industrial scale self-censorship.

She flicked her bag open, pulled out a visiting card and snapped the bag shut, as if putting a period on their past relationship.

'Just so you can find me if you should ever need to. Now let's go and seek out Paul in this throng.'

***

'DARLING, I'D LIKE YOU to meet Nick Hellyer, an old acquaintance from my days with Mertens.'

'Charmed, I'm sure.'

Proudfoot looked hot and uncomfortable in his full dress uniform, but Nick sensed an ice-cool mind in play.

'Funnily enough, your name's not entirely unfamiliar to me, old chap. Have heard the odd whisper about goings on in Coimbra, so perhaps we could have a quick word.'

The 'word' took place in the same grey summerhouse he'd sat in with Aisha. More like a bloody interrogation, actually. His questioner's persistence made it increasingly obvious why Quinlevan had instructed Nick to stay clear of the embassy. The attaché sat twiddling his metal spectacles, all goodwill and bonhomie on the surface. The smiler with the knife under the cloak.

Proudfoot dragged Nick to and fro over the work in the laboratory.

'Would I be right in thinking you're making substantial progress with the vaccine? And that the field trials have a high success rate?'

Nick resorted to silence and evasion.

'Your reluctance to engage directly, Dr Hellyer, disturbs me. Laidlaw's work is potentially of the greatest importance, and we all have to support the Portuguese in their struggles against the rampant communist aggression in Southern Africa. How could there possibly be any harm in a soft word in my ear?

We're on the same side, aren't we? Work for the same firm, if you understand me. HMG is super interested in what is undeniably a British first. And the product could well have multiple applications elsewhere.'

'I'm not sure how to satisfy you further, Colonel. I've told you everything I know, and I've explained the limitations of my role.'

'With respect, I find that rather hard to accept. In truth, quite impossible to do so, because I'm well aware of exactly what you are.'

***

NICK JOINED THE WINDING queue in the soft evening light, intending to thank the ambassador for a memorable evening. Instead, he received a thump on the shoulder from a short fifty-something tanned man with sharp grey eyes.

'Never forget a face. Wonder where we last ran into each other. How you doing, buddy?'

It was the first time Nick had set eyes on the man.

'Ben Levi, Israeli embassy commercial section. Let's meet up for a drink and catch up on old times. How about tomorrow? Or even tonight – I'm not going on anywhere.'

Aisha and Proudfoot swooped to his rescue and spirited him to the front of the line.

She vanished with the faintest of cheek kisses. How come she'd picked another bastard of a husband?

And an even more dangerous one.

CHAPTER 4

Coimbra, Portugal, 1 November 1973

THE MOUNTED GNR PARAMILITARIES descended on the student protestors massed outside the eight-hundred-year-old Sé Velha cathedral. Floodlights picked out the five delicate receding stone arches over the main entrance, and illuminated the advance. The horseshoes clanked and slithered on the steep cobbles, while their riders, whose long clubs dangled from their right hands, fought to control the reins with their left.

Augusta gripped Nick's upper arm tight.

She'd suggested the midnight performance of Coimbra *fados*, traditional student songs.

'All *fados* have to pass the censor, and all performances must be licensed,' she'd told him. 'Tonight's unlicensed one is a protest against last month's rigged elections. The opposition parties all withdrew immediately prior to the vote because of government suppression of any discussion of independence for the overseas provinces. In the end, all 150 seats were won by the government, which claimed a turnout of seventy per cent of the electorate. The students quite rightly don't swallow it, and neither do I.'

Guitars struck up, and the misty breath of the black-gowned

singers hung in the air as the first verse of the most-loved Coimbra *fado* echoed around the dank cathedral square.

> *Coimbra is a lesson*
> *Of dream and tradition*
> *The teacher is a song*
> *And the moon the faculty*

The Lusitanos, nostrils flared and saliva pouring from the bits in their tightly reined mouths, advanced again. Their hooves struck fire on the cobbles, and the riders' clubs swished through the air. Nick squeezed Augusta's hand and pulled her towards him.

The *fado* slowly died away, replaced by a deep chant that grew to a booming crescendo off the cathedral walls.

'*A Guar*-da *Republi*-ca-*na. A Guar*-da *Republi*-ca-*na. A Guar*-da *Republi*-ca-*na.*'

The stressed syllables rendered the chant both provocative and intimidating.

Augusta glanced at Nick. 'Taunting the GNR. Be prepared. Going to get rough now.'

From between the horses, helmeted riot police wielding short batons sprang forward and attacked the crowd, most of whom were already attempting to retreat down the narrow steps behind them. Two teams of officers worked systematically along the front row from each end and met in the middle.

Nick looked frantically over his shoulder for a way out, but they were hemmed in. He stuck his arm out, blocking the baton aimed at Augusta.

'Leave her alone,' he shouted in English.

'*Desculpe, turistos.*'

The policeman stayed his baton, and Augusta pulled Nick into the retreating throng driven by the relentless approach of the GNR.

They fled down the steep flights of steps to the lower part of the city. Nick tripped and fell. Curled into a ball and stared up as panicked students hurdled his body.

The crush eased a little, and Augusta dragged him back to his feet.

At the tram stop, Nick took stock of his filthy, torn shirt and grazed elbows. 'Heck of an evening that – such an audience response! What the hell could they do for an encore?'

'Why don't you come to a concert with us tomorrow and find out?'

***

FOUR MONTHS EARLIER, AUGUSTA had invited Nick to meet her husband. At a restaurant famous for its *frango assado* in Malaposta on the outskirts of Coimbra, he'd been greeted warmly by Captain Mario Mendes.

They'd sat on rough wooden benches, shaded from the heat of the sun by faded parasols advertising Super Bock beer. Nick, mouth half-full of blackened piri piri chicken wing, had shaken his head. 'Augusta, I can't believe it. I assumed the shared surname was a coincidence.'

'I honestly hadn't taken on board that you two had already met until he returned this time. He can't tell me everything for obvious reasons, and we've had plenty of other things to occupy ourselves with, as I'm sure you can understand.'

'Sure, but I'm just blown over. Really great to see you again, Mario. Are you back for a while now?'

'Until the next tour, that is. I'm stationed at a special-forces brigade in Santarém so I can never be quite certain what the future holds.'

'Not an easy situation for either of you.'

'You don't understand, Nick. It's not about us as individuals. The problem we face as a country is fundamental. It's basically an unwillingness to confront the reality that Portugal has been controlled by a fascist regime since Salazar took over in 1932. He died of a stroke in 1968, ironically through the collapse of a British-made deckchair.' The captain had thrown up his hands. 'I'm sure your people had nothing to do with it – we can leave collapsing furniture and exploding cigars to the Americans. Marcello Caetano, his successor, despite vaguely liberal gestures, is pressed from exactly the same mould. A dictator.'

And now here they were together again. They leant against the rear wall of the crammed upstairs hall of Ateneu, an intellectuals and workers collective, up a dank cobbled alley not far from the Sé Velha. A fug of tension hung in the air of the dimly lit, whisper-filled room.

Nick peered around. 'So damn gloomy in here. Can hardly see a thing.'

'Exactly the point, my friend,' Mario replied. 'Nor can the DGS informers – who are certainly here in numbers.'

A single spotlight illuminated the minuscule stage. Conversation ceased and an anticipatory buzz rose. Padre Francisco Fanhais, a thirty-year-old priest forbidden to hold mass because of his political views, began to sing from his most recent album, *Canções da Cidade Nova,* Songs of the New

City, accompanied only by strummed chords from his battered guitar.

Augusta glanced at Nick. 'Can you follow?'

'He's going really fast.'

'Sailor of the sea of fear, hear for an instant my secret, walker in the cold night, hear for an instant my happiness.'

Many of the lyrics were bitterly critical of the regime. Fanhais had slipped back into the country from self-imposed exile in France for this one concert, and would return there immediately after.

At the conclusion of his set, the singer raised a clenched fist, gave a low bow and vanished from the stage and the country.

Nick caught a whisper from Mario. 'Surprise wine-tasting in Sangalhos tomorrow – we'll pick you up at ten. *Hora britânica.*'

'Which means?'

'On time. As opposed to Portuguese time, which as you must have already learnt is at least half an hour later than the appointed hour.'

***

Two floors underground in the cellars of Caves Aliança in Sangalhos, a small town thirty-five kilometres north of Coimbra, they entered a simulacrum of a medieval Irish castle banqueting hall – an incongruous marketing folly from the region's largest wine producer. But a most secure venue for the day's purpose.

Three dozen officers had already taken their seats around a massive oak table where wooden platters of sliced cold roast suckling pig and baskets of bread rolls alternated. In front of each guest, one of three tall glasses had already been filled with deep-red sparkling wine.

Augusta, the only woman present, handed Nick a heavy holdall, its leather brown and faded.

Mario stood beside him. 'I've shared my belief with my colleagues that you are trustworthy and could be of service to us. A few welcome your presence, some are tolerating it, but most are hostile on the grounds of secrecy, I'm afraid. Nevertheless, you have the unique honour of being the only foreigner ever to attend a meeting of the MFA, the Movimento das Forças Armadas. One hundred and thirty-six of us got together at the Roman Temple of Diana in Évora in the Alentejo just over a month ago.'

'But why these intriguing – to say the least – meeting places?'

'You need to realise that we have no freedom of assembly in this country. Groups of any size are forbidden to get together without a permit, unless it's for social purposes. So we billed the Évora meeting as a farmhouse barbecue, featuring marinated pork with hazelnuts. Here, we're tasting the sparkling wine for which the area is justly famous.'

'And the purpose of the Évora meeting?'

'I told you about the disquiet over the wars and the fast-tracking of the milicianos. It amazes me how officers on a political spectrum from ultra-conservative to hard-line communist have become united in their aims. We've moved on from military-promotion issues to ending the wars, and quite conceivably to regime change.'

Nick crammed his mouth with suckling pig. Gold dust. 'Who's here?'

'For obvious reasons, I can't identify any of those present today. I can assure you, though, that they're drawn from all sectors of the armed forces.'

'Go on. Point out just one for me.'

'See the older grey-haired guy at the end of the table, big nose, thick eyebrows? That's Captain Otelo Saraiva de Carvalho, a paratrooper just back from Guinea, and one of our leaders. Born in Mozambique. A regular officer like me.'

Nick glanced discreetly over at the officer, whose strong hands were tearing open a huge bread roll.

'Our MFA process is very democratic and therefore inevitably drawn out – we vote on everything – so you'll have to withdraw just before our formal meeting starts. And this could, and probably will, take hours. Subsequently, we may well have a request for you.'

Nick reloaded his plate and glass, and Mario shepherded him out to a comfortable bench in the foyer. Nick sat back, finally on the trail of something significant to pass back to Quinlevan. He pulled a weighty red bound volume from Augusta's leather holdall. A folded sheet of paper poked out of the front.

> *I'd like to present our national poet – a combination of Shakespeare and Milton in our psyche. 'Os Lusíadas' by Luís Camões, published in 1572, tells the story of Vasco de Gama's discovery of India, the start of our history overseas. It may help you understand how we arrived at our current situation. I'm sure your Portuguese is up to it – 88,000 lines long, though.*

He'd only skimmed a third of the book by the time Mario returned.

'I regret that my colleagues are still suspicious of the British embassy in Lisbon, which is seen as hand in glove with the regime. So I have nothing to relate to you or to ask of you at this moment. But can I offer you a souvenir of today – a reward for your long-suffering patience.'

Mario's right foot pushed forward a cardboard carton containing a half-dozen straw-wrapped bottles of red sparkling wine.

***

NOVEMBER 5TH PROVIDED AN opportunity for Nick to deepen his relationship with the captain and his wife. On the advice of Senhor José of the Casa da Inglaterra, he took a forty-five-minute taxi ride to a run-down barn in Lousã. There he acquired five one-and-a-half-metre-long rockets. Firework displays had to be officially licensed and, unsurprisingly, illicit manufacture for clandestine shows had flourished. The red cardboard tubes of the rocket heads had been packed with the contents of emptied shotgun cartridges that lay strewn across the dirt floor among straw and chicken droppings.

Augusta and Mario arrived at sunset.

'Turn around and close your eyes,' the captain said.

A finger of fear stabbed Nick. He obeyed, anticipating the chill of a pistol nozzle on his neck. Gentle hands covered his eyes, caressed his face and slid down. Arms embraced him. He broke free.

'Patricia!'

'Don't you remember my telling you about my only friend in Coimbra?'

The four of them moved to the garden and lounged against a low-whitewashed wall.

Patricia moved closer to him. 'Augusta's unwittingly kept me up to date with your news.'

What on earth was she doing here? And how come she'd never mentioned Augusta's name? Strictly professional relations, Quinlevan had said.

'You do understand why I couldn't write,' Nick said, unable to resist adding, 'unlike Al.'

She gave him a quick squeeze. 'Enough of that. Now show us what this party's all about. I love the idea of celebrating a revolutionary.'

***

Nick released his thumbs, and the cork flew into the air, leaving a blood-red trail of bubbles in its wake.

The first rocket soared high over the centre of the city. The explosion reverberated across the Mondego valley. Their own cheers were followed by whoops from adjoining houses and balconies greeting a second and then a third rocket. Each flash illuminated the drifting white clouds of smoke from its predecessor.

Quite unlike any Guy Fawkes Night he'd ever experienced. His speculations about Patricia's presence hung like the vapour from the rockets in the moonlight, interrupted only by the roar of revving engines and the urgency of sirens. He glimpsed reflections in his neighbours' windows of blue lights from GNR vehicles pouring out of their barracks a few hundred metres away up the hill.

He turned to Mario. 'Guess they think you've already made your move.'

'We're going to be a little more subtle, don't you worry. But you can see how little it takes to spook the bastards. Best to get indoors though.'

Nick hid the remaining two rockets in the garden shed and joined the others in the flat. Augusta and Mario stayed until the GNR had returned to barracks.

***

TWO HALF-EMPTY GLASSES OF sparkling red wine stood by Nick's bedside table. He half-guiltily watched Patricia undress in the candlelight. She brushed her hair, tossed back the mane and joined him.

'Now, give me your own explosion, lover. It's been far too long for both of us.' She held up her breasts and flicked the nipples. 'Suck them … That's right. Not strong enough. Use your tongue more … Better. Much better. Both together now. Bite and chew. Yes, yes, yes.' Her pelvis ground against him, and she reached down and pulled him inside. 'Now fuck me hard … Harder. Harder. Come on, come on, you can.'

Her flailing arm caught the candle as they came violently at the same moment, and Nick lurched out of bed to catch it. He failed, but the candle doused itself anyway, spraying a line of white wax across the rug. He crawled back into bed.

'No danger. Though I wouldn't have been surprised if the GNR had come charging out again in rapid reaction to your cries.'

Patricia emptied her glass in one swig and sighed as she lay back. 'Still a star student then. But I may have to keep you up to the mark next time. Backsliders get punished.'

He lay on her shoulder. 'Tremendous to hear you mention next time. How long can you stay?'

'A week – if that's all right with you.'
'Plenty of next times then?'
'If you're up for it.'
'I'm ready now.'

***

HE RE-ARRANGED HIS TIMETABLE at the laboratory so they could make a couple of day excursions out of Coimbra. The first was by bus to the coast at Figueira da Foz. At low tide they zigzagged hand in hand across the vast expanse of beach. Nick rolled up his jeans and started to paddle, mesmerised by the invisible division where sky met sea. A larger wave drenched him and he splashed back to Patricia.

'The water's so cold.'

'What do you expect, darling? This is the Atlantic, not the Mediterranean.'

They walked for hours along the shoreline, stopping for a sand-strewn *prego* – steak sandwich – at a beach bar. Late afternoon, on the way back to the bus station, wind-blown and sunburnt, the taste of salt on their lips, they passed the Coliseu Figueirense – the bullring.

Patricia grabbed his arm and pointed to a poster. 'What luck! There's a corrida today – just starting. Shall we?'

'Not sure. I read Hemingway's *Death in the Afternoon* years ago and, to my great surprise, was fascinated and appalled in equal measure by his evocation of the moment of truth. To be frank, I don't feel any great blood lust just now. Sorry.'

'No need to worry. In contrast to those of our neighbours, Portuguese corridas are works of art. Displays of skill and courage. For a start, the bull trots out of the ring almost unscathed at the conclusion. Come on – why not give it a go?'

'Tell me why you're so keen.'

'Part of your Portuguese education. And because we don't have bullfights in Madeira – I used to watch them on TV as a teenager. Once went to one in Lisbon when I was a student.'

They walked down grey concrete steps that softened the deep-red and mustard of the steeply raked arena, and took their seats. The first bull of the day was already shaking its head and swaying its heavy neck from side to side as it peered across the smooth golden sand at a figure on horseback at the far side. Mounted on the grey pure-bred Lusitano stallion was a *cavaleiro* in a red embroidered eighteenth-century frock coat who held the reins in his left hand, and a short multicoloured stick with a sharp metal point high in his right.

'Called a *bandarilha*.'

The rider launched the horse across the arena and past the bull. Planted the *bandarilha* in its neck, turned abruptly and sped away. Two men with matador-style capes but no swords distracted the bull until the *cavaleiro* returned with the next *bandarilha*. After six passes, the rider exited the ring on his high-stepping horse, waving his circular black hat to acknowledge the cheers and loud applause. The exhausted bull remained alone in the centre.

A team of six men wearing white shirts, pink waistcoats, knee-length khaki britches and long white socks emerged from one of the barricades.

'The *forçados* – not professionals like the horseman, but local amateurs.'

The men formed a spaced-out line, one behind the other, and advanced towards the bull. The leader broke the tense silence with a cry of *Oy! Toiro!* as he raised both arms, mimicking bull horns. He edged towards the bull until he'd put a good ten metres between himself and the others. The bull snapped and charged, *bandarilhas* dangling from its neck. The lead *forçado* held his ground as the bull lowered its head, then leapt forward between and over the leather-sheathed horns.

Nick felt the force of the impact in his own belly. The momentum of the charge carried bull and man towards the rest of the team. They wrestled with the beast's shoulders, legs and tail, and brought it to the ground. A great cheer went up. The *forçados* released the bull and scattered over to hide behind the barricades.

The animal nimbly regained its footing and thundered into one of the barricades behind which the heads of its tormentors were visible. Cowbells tinkled. Three castrated old bulls trotted into the ring and gently shepherded the bull out.

Nick realised his shirt was soaked with sweat. 'Wow. And, as you said, the bull survived.'

'In the ring only, darling. Usually they're slaughtered and the meat given to the poor.'

'They can't fight again?'

'No, they've learnt too much from the encounter. A few very brave ones provide breeding stock for the next generation and live out their lives peacefully on bull ranches.'

'Is that it?'

'You mean the fate of the animals or the spectacle? This was only the first bull. There are five more to go. Can you take it?'

Nick sat back, shaken by the drama, the immediacy, the skill of the horsemanship and the courage of the men. 'Like the bull, I'm a learning animal. Never know when I might have to face one. Bring it on.'

***

ANOTHER DAY, THEY TOOK a shorter bus journey to the ruins of the Roman city at Conimbriga, only sixteen kilometres from Coimbra. At first, they had the site virtually to themselves, and Patricia proved to be a knowledgeable guide, having volunteered in excavations in her student days. She pointed ahead.

'What appears to be the outer wall is in fact a newer one that was built across the city in the fifth century when it was under attack from the barbarians. The inhabitants razed almost half their buildings to create it. In the end to no avail. The tide of history was against them.'

Could be a symbol for the Portuguese in Africa, Nick thought. However much both sides sacrificed, there could only be one conclusion.

They had tea and *pasteis de nata*, custard tarts, on the museum café terrace in the late-autumn sunshine.

'Thank you so much for bringing me here,' he said.

'Such a peaceful place now. I love the mosaics most – the preservation is incredible.'

She was right. With the covering sand expertly brushed away, they'd looked as if they'd just been laid.

What couldn't be brushed away were the implications of Laidlaw's research.

***

THE NEXT MORNING IN Golegã, a hundred kilometres south of Coimbra, Laidlaw clambered out of the cramped back seat of the dusty beige Renault R-4 that Patricia had borrowed from Augusta. He stretched his arms.

Clara had organised what the professor had dubbed the 'works outing' to the centuries-old National Horse Fair in the Ribatejo. It was the Feast of St Martin, the most important day of the fair, a traditional market at which bullfighters, the army and the GNR acquired most of their horses.

And it was Patricia's last day.

They jostled with excited family groups, officers in parade uniform and farmers in their Sunday best. Nick became immediately gripped. Like being transported back to the eighteenth century – a different world governed by different rules.

Improvised tented booths selling roast chestnuts and *água-pé*, a foretaste of the new season's red wine, ringed the sand-covered central square. Clouds of dust hung in the air as majestic thoroughbred Lusitanos high-stepped on parade. Their erect riders wore distinctive broad-brimmed black hats. A procession of open carriages, each pulled by two horses, circled. The immaculately turned-out passengers sat sideways facing each other.

They joined the queue in one of the booths, and Nick slid his arms around Patricia's waist from behind and whispered in her ear. 'Feels like a film set. The question is, my darling, are you the heroine?'

'Silly boy. We girls are going to check out the action.'

She gave him a fleeting caress, and slipped out of the packed tent with Clara, both women armed with glasses of water.

Laidlaw tossed back his tumbler of *água-pé*. Most reached his mouth; the rest dribbled over his blue-shirted belly.

'Let's have a refill and get out of this blasted crowd.'

Outside, the professor mopped his brow with a large linen handkerchief. The glass in his other hand tilted and spilled, spattering the sand with drops of blood-red wine.

'Not the ideal place to inform you, but there could be ears anywhere. Can't be too careful. The best possible news. We've finally got the all-clear for human trials in Mozambique. Almost immediately. Absolutely essential, of course, that you accompany the team – make-or-break time, you see. Now, are you in or out?'

The moment Nick had been dreading. The experiments on humans Laidlaw had done in secrecy at an unknown location were to be replicated with official approval. He couldn't go through with this. His role encompassed espionage, not complicity in mass murder. Every part of him resisted being dragged deeper into shifting quicksand, ever further away from his conscience. Yet he had his orders and couldn't deny that part of him wanted to seek out the truth. Still, it would be wrong to appear too keen.

He paused, drew a deep breath and put on a brave smile. 'In.'

'Knew I could trust you, Hellyer. Trust – now there's a word. Difficult thing, don't you see? Never can know what another's actually thinking, eh? Fancy another one while we watch the show?'

They stood shoulder to shoulder. White dust from the Lusitanos' hooves powdered their glasses. Laidlaw applauded.

'Most important project of my life. Bet everything on it. Anyway, look, here come the girls – wonder what kind of mischief they've been getting up to.'

The taller Clara limped slightly as she half-dragged a bright-eyed Patricia along behind her. Clutching paper bags of burning hot chestnuts, they navigated the crowd. Laidlaw ignored Clara, stared directly at Patricia, put his head back and raised his voice.

'Welcome back – but I can see from your face you're really worked up. Something fishy going on, is there? Is it the chestnuts or the stallions that turn you on? Or have you been trying to pump Clara about our project? If that's the case, I absolutely won't stand for it. Totally top secret.'

Clara took her glasses off and touched the glowering man's arm.

He flinched. 'Don't try and smarm me.'

'What's up with you, Professor? You're totally mistaken on this one. You know I'd never share our work with anyone outside the group. Patricia and I have just been soaking up the atmosphere and discovering that we have much more in common than we knew.'

She glanced at Patricia, who smiled back warmly.

Clara stroked Laidlaw's forearm like a mother soothing a cantankerous child. 'Just girl talk. Nothing for you to worry your head about.'

'You're extremely lucky to have such a charming colleague.' Patricia smiled at Laidlaw. 'I hardly know you, Professor, but don't spoil a great day out. I'm so grateful for your invitation to this frankly mind-blowing fair.'

Nick glimpsed a scarlet flush below the open collar of Patricia's white blouse as she bent down to reclaim her discarded paper bag.

'Shall we have a wander around the stables? Check out the horses at close quarters?'

Laidlaw shook his head, scuffing the sand with his right foot. 'Not at all sure about that, Nick. Staying on doesn't feel right somehow now. Sorry. Suddenly got a creepy feeling about this place.'

'Well,' Patricia said cheerfully, 'if you're quite sure you've had enough, why don't we return via Fátima? We could even visit the sanctuary if you'd like, although there'll almost certainly be thousands of pilgrims.'

Laidlaw's face brightened. 'Great idea – I've always wanted to go there. As a scientist, obviously I don't buy into the myth about the Virgin Mary and the children. But her message is still so valid.'

On their way back to the car, Patricia hissed in Nick's ear. 'I did not cross-question her about their work, I promise you. Yes, he sensed something in the air between Clara and me, but he got hold of completely the wrong end of the stick. Paranoid. *Cuidado!* Watch out for him.'

They skirted the parading horses at the edge of the square, and Laidlaw caught his foot on a tree root. He lurched forward, fell heavily against Patricia, propelling her into the path of a high-stepping white stallion. Nick leapt forward, grabbed her arm and dragged her back. His rapid movement spooked the horse, and it reared terrifyingly high above him, almost unseating its rider. As he dodged the thrashing hooves, Nick caught the biting slash of a whip across his face. The stallion skittered sideways towards a chestnut-stall queue. It scattered as the rider struggled with the horse. He eventually brought it under control, gave Nick and Patricia a cold stare and rejoined the parade.

Nick put his arm around Patricia as they returned to the car. She was still trembling and gave him an extra-strong squeeze.

'That shove. Deliberate.'

***

LAIDLAW'S VOICE BOOMED FROM the back seat as they approached the sanctuary in Fátima. 'Glad you survived that little mishap, Patricia, and I'm sure Nick will recover from his slight wound soon enough. Do please forgive my earlier grumpiness. Don't know what came over me. An excellent suggestion to come this way, but really no need to stop here on my account. As you said, the sanctuary's swarming with pilgrims. Just seeing it means so much to me. I do struggle with the notion of the actual apparition in 1917, but the Virgin's warning about the threat of the Bolshevik Revolution is as relevant today as then. We must all combat communism now because time is slipping through our fingers.'

Nick closed his eyes. He had sworn an oath on his knees in front of *O Magnifico* to fight that very fight. How wrong he'd been to mistake Laidlaw for a high-flying, rigorous but essentially clumsy and socially inadequate academic. The man had just revealed a mission, a goal that justified the potential horrors of his research. Yet even if Nick couldn't defeat the man's twisted logic, he might at least prevent the outcome. But only if he bided his time and swallowed his principles.

The Renault R4 wound slowly from the town centre down towards the main road, passing hundreds of pilgrims trudging in the opposite direction, bound for the shrine. Nick twisted his head to follow the progress of two elderly, dark-shawled women half-crawling up the slope. Bloodied cloths barely protected their knees. A memory flashed – the discarded bloodstained dressings in the mine crater in Tete.

Both self-inflicted wounds – this one personal and religious, the other national and political.

***

PATRICIA ENTERED THE BATHROOM as he was dressing his cheek wound with strips of Elastoplast.

He caught her expression in the mirror. 'Can you really be sure?'

'Definitely. And I think Clara would bear me out – she's by no means anyone's fool.'

'So she and Laidlaw aren't—'

'One track mind – no, of course not. Quite the opposite. You're not very observant about women, are you? She wants to fuck his brain, not his body. She's collaborating with him because he's a groundbreaking world-class scientist and she's persuaded that one day his vaccine work will be recognised. Being part of his team could dramatically improve her own career prospects.'

'Did Quinlevan send you, then? To check up on me and worm what you could out of her?'

She ignored the comment, ripped off the Elastoplast strips and redressed his wound with quiet efficiency. 'What do you think? Q has no inkling of Clara. And as for you, yes.'

***

THEY LAY ON THEIR backs, sleepless through most of the night. In the morning, Nick brought fresh rolls and coffee to bed. They made lustre-less love. Afterwards, Patricia leaned back against the bedhead.

'You can trust Augusta and Clara completely, even if you've lost your faith in me.'

Nick dropped his half-empty cup onto the bedside table. 'I truly hoped you'd come here for my sake, not because you'd been ordered by Quinlevan to sleep with me.'

She mock-punched him in the ribs. 'It's both, darling. Do try to understand.' Her lips brushed his forehead. 'Time to go.'

***

THE LITTLE TRAIN CHUGGED away from Coimbra A. Nick blew kisses and waved goodbye to both Patricia and his illusions.

The professor proved considerably more forthcoming about the arrangements for the Mozambique expedition. He and Nick would initially fly to Lourenço Marques, the capital. The Portuguese air force would subsequently airlift them to a secret location in Tete. Clara would go ahead direct with the gas and protective equipment via a military plane.

'That's a massive responsibility for her, Professor, if I may say so.'

'You may, but your observation would be completely incorrect. Clara's a damned sight tougher than you might think. You've observed her gait, I imagine. Childhood polio. Gave her an exercise drive – running every day, lifting weights. Strong as steel. Mentally and physically. You wouldn't want to mess with her, I assure you. I can rely on her totally to handle the logistics of this mission.'

Laidlaw briefed Nick on everything but one vital detail – the identity of the experimentees.

'Volunteers, I'm assured. You'll see that on the ground,' was all he would vouchsafe.

***

ON DECEMBER 2ND, MARIO dropped by late in the evening.

'Got any of that red *espumoso* from Sangalhos left? I have some important unfinished business to discuss with you.'

They sat cramped together on narrow wooden stools on Nick's bedroom balcony overlooking the Mondego valley.

'Cheers! Safer to be out in the fresh air. By the way, this has nothing to do with the incident at the horse fair – Patricia filled Augusta in about events there. Though I must say, the scar does make you look rather Prussian.'

Nick ignored the remark, not the first he'd received on similar lines.

'The reason I'm here is that a number of my fellow officers have finally come around to my view on opening an alternative means of communication with your government. In other words, going via you to London rather than through normal diplomatic channels. What would you say to a meeting with your superior on Monday week in Obidos? The aim would be to align the MFA and the UK. And for me, it represents a giant step forward. I suggest you stay at the Pousada and I'll contact you there.'

The following morning, Nick rang the London number Quinlevan had given him and demanded a crash meeting.

'Copy. Hire a car and pick me up at Lisbon Airport on the 10th.'

***

Nick squeezed his run-down, hired red Ford Escort through the gate in the high grey medieval walls and trundled over cobbles through narrow streets. He parked outside the church by the hotel. A converted thirteenth-century castle, the Pousada dominated both the town and its approaches from the sea.

Quinlevan stared up at the hotel and shook his head. 'Not sure at all whether Service Conditions Department will wear this kind of extravagance. Must be way over the subsistence allowance.'

Nick handed Quinlevan his bag, pushed down the locking button on the driver's-side door and slammed it shut. 'Shall we get together in my room at six? I can brief you fully. Going to be worth every penny, I promise.'

At the appointed hour, they sat side by side like two freshly met insecure lovers on the narrow single bed in Nick's turret room.

'Apologies for not wanting to debrief in the car, sir, but I haven't driven in yonks and needed to concentrate. Especially as we're on the wrong side of the road here. Laidlaw's building on the successful trials of his sarin vaccine on animals and will begin tests on humans in Mozambique very soon – at a secret military facility in Tete. From covert computer data I've glimpsed, this might not be the first time he's tested on humans, but for obvious reasons I've not been able to challenge him. Plus, he claims never to have done so. Most importantly, I'm down to accompany him.

'Where's he getting the gas from?'

'That's not the point, sir, if you'll forgive me. It's more about how far I can continue with this masquerade. Do you expect me to participate in the impending deaths? Become an accessory to murder?'

'Only way to stop him is to find out the truth. May all be bluff and bluster. I order you to go with him.'

'And if I don't?'

'You're the only asset we have on the inside I can trust. Well understand your reservations, of course, but from where I'm sitting, your participation's the only conceivable way forward.'

Nick sighed.

Quinlevan ignored him. 'And the gas?'

'They're making small quantities in the lab. But he's mentioned a much larger, newly-constructed production facility nearby.'

'Get even closer to him and identify the exact location.'

'Talking of staying close, sir, why on earth did you send Patricia to Coimbra? Laidlaw sniffed her out pronto. Faster than I did, to be honest.'

Quinlevan's back straightened. 'And from what she's reported back, he had a damn good try at wiping her out as well. Can't you recognise a false trail when you see one? Her actions will have unequivocally established you more firmly in Laidlaw's good books.'

'That's not the way it appears to me. And, to my mind, you're treating her with a gross lack of respect.'

'Be that as it may, it's all part of the game, my boy. Now what else? Why here?'

'A delegate from the MFA wishes to meet you this evening, conceivably with a momentous request.'

***

AFTER A STRAINED DINNER together, Nick sprawled listlessly on a lumpy nicotine-yellow sofa in the foyer, then wandered over to the open doorway by reception where Vitor, the smartly turned-out hall porter, was running fingers through his heavily oiled thick black hair as he followed the football commentary on the radio. The porter filled him in on the latest setback in the progress of Benfica to world domination.

'*Falta da luz no Estadio da Luz.*' Blackout in the Stadium of Light.

Nick peered into the gloom. No sign of a power cut, although the walls of the castle stood deep in shadow. He felt powerless. Stuck in the middle again, this time between Mario and Quinlevan.

A hiss and wave came from an indistinct figure across the square, and a hand gestured towards the entrance of one of the narrow stone staircases leading to the battlements.

He and Quinlevan climbed to the top. Mario put a finger to his lips. and beckoned for them to follow. The captain led them up a further staircase and into a small sentry tower with gun slits at the end of the battlements.

'Low voices now and I'll do the talking.'

Quinlevan characteristically ignored the direction. 'But who are you?'

Mario pointed towards the uncurtained windows of a fluorescent-lit low modern building beyond the town walls. 'Regard the Obidos Sports Club, where eighty officers from all sections of the armed forces are currently enjoying a seasonal chestnut-eating session.'

Quinlevan threw up his arms and turned to leave. Nick leaned back against the cold stone in silence. Damn the major's histrionics.

'We have neither time nor room for attitude striking,' Mario said. 'This is a formal meeting in, I admit, a somewhat unconventional location. I represent the MFA, Movimento das Forças Armadas. We would like to initiate a direct channel of communication with your government and thereby ensure your support in any eventual regime change.'

'Why on earth not go via our embassy?'

Mario glanced at Nick and shook his head. 'No, it has to be this way. We're the ones taking all the risks, not you. Your embassy is in the pocket of our government. I would be most grateful if you could relay this request for dialogue to the highest level.'

'Bit of a facer, what? I mean, how can we have confidence?'

Mario shifted his feet in the tiny space. 'That I'm speaking to you now is surely evidence of the personal trust I have in Nick and, by extension, in you and those behind you.'

'Not at all that simple, I'm afraid. In fact, dashed complicated. Her Majesty's Government may not need to be privy to the burden of what you've disclosed quite just yet. I suggest we keep this encounter strictly entre nous for the time being. If events turn out as you predict, then I can and will brief accordingly.'

Mario stamped on the stone floor. 'What on God's earth does that mean?'

'That it would be premature and inappropriate for me to offer any support at this particular moment in time. But that support might well be forthcoming if events evolve as you hope. Kindly remember that I'm a mere military intelligence officer, not the foreign minister.'

Mario flashed a smile, and his shoulders slackened. 'So the oldest ally might well turn its gaze away at the right moment.'

'You could certainly put it like that, although more official channels would almost certainly deny it.'

'I must return to the group now, you understand. And I'll only share this conversation with a select few. I'll stay in touch via Nick.'

They shook hands and Mario disappeared down the stairs.

Quinlevan stayed quiet for a few moments as the pitter-patter of footsteps dissipated, then said, '59 and 61. Previous coup attempts – both complete failures.'

'Could be different this time, sir. But as for me being the point of contact, but not via the embassy, post or telephone on your own instructions – would it be a good idea to start training carrier pigeons?'

'Very droll, but understand this: in no way do I under-estimate the value of your poison gas-intelligence and this potential coup breakthrough. But for that very reason, we have to hold you at arm's length to raise you above suspicion.'

'Don't attempt to sell me that clapped-out high-speed Morse code transmission thing again. Just about worked in Egypt over six years ago but it was highly dodgy even then.'

'No need to lose your rag, dear boy. You must place your confidence in me. On my return, I'll ensure you take delivery of three pieces of kit – the first for your safety on the African trip, the second for use in this country and the third for communications. You're already familiar with the first two; the courier will instruct you on the third. Codename: Midnight Bike Rider. Now let's get some shuteye.'

***

As the sky lightened, Nick and Quinlevan negotiated the steep hotel steps down to the Escort. Vitor led the way, having insisted on carrying their small overnight bags.

'Shit.'

Nick patted first his trouser pockets and then his jacket, peered through the car window, and clocked the keys on the passenger seat. Just where he'd dropped them the previous day when he'd pushed down the locking button and slammed the door shut. Disaster.

Quinlevan consulted his watch, tutted and shook his head. 'Perhaps I should get a taxi.'

'If I may make a suggestion, sir,' Vitor said. 'A solution can be at hand.'

He whistled. A side door banged open, and a bent, elderly, walnut-faced man in rough khaki shirt, apron and trousers emerged.

'Alberto will almost certainly be able to resolve your problem.'

Nick followed the man through the ancient blackened doors of the deserted church. Alberto crossed himself and led him up the aisle, past the white columns and blue-tiled walls and into the raised sanctuary. He pulled a dilapidated cardboard box out from under the embroidered cloth covering the altar and grinned. A gold tooth flashed.

Back at the car, Alberto used a short broad-bladed knife to lever open the rubber window seal and slid a twisted wire coat-hanger through the gap. Seconds later, he'd unhooked the locking button.

Nick held out some notes to his saviour but Vitor waved a finger.

'For many years, Alberto was one of Lisbon's most successful car thieves. Upon his retirement following his most recent release from prison, our priest agreed he could store his work tools here, providing they were used only for the common good. A question of trust.'

Trust. Nick drove his superior to the airport in silence. Whom should he trust? Quinlevan, his recruiter, boss and mentor? He had little choice in the matter, despite the obvious manipulation. Patricia, his dance partner, teacher and lover? He so wanted to but his conjectures were mired in their work/love crossover and his insecurity about how much she'd concealed or revealed. The professor, his target? Not at all, given the computer printouts, though he'd have to put on a masterly show of trusting him. Clara? Yes, certainly. Without doubt a strong woman. Patricia had vouched for her, and based on his own observations he had full confidence. Augusta? Had she deliberately obfuscated the connection between himself and Mario? He hoped not, and so wanted to give credence to her testimony. Mario? The crux of the matter was this. He had to.

The existential question, however, remained: Could he trust himself?

The major had spent much of the transfer dozing, only rousing on arrival at the airport.

'On reflection, rather regret I played it downbeat with your contact, whatever he's called. This coup could very possibly be a global game changer.'

'Mario Mendes.'

'Couldn't really get a handle on the chap, mind you. Bit of a slippery fellow. But push him along with reassurances, however worthless they may prove to be. Do keep your nose clean and come back from Tete with stunning revelations for us one way or the other. Now you're going to have to keep your eye on two balls at the same time.'

Bonecas again, but in duplicate.

***

AT THE CLOSE OF the following week's play reading in the Casa da Inglaterra, Price took Nick aside.

'I'm afraid I may have unthinkingly given your address to someone who popped in earlier. Claimed to be a friend from Cambridge but didn't leave her name. She told me the Council were funding her research into Eça de Queiroz's links with the UK. I do hope you approve.'

Nick had greatly enjoyed Queiroz's *El crimen del Padre Amaro*, but knew for a fact that its author had spent his two years in the UK in Newcastle, not Cambridge.

He arrived back home, moved a straight-backed kitchen chair beside the front door and sat in the darkness.

Mossad? The Egyptians? He wiped his clammy hands on his thighs and rested them there, trying to control his breathing.

A tentative knock came at ten. He waited. A second, more confident rap followed. He pulled the door wide open and snapped on the light, poised for combat.

And froze.

Anna. Unmistakably. She stood there, hand in mouth, red curls bouncing. They'd acted together at the Footlights in their undergraduate days and been eager fumbling first-time lovers.

'Steady on, Nick,' she squeaked. 'It's just me. Is this how you greet all your old friends?'

'So sorry, Anna. Do forgive me.' He ushered her in. 'Complete surprise. I'd been expecting a visit of a completely different kind. How lovely to see you again, sweetie.'

Her eyes flicked around the room as she perched on the edge of the small sofa. 'I know I ought to apologise for dropping in on you like this,' – her voice was pitched higher than he remembered, less throaty – 'but you did scare the fucking shit out of me just now.'

Nick poured two liberal glasses of port. Spilled drops on the carpet as he passed over her glass with a trembling hand.

Anna took a sip. 'Now, Nick, my old dear, do tell me why you lurk behind your front door in attack position. I don't recall you being the aggressive type. In fact, quite the opposite. You always came across as sweet and a little timid … as well as very lovable, of course.' She attempted and almost managed a calming smile, like some game bird poised to take to the air in a bid to escape encroaching beaters.

A late evening of mutual sharing followed. She filled him in on her Queiroz project, which was entirely believable despite his initial suspicions, and her insecure life as a researcher dependent on part-time Cambridge University teaching contracts. In return, Nick sold her a package of lies about a nervous breakdown and delusions, hinting at threats of violence and even kidnap. She silently took in all his stories, twitching nervously from time to time. Upon her departure, the air became heavy with mutual false promises of keeping in touch.

What had come over him? Was he becoming as paranoid as the professor? She'd been scared witless and had scarcely credited a word he'd uttered. And why on earth should she? Anna inhabited a different world, the one he'd left so abruptly six years earlier.

His bedside phone rang at midnight.

'Here is Yamaguchi. Just leaving the border at Guarda. See you in a few hours.'

'I beg your pardon?'

'You must remember me. Your old biker mate.'

Too many old friends, all of a sudden. But he'd most certainly never been a rocker – mods had been much more his style.

But it was midnight. And a bike rider had called him. Quinlevan's courier.

***

THE DEEP THROATY BURBLE of a Harley-Davidson woke him at four. Bloody hell, the GNR would be out again on the prowl within seconds.

Nick switched on the outside light, illuminating a heavy figure unstrapping panniers from the huge motorbike. He welcomed the broad-shouldered leather-clad biker into the flat and offered tea or coffee. The man pulled off his dark-visored helmet, shook out long black-brown streaked hair and held out a hand. 'Yamaguchi. Large brandy, please. No ice.'

Nick filled two tumblers and handed one over. 'So what are you doing here?'

'Anglo-Iberian Rally participant.' Yamaguchi pointed to the large ninety-nine in yellow on the back of his jacket.

Nick raised his glass. 'Cheers. I mean what are you really doing here?'

Yamaguchi pulled out goodies from his panniers – a familiar Walther PP semi-automatic with spare magazines and swivel ankle clip. The biker rolled Nick's right trouser leg up and strapped on the pistol.

'Thank you so much for reminding me how to do that.'

Yamaguchi ignored the sarcasm and opened a larger carefully wrapped package.

'Plessey transceiver. Two encrypted pre-set channels. Voice transmission. Rolled whip aerial mast. Stick it out of the window or, to be more discreet, throw this wire out over a tree.'

He showed Nick how to use the radio with all the patience of an adult instructing a recalcitrant child.

'Got it now? Make a test transmission, please. They'll be waiting.'

'What shall I say?'

'How about "Test"?' Yamaguchi was impassive.

Nick picked up the microphone, stretched out its curled aerial cable and tossed it out of the window. Pressed transmit and said, 'Test.'

The response was immediate. 'Test matched.'

Yamaguchi frowned. 'Matched?'

'An English cricketing reference, which would take far too long to go into now. And the third item?'

The courier's final package contained two half-kilo blocks of tightly wrapped Semtex. He helped Nick saw through the underbed floorboards, secreted the radio and plastic explosive in a cache between the joists, then rubbed dirt into the raw cuts and covered the floor with an old rag rug.

'And your next stop?'

Yamaguchi laughed for the first time. 'Nowhere – this trip only for you.'

As the rumble of the motorbike died away, Nick returned to bed, reassured that Quinlevan had been true to his word. But the pistol remained strapped to his ankle. Just in case another visitor showed up.

CHAPTER 5

Mozambique, 8 December 1973

'FIRST OF ALL, WE have an appointment in the capital.' Laidlaw wriggled his ample rump further back into the business-class seat on the TAP 747B flight from Lisbon to Lourenço Marques. 'Once that's dealt with, the Portuguese military will fly us north to conduct the experiment with their guinea pigs. Not actual pets, you understand.' He chuckled. 'And once my thesis is proved, as I'm convinced it will be, we can go into full production of the vaccine. I promise to introduce you to the new manufacturing facility first thing in the new year. Almost ready to roll, very discreet and not too far from base – you'll adore it.'

The atypical in-flight unburdening had made Nick twitchy enough; the Hotel Polana in Lourenço Marques left him in no doubt as to the power and wealth of Laidlaw's backers. The enormous three-room suite contrasted sharply with the slightly run-down single from his previous visit – extravagant art deco styling, huge slowly rotating fan in the high ceiling, and a spacious white-marble balcony that looked out over the azure Indian Ocean.

'So, who's paying for all of this, if that's not a state secret?' Nick poured coffee for the professor, who'd joined him for breakfast on the balcony.

Laidlaw dunked his roll. 'What, you mean the flight and this swanky suite?'

'The whole shebang – laboratory, equipment, factory, research staff, you and me, the lot. The university alone can't possibly be funding a project of this size and complexity. Therefore, it must be either the Portuguese military or a conglomerate.'

Laidlaw paused and inspected Nick closely, as if he were a newly-discovered botanical specimen. 'Unusual question coming from you, but I'll give you the decency of a straight answer. Yes, the funding comes from both. Although – how can I put it – another party has also expressed a not unsurprisingly keen interest in developments. Shall we go and meet them?'

***

THEY LEFT THE BLINDING sunlight and entered a small, dark, first-floor oak-panelled meeting room. Colonel Paul Proudfoot was lounging on a gilt sofa. He uncoiled himself and greeted them.

'See you've got your toy poodle with you. Though to give him credit, I couldn't squeeze anything out of the boy the first time we met.'

Laidlaw poured glasses of water. 'I need Nick to interpret for me during the experiment. It's essential that the results stand up to rigorous scientific scrutiny, and, as he'll be there anyway, I saw little point in excluding him from this meeting. We can't afford any misunderstandings on the test site, and you're very well aware that I don't speak the lingo. He's shown himself to be a highly competent interpreter. I can assure you his presence is very much in both our interests.'

The military attaché licked his lips as if he'd just swallowed a particularly fine sweetmeat and didn't want to miss any residual flavour. He reclined, arched his back, folded his hands behind his head and stuck his leather-booted right foot onto the coffee table.

'In your interest, not mine. All I require is a serviceable weapon. A world-beater. How you get there is solely your concern.'

Who did these two guys think they were? Talking over his head as if he were a child, while behaving like billy goats themselves. He loved it on one level – just the scenario that Quinlevan had engineered – but on another, dreaded where it might lead.

The poodle curled up in a ball, put a paw over its eyes and feigned sleep.

Proudfoot removed his boot from the table. 'Accept the reality of the situation, Professor. The change of UK government policy constitutes an admission that your research at Nancekuke flagrantly contravened international law. Difficult situation. My masters in the MoD, paradoxically, have long been cognisant of your work's enormous potential significance. They earnestly desire that, far from terminating your quest, you should be free to pursue it to a satisfactory conclusion. And they've succeeded in that aim because, with surprisingly little persuasion, the Portuguese government have become our proxies. You do the development for them and deliver the goods, and they get a weapon that changes the balance of power in their African wars. As a concomitant, the UK will achieve access to technology that could dramatically redraw the parameters of modern warfare.'

Laidlaw leaned forward, palms steepled like a supplicant. 'Most grateful indeed for your department's pro-activity, but I must have your word that I'll be free to publish the completed research.'

'You might not be able to immediately – I imagine you'll need further data from actual use in the field to validate it. Might be wrong – your patch, not mine. But eventually you will, and, I'm sure, to worldwide acclaim. The highlight of your illustrious career – a strong Nobel candidate. Why not?'

Laidlaw soaked up the flattery, shoulders relaxing, hands unwinding.

Proudfoot patted the gilt sofa. 'Now, come over here and guide me through the plans for the trial step by step.'

Thigh by thigh with Proudfoot, breathing heavily, Laidlaw proceeded to outline a far more detailed technical appraisal of the operation than he'd vouchsafed on the plane. Nick remained apart, propped against the panelling, studying his toecaps and playing deaf, dumb and stupid.

'Right.' Proudfoot sprang to his feet, all military action man. 'See you in the foyer in half an hour.'

***

DAMP HEAT BLASTED IN through the half-open driver's window of the dark-grey British embassy Land Rover as they sped past ramshackle huts on the roadside. Half-naked children squatted in doorways as mothers rushed to protect tin baths of freshly laundered clothes from the clouds of dust thrown up by the vehicle.

The Land Rover bypassed the passenger terminal and drove through barbed-wire gates into a military area. The sign read:

Força Aérea Portuguesa. Armed guards rigorously checked IDs, and the vehicle swung across the tarmac to a dispersal area where a dark-green FAP Dakota awaited.

At the foot of the steps at the rear of the aircraft, Captain Mario Mendes greeted them.

'I have the great honour of being your escort.'

The captain saluted Colonel Proudfoot, then bowed and shook Laidlaw's hand. He looked at Nick and raised an eyebrow.

'May I introduce Dr Hellyer, Captain. He's my interpreter.'

'So I shall test him, with your permission. *Muito prazer a conhecer pela primeira vez, Senhor Doutor.*'

'Pleased to meet you for the first time, Doctor,' Nick said.

'Perfect. He passed with flying colours. Congratulations, Professor, on your interpreter's skills. Englishmen like him are few and far between.'

Flying colours. The same words Patricia had used in a different context. Mario had gone over the top surely; Proudfoot would twig.

But he didn't.

Laidlaw clapped Nick on the back and grinned at the colonel. 'There you are, Proudfoot. The genuine article.'

The captain extended a courteous arm towards them. 'Now, would you like to board?'

They were the only passengers on the tired freighter and sat on a line of inward-facing metal seats in the bare lime-green interior. The whine of the engines became a deep *chug-chug* and then a roar. Nick's whole body vibrated, and meaningful conversation proved impossible until they'd reached cruising altitude.

Laidlaw and Proudfoot shared a solid conviction of the sanity of the madness they were engineering. But what role could Mario of all people be playing here?

Nick leaned across. 'Why's the Dak green, Captain? Aren't they usually shiny bare metal?'

'FRELIMO recently acquired Soviet surface-to-air missiles. Green's much less likely to attract their attention than silver.'

Great. The odds of being shot down en route had been marginally reduced.

***

THE FOUR-HOUR FLIGHT WAS choppy and the aircraft side-slipped on approach in case of up-coming fire. Mario offered a relieved smile as the Dakota landed and taxied along a jungle dirt strip. It settled by a wooden hut with a corrugated iron roof.

'Welcome to Tete, gentlemen.'

Proudfoot was last off the plane. 'Where are we exactly, Captain?'

'The nearest settlement is Furancungo, not far from the Zambian border. We have a battalion stationed there to catch guerrilla infiltrators, and they'll be providing the subjects for your experiment tomorrow.'

A Panhard armoured carrier bumped through thick forest to a wired compound in a large clearing. Nick stumbled out and spotted Clara dozing against two wooden crates, both arms clutching her army rucksack like a teddy bear. No business class and luxury hotels for her.

She sprang to her feet, rubbed the sleep out of her eyes and put on her glasses. 'Everything's in place, Professor. So good to see you made it safely.'

Laidlaw dabbed at a trickle of sweat on his forehead with a sodden linen handkerchief. 'Thank you so much, Clara. Can't imagine what I'd do without you.'

Mario gestured towards two camouflaged tents, explaining that Laidlaw, Nick and Proudfoot would share the larger one, while Clara would sleep in the single.

'You'll be our guests tonight in the officers' mess, but first permit me to offer you a short tour.'

In the adjacent main camp, two spindly middle-aged men were sweeping the beaten earth with twig brooms between neat rows of tents. They stepped back respectfully to allow the group to pass. Mario thanked them.

'These former terrorists deserted to us at the time of their capture. They made the right choice – secured their lives. Now you're about to meet some of those who got it drastically wrong.'

The captain marched over to a fenced-in corner of the camp where a high khaki canvas canopy tied to tree trunks shaded its shackled occupants from the sun. Dejected bootless guerrillas dressed in a ragtag of fading military camouflage uniforms lay listless on the red earth. They seemed withdrawn, perhaps conserving energy, hoping for the best, but fearing the worst. Nick empathised with them – after all, they were thinking, feeling fellow human beings who'd chosen to join the FRELIMO struggle to free their country from colonial oppression. Regardless of the means they used, the contrast between their motivation and his own was inescapable. What did he truly believe in? Whose cause was he fighting for? Even Laidlaw had a motive.

Two alert black-uniformed special group soldiers with yellow scarves and berets guarded the guerrillas.

Mario stood with hands on hips. 'Most of these men are terrorists who pretended to come over to us but subsequently either refused or failed to divulge their infiltration routes. The others have denied any FRELIMO affiliation at all, despite being captured in combat. So this is the pool in which you'll be fishing tomorrow, Professor. Now, let me lead you to supper.'

They sat at a long-benched table in the mess tent. Mario had positioned his group a little apart from the other officers. Once they'd wiped their plates clean with chunks of bread, Proudfoot, Laidlaw and Clara discussed the arrangements for the next day.

Mario nudged Nick. 'Cigar?'

'I don't.'

'You do now.'

They pushed through the mosquito netting and out into the humid night.

Nick gazed up at the starry southern African night sky, so much clearer than the hazy glimmer of London. 'What are you doing here?'

'My country or me? Or is that a philosophical question? In which case you need a priest, not a soldier.' The captain drew on his cigar. 'Overwhelmingly, the driving force for our military presence here has been economic and geo-political.'

'I meant you personally, as you're well aware.'

Mario puffed out smoke. 'Okay. The MFA are seriously concerned about your professor, and that's why I swung things in Santarém to get here. My fellow officers and I have other more urgent preoccupations at this moment, but the development of nerve gas for use in combat is something we absolutely cannot tolerate.'

'So why on earth are you facilitating this trial then?'

'I could ask you the same question. The short answer is that we have to be sure about what's going on before we can act. Or you can act on our behalf. The longer answer is that we cannot prejudice the greater goal of our movement. The involvement of your government, tacit or not, in this nerve-gas development muddies the waters.'

So Mario regarded him as the MFA's escape route from their quandary. His message: get the Brits to sort themselves out so we can focus on our own prime objective.

They returned to the smoky mess tent. Clara was surrounded by a group of shouting officers; Laidlaw and Proudfoot peered over their shoulders. Shirtsleeves rolled up and lines of sweat streaming down her cheeks, Clara was elbow-wrestling a chunky young officer. She stared at him, lips pursed, and shuddered under the pressure of his strength. But slowly, slowly, forwards and backwards, she forced his arm down. White knuckles hit the table and she released her grip. A deep sigh and a cheer came from the crowd. Clara patted the junior officer on the head with a smile, and they shook hands.

'What on earth was that all about, Mario?' Laidlaw shouted. 'She could have got seriously hurt. Can't possibly risk that.'

'Apparently, the gentleman concerned had less than positive opinions about Benfica's prospects in the next round of the Portuguese Cup. And as Clara's youngest brother's an apprentice with them, she felt obliged to challenge him. A matter of honour, so to speak.'

Nick pushed through the crowd to Clara. 'You're amazing. Where on earth do you get that strength from?'

'I've always had to strive harder than others to make up for my physical disability … school, university, you name it. I've learnt how to stand up for myself, and tonight I refused to let that boy patronise me.'

That was Clara all over. It hadn't been about football but about attitude and principle. She could teach them all a thing or two.

***

EARLY THE NEXT MORNING, Mario led them to the fenced-in corner of the compound. The shackled men were now guarded by four special forces troops. The soldiers gestured with their G-3s, and the prisoners reluctantly climbed to their feet.

'You're on the spot now, Nick,' Laidlaw said. 'Order all those who have borne arms to step forward.'

He did. No one budged, just stared straight ahead. Then three shuffled forward, heads down.

Laidlaw swivelled towards Mario. 'Not at all the cohort you promised.'

The captain gave an order to the soldiers, who raised their sub-machine guns and fired briefly in the air. The men glanced at each other, then fifteen more shuffled forward.

'Explain that we're offering them the chance of a lifetime,' Laidlaw said. 'Request their consent to take part in a scientific experiment. If they co-operate, they'll have a future with the Portuguese armed forces. No need to pass this on, but it's essential I get a dozen participants, a representative sample of age and stature.'

Nick obeyed, chilled in the tropical heat.

'Right, let's see what we've got.'

Laidlaw told Nick to order the men to line up and stand to attention.

The professor halted in front of each one as if he were inspecting a presidential guard of honour and looked them up and down. The guerrillas hung their heads. Laidlaw patrolled the line again, tapping one then another man on the shoulder and beckoning him forward until he had his twelve. His clammy fingers left sweat marks on the dust-infused uniforms.

He'd selected matching pairs – teenagers, men in their twenties, others in their thirties.

Half would die.

The guerrillas shuffled towards two small newly-erected medical tents. Each pair stepped forward; each man was directed into one of the two tents.

Sterile green cloths covered folding tables. Clara had laid out syringes in pencil-case-like black travel packs. Nick interpreted for Laidlaw, and Clara noted down the men's personal details. The subjects were then vaccinated. Those in one tent had their arms stamped with an indelible blue; the others received a red cross.

The irony of that latter mark wasn't lost on Nick.

They returned to camp, and he excused himself from supper. That night, he lay sleepless in the hot tent, running through scenario after scenario. Each one more horrific than the previous.

**

THE NEXT MORNING, A Panhard was loaded with the crate packed with kit. Clara, Laidlaw, Mario, Proudfoot and Nick climbed aboard. A Unimog followed, carrying the twelve subjects seated back to back, overseen by special forces soldiers.

They drove ten kilometres to an abandoned church. The building was partly burnt out, though the doors, roof and windows were still intact. The shackled men lurched from the Unimog, the soldiers urging them to jump and catching them as they landed on the ground. The guards hustled them into the church and roped them to what was left of the pews in the chancel. One voice began to sing; others joined in. The chorus rose – a deep chant of resistance, a FRELIMO anthem that swelled and filled the empty building.

Not a Christian hymn, but a cry for freedom.

Clara crowbarred open the crate and pulled out gas masks, protective equipment and a heavy grey cylinder of sarin, which she lugged into the church.

Laidlaw, Clara, and Proudfoot dragged on yellow capes, masks, trousers, gloves and boots. Nick hesitated, his gaze drawn to the lines of bound men, all too aware of their petrified attempts to make eye contact.

'Get on with it man,' Laidlaw bellowed to Nick. 'Time to put the gear on.'

Nick shook his head. 'Reconsider. It's not too late. We could still back out of the test, let them return to the camp. Can't you see this is total madness?'

'Reconsider what, sonny boy? You knew what we were planning, and you went right along with it. You're into this experiment up to your neck, whether you're inside or outside the church.'

Nick walked away.

'I'll deal with you later.' The professor slammed the high dark doors behind him.

***

MARIO AND HIS MEN lay flat on their backs smoking in the shade of a fruit tree fifty metres away. Nick dropped to the ground by the captain.

'Why on earth didn't I act to prevent it sooner?' He glanced at the soldiers.

'Don't worry,' Mario said, 'they don't understand English. Just think about it for a moment. How on earth could you have stopped Laidlaw?'

'Those men in the church are human beings with their own families and lives. They're not lab rats. We're both complicit in a war crime.'

Mario raised himself onto his elbows. 'You're a spy. I'm a soldier. We both have to take responsibility for our actions. But consider the broader picture. Had you acted now to curtail the experiment, you'd have blown your cover, unless you'd killed Laidlaw. And me, I'd have been court-martialled and the MFA compromised. Both of us are here to observe and report, not act. And that connivance draws us even closer together. I can assure you, based on my personal experience of African wars, far more horrific crimes have been committed.'

Nick stared at his dust-covered boots. Sullied. Filthy. As was he.

'Now you can better understand the internal forces the MFA are combating. I have no brief whatsoever for how to deal with these guerrillas who've killed and mutilated my comrades, however much I may sympathise with their libertarian aims. But I disagree profoundly with the proposed indiscriminate use of poison gas on them. And your government isn't just complicit in this project; it's actively encouraging it.'

Nick lay down beside Mario, rested his head on the hot sandy earth and closed his eyes. Images of the experimentees convulsing, collapsing, paralysed, unconscious and dying assailed his mind. Just like the piglets at Nancekuke.

A column of ants crawled up his neck and into his right ear. He sat up abruptly, and the church doors crashed open.

The professor ripped off his mask, pointed towards the survivors, and roared, 'Come and see! All blue crosses. It's conclusive! Our vaccine works. Glory!'

Nick peered into the blackened church. Corpses lay twisted on one of the pews, foam drying on their cracked lips. Some had fallen forward; others were held erect by their ropes. A voice cried out from the line of petrified, curled-up survivors.

A grim-faced young man held out his arms. 'In the name of God, please save us.'

A rhythmic groaning and wailing broke out among the others.

He should have stopped it. He could have stopped it. But he hadn't. He didn't have Mario's moral defence of fallen comrades. He had no excuse. Guilty as charged.

Clara, still in protective clothing, but with mask pulled down and pearls of sweat on her forehead, worked along the line of survivors with a flask of water. Mario ordered his men to remove the corpses. The soldiers propped their G-3s against the wall, pulled out knives and cut the restraining ropes.

Proudfoot, who'd been squatting outside the church doors, rose and grabbed one of the rifles. 'Best we have no witnesses, don't you think, professor?'

Mario barred his entry.

Proudfoot turned the gun on him with a sneer. 'I wasn't referring to your men, captain. We're both fighting on the same side. I'm about to shut the mouths of these guerrilla leftovers, and you can be my witness that I acted in self-defence.'

Laidlaw moved and stood shoulder to shoulder with Mario. 'No, no, you can't possibly. You must understand. Would make the whole experiment totally pointless. The survivors are essential for peer validation of our subsequent trial.'

'I'm not preparing a paper for an academic journal, Professor. This is a fight to the death against terrorist insurgents. And there can be only one winner.'

Proudfoot pushed Laidlaw away, twisted the captain's arm behind his back and marched him into the church. The military attaché thrust the G-3 deep into Mario's fleshy neck. 'Tell your men to drop their knives.'

Nick shadowed Proudfoot as far as the doorway. The 'we' sank leadenly into his consciousness. Confirmation of joint complicity.

Mario ordered his men to stand back. Proudfoot ranged the G-3 along the row of survivors, prolonging the moment. Savouring it. Bastard.

Only one thing to do.

Nick's hand slid down to his ankle holster.

He shot the colonel in the right buttock at a range of eight metres. The sergeant instructor at the Roman Barracks would have been proud of him.

Proudfoot screamed, swivelled, staggered over to Nick and clubbed him to the floor with the stock of the rifle. The attaché kicked the Walther away and stood over him.

Nick's vision blurred, and he fought to concentrate through the throb of agony. What the hell had he just done? Yes, he'd saved lives and should be proud. But if he submitted now, it would have been in vain. He tried to get up, but Proudfoot's boot slammed into his chest.

The assault cleared his thoughts. Shit scared, sure, but he'd done the right thing. And he'd take the consequences. He stared up along the barrel of the G-3 and mouthed, *Go on – do it.*

The colonel lifted his boot from Nick's chest and stepped back. 'At your own request then, poodle.' He looked over his shoulder at Laidlaw and Mario. 'Time for the traitor to receive his comeuppance.'

A sharp crack echoed around the church as Nick booted the colonel in the right knee. Proudfoot lost his balance. Nick scrambled to his feet and head-butted the colonel as he toppled.

When the man's head hit the tiled floor, a deep murmur from the survivors bounced off the walls of the church. Nick holstered his Walther.

Mario retrieved the G-3. 'Going to radio for medevac.'

The soldiers cut the survivors free and led them into the blinding sunshine. They returned and carried the corpses out of the church, stepping over Proudfoot's prone figure on the way.

Clara made an improvised pillow from her jacket. The colonel began to come around and she proffered him water from her flask. Proudfoot thrust her arm away and raged, threatening vengeance on each and every one of them. Clara's cry for help was answered by the soldiers, who grasped the colonel's shoulders and legs and dragged him out of the church. They laid him on his side on the hard-beaten, sand-covered ground, his head supported by Clara's jacket, and watched over him.

Nick and Laidlaw sat like mourners, side by side on a charred pew.

'I'm indebted to you, Hellyer. Never thought I'd say that.'

Nick stared at the carefully stacked pile of corpses by the doorway but said nothing.

Mario returned. 'The helicopter's on its way. It'll take the colonel to the military hospital in Tete.' He pointed out of the church doors to the survivors, who sat in a circle in the shade of a baobab tree. 'More immediately, Professor, what do you want me to do with those men?'

'Honour your promise to them, Captain. I'm sure they'll serve you well. And from a scientific point of view, I'd be extremely interested in how they do and if any side effects become apparent. So do please keep them in a discrete group … if at all possible.'

'Not my call. I'll pass on your request to the battalion commander but can't make any promises. You're an extremely odd fish, Professor, if you'll forgive me for saying so. Six men just died in your so-called experiment, yet you show no signs of remorse.'

'Don't come the wishy-washy liberal with me, Captain, if you don't mind. How many men have died at your own hands, or as a result of your commands? Dozens? Hundreds? What's the difference?'

Mario grunted. 'A huge ethical one. We're fighting a dirty war against a ruthless enemy so it's kill or be killed.'

'Look, what I've just proved is how your government can end these futile wars much more speedily, thereby saving the lives of many thousands of combatants on both sides. Just as the A-bombs at Hiroshima and Nagasaki shortened the conflict with Japan. Can you not see it in that light?'

'Conceivably, if I believed the struggle was worth winning in the first place.'

Mario turned and left. Laidlaw's promise to 'deal with him later' was forgotten it seemed.

'Won't ask where you got that gun from, but I'm glad you took him out of the frame. Bullied his way into the programme with shedloads of money. Wanted results without formal commitment. Absolutely essential to follow up the experimental subjects, so it would have been a disaster if he'd killed them. Not just a question of monitoring possible side effects. We need to know how long the immunity lasts.'

'You mean gas the same men again and see if they survive?'

'Exactly: same subjects, same procedure. But in the meantime, we can go full steam ahead with production in the lab and at the new sarin gas plant.'

The ruthless inhumanity of cold scientific logic. Nick caught a deep rumble of what could have been thunder, more likely a mine, and shivered. Although he had the information Quinlevan sought, he grasped the pew tight, steadying himself on an alternative reality train hurtling towards unseen buffers.

The clatter of an Aérospatiale Alouette III helicopter announced the arrival of the medevac team. Sergeant Para-Nurse Maria Teresa Gonçalves climbed out and introduced herself. Her camouflage uniform was half-unbuttoned, revealing a white T-shirt. Aviator sunglasses hid her eyes. Ignoring Nick and Laidlaw, she pushed the restraining soldiers away and knelt by Proudfoot.

'Deep, non-threatening flesh wound, significant blood loss and slight concussion. Hence his delirium.' She stood up and faced Nick. 'Captain Mendes has informed me that you shot him from behind. That's an unusual way of dealing with a fellow countryman, to say the least. Care to explain?'

'One of those stupid accidents – gun just went off, I'm afraid. These things can happen, you know.'

His account couldn't have sounded weaker if he'd tried.

The nurse raised her sunglasses and perched them on top of

her beret. 'Self-firing pistols, whatever next? And the neatly arranged pile of corpses outside – also an accident?'

She helped lift the wounded man on to a stretcher and Mario came over to assist.

'In a moment, Captain.' She turned to Nick and Laidlaw, and spoke in a calm, confident but cutting tone. 'I'm a nurse and I'll treat anyone, irrespective of how they've been injured or by whom. But something here stinks. Literally.'

She raised her end of the stretcher. The helicopter pilot helped strap the casualty to an outside frame and they took off in a twisting swirl of dust and leaves.

As the clatter faded, Laidlaw roused himself. 'Strong woman, that. Got to admire her. Quite wrong, though, in one detail. Nerve gas leaves no odour behind, only silent death. What she could smell were the faecal consequences.'

***

No one spoke on the return journey to the encampment. Nick's brain replayed the images of the gassed guerrillas' faces. Clara had retreated into herself, her mind no doubt reliving the same horrors. He tried to insert himself into Laidlaw's mindset, imagining an oscillation between exhilaration at the vindication of a life's work and real concerns about how the project could be driven to fruition.

Two frustrating days later, Mario returned from Tete. 'You're flying out tonight, so get your things together at once. We're going to call in at the hospital on the way to the airport. Unfortunately, I'm the bearer of very bad news.'

Laidlaw and Clara stayed in the transport while Mario ushered Nick into Tete Military Hospital. The appalling conditions were closer to World War I than the 1970s. Wounded soldiers lay on trolleys in ill-lit corridors littered with discarded bloodstained dressings and rat droppings.

The captain led him into a ward that reeked with the stench of rotting flesh and hummed with well-fed flies. Maria Teresa Gonçalves, now in a pristine white uniform, lifted a bed sheet. Proudfoot. Naked. Dead.

'My understanding is that things took a turn for the worse while I was away on other missions. His wound became badly infected, and in this climate … He suffered, but only briefly until the delirium took over, I'm told. What more can I say?'

What indeed? What could anyone say? He'd acquiesced in the gassing of the guerrillas, although he'd succeeded in preventing the slaughter of the survivors. Now he'd been the indirect cause of another death. Whichever way you looked at it, his hands were well and truly soiled.

Mario stood formally to attention at the foot of the bed. 'I will inform your embassy of this most unfortunate occurrence. They may wish to arrange repatriation of the body, since I regret that the colonel cannot accompany us on our flight this evening. Far too many formalities to complete.'

And so only Laidlaw, Mario, Clara and Nick clambered aboard the ageing FAP Boeing 707 freighter at Tete Airport. Each appropriated one of the four rows of seats at the rear and stretched out in preparation for the late-evening take-off.

***

THEIR ROUTE TOOK THEM via the Azores for refuelling and, as the 707 taxied across Lajes Field in the dawn light, Nick glimpsed an all-black unmarked B-52 on a hard standing. So the Yanks had achieved their goal.

From Lisbon Airport, an army jeep drove them back to Coimbra. Nick was dropped off first.

He opened the floorboards, pulled out the Plessey transceiver, stuck the whip aerial out of the window and sent a test transmission.

'Receiving you. Go ahead.'

'Confidential telegram for Quinlevan.'

'Copy. Continue.'

'Sarin vaccine test: positive result. Laidlaw initiating production of further serum. Also activating bulk gas facility at still unidentified location. Proudfoot dead of infected bullet wound at site of trial. Mendes from MFA our surprise liaison officer. Observed Lajes Field operational. Await instructions.'

'Received and understood. Stand by.'

The transceiver leapt back into life half an hour later. 'Reactivate for response 12.00 hours your time 24th December.'

In a week? He'd put his life at stake, nailed the bad guy and given his boss two game-changing secrets, only to be stood down like a lego soldier. An invisible hand wrung his intestines.

He got up from the bed, touched his toes, straightened and inhaled sharply. Come on, this was what he'd signed up for. No getting out of it. He took another deep breath. Nor could he put off one remaining responsibility.

'Aisha. It's me. I'm most terribly sorry. It—'

'The embassy informed me you were present at the scene.'

'I have to talk to you face to face. I can't go through what happened on the phone. Feels all wrong.'

'And I don't feel in any state to cope with you in the flesh. I'll ring you back.'

Half an hour of suspense. He fingered the card she'd given him. The phone trilled. She had one word for him.

'Come.'

***

THE ELECTRIC TRAIN TO Cascais and a short walk uphill brought him to the embassy villa. They held each other for a moment in the hall, then she gently pushed him away and led him into the lounge.

Nick hung stiffly on the edge of an easy chair. 'So how much have you been told?'

'That he suffered a bullet wound while on operations in Tete. That they evacuated him by helicopter to hospital. That he died there. Now give me the real story. Tell me exactly what happened.'

But which version? Proudfoot had shot himself. Or the gun had gone off by accident as Nick had told the para-nurse. Or guerrillas had ambushed the colonel. Or one of the gas-experiment survivors had grabbed a gun. Or it had all been a spoof to enable Proudfoot to lead a new life in Johannesburg under an assumed name …

Or the truth.

'We went there as part of an Anglo–Portuguese trial of a nerve-gas vaccine on humans. The concept was beyond appalling, and I take full responsibility for my own limited participation … something I will always regret. Six of the experimentees died, and your husband proposed to eliminate the surviving subjects to remove evidence. I could see no other option than to plug him in the arse to prevent the slaughter. Softest part of the body, and the shot hit far away from his gonads. Well-chosen spot and not dangerous. A flesh wound that prevented him from committing murder.'

'But apparently this flesh wound turned out to be fatal.'

'Yes, he developed a severe infection – if you want me to, I can describe the catastrophically poor hygiene in that hospital. I admit that he died as a result of my action, but most certainly not from my intention. I could have shot him clean dead. Easily. And rightly so in the cause of saving further lives. But I chose not to. You must understand that your husband showed no compunction whatsoever in his intention to murder the surviving men. A highly competent nurse in the hospital in Tete showed me his body, so I can assure you it was indeed his.'

'Thank you. How much I choose to believe is my own concern. It matters little whether I think you're shooting a line or not. The embassy has informed me that they'll repatriate his body. But where to? I have no home in the UK, and when we got married, he told me he had no living family.'

'Let him rest where he fell, Aisha.'

'I suppose you're right. I don't have the slightest idea what to do with myself. Going back to the Lebanon doesn't appeal. And as for living in Britain, for what purpose? I have to move out of this place soon to make way for new occupants. The embassy tells me I'll eventually receive some kind of widow's pension.'

Nick sat next to her and stroked her hand. The gesture was as much to soothe his inner turmoil as to comfort her. He mustn't do it, mustn't say it. Wrong on so many levels. But he made the offer. More out of guilt and pity than love.

'Why not come and stay with me for a bit? Let things settle. We could learn to get along.'

Aisha closed her eyes. A half-smile flickered across her face and vanished. She pushed his hand away and rescued him from himself.

'My first husband correctly identified you as a spy. And you've just as good as admitted that you killed my second. Why on earth should I move in with you? No. You can stay tonight, of course, but nothing more. The first train back to Cais do Sodré in Lisbon leaves at five thirty.'

***

IN THE EARLY MORNING, they drank freshly squeezed orange juice and bitter black coffee in the small blue-tiled kitchen. No promises, but a strong warm handhold over the cracked yellow Formica table.

'Now just leave,' she said. 'I simply can't deal with you. Go.'

So he did. Lineside telegraph posts flickered through the window of the rain-spattered train to Coimbra, turning the scene into a jerky black-and-white movie. The repetition was almost hypnotic – frames spooling blurred images of academic, spy, lover, killer, academic, spy, lover, killer …

***

LAIDLAW SUMMONED HIM. 'I have much to thank you for. Haven't told you the half of it. Our late lamented friend was blackmailing me, using past allegations to force me to share the experimental results.'

Nick eked out the subsequent silence until Laidlaw broke.

'Years ago, a trainee colleague claimed I'd sexually assaulted her. Nothing came of it, but once Proudfoot had dredged the affair up again, he had me pincered. So I'm delighted that as a direct result of your decisive action my allegiance can now be to the Portuguese state only. I'll induct you into the new manufacturing facility in the new year – almost complete and ready to go.'

A turn-of-the-year gift for Quinlevan.

His own Christmas surprise came rather earlier.

CHAPTER 6

Coimbra, Portugal, 24 December 1973

T HE HAMMERING ON HIS door jerked him awake at four in the morning. He pulled the Walther from under his pillow, but thought better of it and put the gun in the hiding place under the bed.

The banging resumed. Could be anything. A fire? Burglars didn't usually signal their approach.

Mouth dry, he wrapped himself in a sheet and crept along the dark landing towards the vibrating door.

It crashed open. Head pulsing, chest throbbing, he raised his arms and tensed for combat. The sheet fell to the floor.

Loud guffaws came from his uninvited guests who leant back against the doorjamb on the well-lit landing. Two smartly suited, fit-looking middle-aged men. DGS agents without a doubt. The taller man bent down and lazily flicked wood splinters from his trouser leg. He straightened and pulled off his kid gloves.

'Dr Hellyer, feel free to protect your modesty.'

Nick bent to retrieve the sheet, and the tall agent whipped him across the cheeks with the gloves. Nick caught a whiff of sandalwood. Must be the guy's preferred cologne. He focused on the fragrance, let it move him into a pain-free olfactory universe.

So they'd caught up with him. Not an ideal place to be. The hot blood drained from his head, replaced by an icy calm. This would be a mental as well as physical battle.

The other DGS agent pushed past them and started to poke around in his drawers and shelves, his manner desultory, almost bored.

Nick stared at the tall agent's face and was momentarily distracted by the extravagance of his black eyebrows.

'I can see you've already made yourselves at home. How can I help you?'

'We've been keeping a close eye on you, *Senhor Doutor*. You are not who you pretend to be.'

The agent gave him an open-handed slap, spun him around, thrust him into the kitchen and cuffed his wrists behind him.

Nick sat upright on the wooden chair, naked and defence-less, shoulders strained back.

He stared up into the man's face. 'What do you want from me? If you're thieves, I've got no money here. And there's nothing else to steal apart from my clothes.'

'No, my disingenuous friend,' the intruder growled. 'Information, not money or valuables.'

'I haven't the faintest idea what you're getting at.'

'Oh, yes, you surely have.'

Nick tensed his abdominal muscles as the agent tele-graphed a blow to his belly. And while his roar had made more of the pain than was the reality, his stomach still hurt like buggery.

Eyebrows laughed. 'Just a taste of what's to come. In fact, we're going to take you apart – very slowly – until you admit your true identity and purpose.'

Mind over matter. Ignore the present. Who had snitched on him? Surely not Mario or Augusta. Laidlaw? Clara? No. Proudfoot before he died? Yes. He drifted off into further fruitless speculation. Anything rather than acknowledging his dread of the next assault.

The DGS agent hurtled him back to the real world with a stinging belt across the face from his kid gloves.

'Pay attention, *Senhor Doutor*. We've got all night, and then the next day. And unless you open up, all those that follow.'

As the interrogation progressed, it dawned on Nick that the DGS operatives had no clear idea what they were looking for. No inkling of the innocent though potentially incriminating rockets hidden in the garden shed, or the transceiver, gun and plastic explosives nestling under the rug beneath his bed. It was a fishing expedition, and he refused to take their bait. Instead, he repeatedly queried their presence, admitted nothing and referred them to the university, the laboratory, the embassy and the British Council.

The questioning took place in Portuguese – his attempted plea of partial incomprehension was met with a blunt finger jerked in the direction of the open copy of *Os Lusíadas* dominating his tiny coffee table.

The agents were conscientious and persistent in their physical assaults and mental intimidation. But he'd suffered worse at other hands and worked to separate his mind from the pain. The worst thing would be to nourish a desire for revenge, so he rolled with the punches as best he could. His time for settling scores might or might not come.

***

LEAVING BEHIND NOTHING BUT threats, the DGS men departed empty-handed in the blue-grey dawn with the clang of the first tram.

Despite the failed outcome of their visit, the agents had turned him into soiled goods in the eyes of the Portuguese secret state, Nick had no doubt. He made a half-hearted attempt to tidy up and brewed a restorative cup of tea before collapsing on the bed beside the transceiver.

***

HE WOKE WITH A jerk, spilling cold tea onto the green-and-black-checked counterpane. The transceiver had sprung into life promptly at midday.

'We'll send you support to destroy the main gas-production site as soon as you confirm the location.' No preliminaries from Quinlevan. 'Absolutely no need to accept responsibility for the collateral damage in Tete.'

'I ought to inform you that I've just had a night-time visit from the DGS – bit of a fishing expedition. No real harm done. But they left their mark on me and I'm most definitely on their radar.'

'You well know how to watch your back, so do so. I have complete faith in you. Over and out.'

Well, bloody hell. Thanks for the sympathy and the Christmas greetings. As usual, truth and emotion had proved to be strangers to the major.

***

THAT EVENING, AT THE Mendes's apartment, he ate *Bacal-hau da Consoada*, salted dried cod with potatoes, cabbage and boiled eggs, a Christmas Eve peasant dish courtesy of Mario's grandmother. Over coffee, Augusta mentioned the visit to Coimbra of the director Bill Gaskill from the Royal Court Theatre. 'End of January. Might well stir a few things up.'

Nick leaned over the low glass-topped coffee table and melodramatically swept off the dark glasses he'd worn to hide the worst of his bruises.

'Talking of stirring things up, I spent a considerable part of the early morning entertaining a pair of uninvited DGS agents.'

Silence. A coffee cup pushed away and a hard stare.

'Could hardly miss your injuries but didn't want to enquire. How much intelligence do you think they have on us?' Mario's usually expressive face appeared untypically blank.

'Nothing at all about the MFA as far as I could tell. That didn't seem to be the angle. But they're well aware of the experiment in Mozambique, and of Proudfoot's demise.'

'Yes, the DGS have always had a substantial footprint there through their special forces. Did they grill you about Laidlaw's research project?'

Nick shrugged. 'I played broken record about being a mere teacher and translator. But given their questions, I'm convinced they know what's going on in the laboratory. Probably considerably more than I do.'

'But the overarching question is whether you feel you're compromised.'

Another shrug. 'By far the best to assume so. From the little they let slip, it's hard to guess how long they've been on my tail. Although I've got a damn good idea about who tipped them off. Proudfoot.'

'So kindly tell me why you shot your compatriot. It can hardly be on the basis of that suspicion.'

'For Christ's sake, Mario, you know exactly what happened. You witnessed it. No way could I allow him to massacre the survivors. Not because of Laidlaw's bizarre wish to replicate the experiment, but because six of the poor buggers had already died. For what purpose?'

'I'm afraid that's not a proper answer to my question. Let me put it another way. Did you shoot him under orders? Otherwise, why were you bearing a weapon?'

'To defend myself. And, anyway, you or I could well have turned out to be the next victims. Further inconvenient witnesses. Let's stop pussyfooting about. What do you and the MFA want?'

'Sabotage the sarin factory, eliminate Laidlaw and get Her Majesty's Government to support the new regime. End of story.'

'I'll be delighted to pass on your requests. However, there's a catch, because funnily enough, I picked up a new Portuguese expression the other day: *Fazer coisas para ingles ver*. Doing things for the English to see. Does that apply to the MFA's relationship with the UK? No doubt a relic of our old alliance. All smoke and mirrors but no real substance.'

Mario ran his hand over his brow and looked Nick straight in the eyes. 'No, we're not putting on a show, if that's what you mean. But I will admit that it could be a few months yet until things come to a head.'

Nick sighed.

Augusta brought in plates of homemade *bolo rei*, Christmas cake with nuts and crystalised fruit, and broke the heavy silence by putting on an LP.

'A test of your listening skills, Nick. Do you recognise where these lyrics come from and who the singer is?'

He listened for a moment.

'Here's a clue,' she said, and scribbled a translation of the opening lines: *The times they are a-changing, as do our desires. Changing our being, changing our trust. The whole world's a flux of change.*

Nick laughed. 'Don't need it. The singer's José Mário Branco and I've got the album – startling black-and-white cover with an eye in the middle. But I hadn't realised the lyrics were by Camões until you lent me *Os Lusíadas*.'

'Full marks. And this song describes exactly where Mario and I find ourselves at this moment.'

***

NICK RESUMED WORK AT the laboratory on Wednesday 2nd January, and Laidlaw honoured his promise to introduce him to the production facility.

Clara drove them out of Coimbra on the winding road to Lousã. He shivered with recognition as she turned off onto the cart track that ran towards the old wooden barn where he'd acquired his rockets. Surreal. But they sped past the barn and halted a kilometre further along by a newly-completed single-storey concrete and raw-red brick structure. The sides were windowless, but there were skylights in the roof and tall windows at each end. A shiny steel chimney reflected the grey-pink clay roof tiles of the surrounding crumbling stone farm cottages.

Laidlaw hopped in clumsy excitement, waving a bunch of keys. He thrust forward. 'Go in, go in. Production hasn't started yet so we've got my baby all to ourselves.'

Clara, clearly on top of every technical detail, gave Nick a whistle-stop tour of the glistening hi-tech facility. The interlacing pipes and the storage tanks, the size and shape of a household hot-water cylinder … all of it was familiar. Yet the setup marked a whole step-change from Nancekuke's sixties technology, which had featured patterns of rust, evident welding fixes and worrying, deeply ingrained stains on the concrete floor as a result of leaks. Here, though, the sun shafted through the skylights and bounced off the stainless-steel equipment. This plant was state of the art. Oozed sterility. And it was all too ready to be fired up.

If the intention had been to impress him, it had more than succeeded.

'Incredible how you managed to create all this in such a short time frame. And in total secrecy.'

'Yes, you've nailed it, Hellyer. Most perspicacious of you. Looks like any small industrial unit. No fences or guards. Their presence would only draw unwanted attention. No need for them out here anyway.'

'You've really worked this through, sir. I'm full of admiration, and grateful to you for sharing it with me.'

While Laidlaw soaked up the adulation, Nick took mental measurements – positions, distances, levels, entrances and exits, weaknesses and attack points.

'We'll be able to manufacture at least thirty litres a day initially. Then we can increase volume – far more than the Portuguese could possibly need at this moment. But, as you're aware, we still have a strong potential purchaser in the UK. Our allies across the pond have been putting out extremely positive feelers, and there have been some fruitful contacts with a certain southern African country – regular prior customers of our Nancekuke CS gas for deployment in their townships.'

Sunshine from the tall window at the end of the building caught Laidlaw's hair, setting it ablaze. Nick smiled and nodded to the professor – a tribute to the man's appalling ambitions and to himself, because a straightforward solution to his problem had become screamingly clear. All he had to do was watch and wait for instructions.

***

ON THE EVENING OF the last day of January, a tall man in a heavy green Loden overcoat and a black Homburg strode into the ground-floor meeting room of the Casa da Inglaterra. The eager buzz of student conversation in the packed house dampened to a whisper.

Bill Gaskill carefully folded his coat over a high stool, cast his hat on top of it, threw a few pages of notes onto the minuscule lectern, and commenced.

'Brecht's *Caucasian Chalk Circle*, which I once had the great privilege of directing, can lead us to insightful conclusions, not only about society in general, but also about ourselves as individuals.'

The dull-grey double entrance doors flew open and a three-man film crew jostled past Augusta and Nick, who stood at the rear beside racks of dripping umbrellas. The powerful camera light drew shadowy silhouettes on the walls as it panned across the audience, many of whom had quickly donned hats and out-of-season sunglasses. Others held up newspapers in front of their faces.

'Bit of a coup for Price,' Nick whispered. 'Media exposure like this should go down well in London.'

'Don't get too excited, my gullible friend – this isn't going to be broadcast on local TV. These bastards are from the DGS, recycling an old trick of theirs to record who's present.'

Once the film crew had departed, newspapers descended and hats and sunglasses returned to bags and pockets.

Gaskill winked at his audience. 'Back to Brecht then, following a scene he might have recognised and relished.'

A roar of laughter and a wave of applause filled the room.

**

LATER, SHELTERING IN THE Praça da República café from the teeming rain, Augusta handed Nick a small brown paper parcel neatly tied with a green string bow.

'A late New Year's present from Mario and me.'

He unwrapped the gift: *Portugal e o futuro – Portugal and the Future –* by António de Spínola, a general best known for combating the insurgency in Portuguese Guinea.

'Thank you so much, Augusta. A lovely surprise. But you must have had a reason for choosing this particular title.'

'We most certainly did. The book itself won't be published until late February, so what you hold in your hands is the advance proofs. You'll form your own opinion, but Mario and I think it's explosive. Read, mark, inwardly digest and feel free to share as much of the content as you wish with your superiors.'

Spínola's book proved to be a grenade lobbed into the heart of Caetano's corporate state philosophy: 'To want to win a war of subversion by means of a military solution is to accept defeat in advance unless one possesses unlimited capacity to prolong the war indefinitely, turning it into an institution. Is that our case? Obviously not.'

Nick read through the night. How long could the centre hold? Something had to give.

He sent Quinlevan a lengthy précis, together with news that Laidlaw planned to start gas and vaccine production at the end of February.

Then an urgent request came through from Mario wanting a meeting near Lisbon on March 5th. Nick forwarded the message, and transmitted his own response: *What's being planned there is a* coup d'état, *a* putsch. *You must come to Lisbon.*

***

ON MARCH 5TH, NICK met Quinlevan at the airport. A taxi drove them to Cascais, thirty kilometres away, their destination a substantial darkened rococo villa set deep in its own grounds. As the cab scrunched back down the gravel drive, Nick yanked on an elaborate copper ring chain, eliciting a mighty peal. Startled rooks cried as they took to the air, only to return to their roosts in the tall eucalyptus trees.

A pinprick of red etched concentric circles in the blackness by the side of the villa.

Mario, cigar in hand and jacket over his shoulders, greeted them warmly.

'Shall we take a stroll? Our architect friend, whose villa this is, has hosted 176 MFA officers today and quite understandably has had quite enough of visitors. Furthermore, what we have to exchange may be better done in the fresh air.' Mario took Quinlevan's arm. 'You're well aware of my identity, so may I enquire about yours?'

'Major Patrick Quinlevan, British Military Intelligence.'

'So you outrank me, a mere captain.'

'As I understand from Nick, "mere" captains are about to change a regime.'

Mario dropped his cigar and stubbed it out with a turn of his heel. 'That is exactly what we're going to do. Today we adopted a slogan: *O MFA está com o povo e o povo está com o MFA*. The MFA is with the people. The people are with the MFA.'

'Fine words, Captain, but how soon is the action going to start? Without a lot more detail, I cannot recommend supporting you at this stage, I'm afraid.'

'But what's your view on Professor Laidlaw's proposed deployment of sarin? Surely opposition to the use of chemical weapons in the African conflict is something we have in common.'

'You're spot on there. But it'll take Laidlaw time to build up a stockpile of gas and ship it, quite apart from organising the vaccination of the troops prior to deployment. I reckon a month, minimum. And I can assure you categorically that we'll have dealt with this problem well before then. Unless you've already done so.'

Mario shook his head. 'Not good enough. It's vital to us that you take the action. There's no way I could lead my men in an assault on a quasi-governmental installation at this delicate stage.'

'Interesting, although you're planning an attack on the government itself.'

'That's the whole point, although I admit there are contradictions. And the professor? Will you also take care of him?'

Quinlevan's grin became even more foxy than usual. 'He's a British national, so that's up to us. As is the timing.'

'We do very much appreciate both your coming and the assurances you've given today, and we'll stay in close touch via Nick. It may not be apparent from your perspective, but from ours, things are moving precipitately, and we rely heavily on your indications of eventual support.'

Quinlevan and Nick negotiated the gravel drive in the darkness and headed downhill towards the railway station. The narrow road took them past Aisha's villa, and Nick glimpsed a crack of light. He paused and squatted to retie a non-existent loose shoelace, then put his head in his hands.

'You all right, Nick? Hard to see in this light, but you did look a bit peaky to me earlier on.'

He straightened and dredged up a handful of coins. 'You go on ahead, sir. Just need a breather and I'll be fine. Plenty of trains. Ticket machines at the entrance, so nice and easy. Hotel's across the road from the terminus.'

'Suit yourself. See you in the morning, no doubt.'

***

NICK'S TAPPED TENTATIVELY ON Aisha's front door. No response. He peered through the triangles of a multicoloured lead-glazed side window and distinguished the outlines of four suitcases. He rapped on the window and a figure came into the hall, face sallow in the yellow glass.

Aisha half-opened the door and peered around. 'What on earth are you doing here?'

'Would take too long to explain. But looks like I'm just in the nick of time.'

She gave a weak grin and pulled her dressing gown tighter across her chest. 'Bad pun, my dear, and not exactly the ideal moment for a laugh. Yes, I'm leaving first thing in the morning for Beirut – it tastes like defeat, in truth I've nowhere else to go. But do come in now you're here. Can hardly turn you away, can I? Let's have a proper farewell drink together. And don't think I'm going to let you wriggle out of a decent explanation for this intrusion.'

She plonked a half-empty bottle of Hennessy VSOP on the lounge table with two moulded kitchen glasses. 'Last of the diplomatic booze. Now tell me.'

They sat together on the sofa while Nick spun a tissue of lies to explain his presence and she half-heartedly pretended to accept them. Meanwhile, another more physical conversation was taking place. Hands clashed and thighs touched as they put down their drinks. The sensation was electric, and she must have sensed it too because they both shuffled away from each other. She flicked her hair back, looked down and then sideways at him. He stroked the inside of her left wrist and caressed the nape of her neck with his forefinger. A long, long pause followed and then, avoiding eye contact, she took his hand and led him upstairs.

***

NICK FLOATED IN A sea of post-coital contentment. Aisha. So tender, so loving. She brought out the more sensitive side of his being. Unlike Patricia, whose lovemaking had turned on his wilder side, though she'd as good as told him that she'd shagged him partly on orders. Could he live with Aisha? And if so, where? Beirut? The Lebanon? Why not? The shadow of Mossad flickered a warning, but perhaps they'd never find him there. Nor would the department. A fresh start, one he'd have chosen.

He rolled his head, nuzzling her firm breasts. At peace, in fantasy.

Aisha ambushed him. 'Good to have a proper ending, isn't it? But now I'm really afraid it's time for you to get your skates on.'

Dashed back to reality, like something discarded from the locked suitcases downstairs. He gave her a chaste farewell kiss on the forehead.

***

'CAUGHT SOMETHING?' QUINLEVAN REMARKED on the way to the airport.

'Think it's called Portuguese flu, sir. Rapid onset.'

'Unlike Portuguese revolutions, then.'

Quinlevan had enjoyed his little joke but the major would turn out to be entirely wrong.

***

NICK UPDATED LONDON REGULARLY every night via the transceiver, relaying information from Mario as well as what he could glean by scouring the heavily-censored newspapers. The weekly *Expresso* was a more outspoken exception.

8 March: four MFA officers posted overseas and two more arrested.

14 March: Caetano reads *Portugal e o futuro* and sacks Spínola.

16 March: Fifth Infantry Battalion. Revolt at Caldas da Rainha, eighty kilometres north of Lisbon. Two hundred soldiers, led by a major and captain, imprison their commanders at 3 a.m. and set out in a ten-armoured-vehicle convoy for Lisbon. Ten kilometres from the capital, combined Seventh Cavalry and Republican Guard units halt them. On return to barracks, all would-be rebels are held by the DGS.

18 March: Inflation thirty per cent. Illegal strikes widespread.

30 March: Laidlaw predicts first gas and vaccine shipment to Mozambique on 21 April. Facility now working seven-day shifts.

The communications traffic remained one way, Nick's only feedback *Copy* at the end of each transmission. It seemed to him that the failed coup attempt had reinforced London's view of the MFA as another busted flush.

An incoming message marked top urgent proved him wrong.

8 April: Destroy the sarin production facility before shipping-capable. Sending operative to assist. Can see no immediate need to act on the laboratory. Vaccine valueless without gas. Acknowledge receipt. Quinlevan.

***

PATRICIA KNOCKED ON HIS door late in the evening of the 21st, a shiny white plastic TAP flight bag slung over her shoulder and a hired green Fiat at the kerb.

'Just to be clear, I've still only got one bed and the cupboard's almost bare. But the essentials are sound – wine and olives aplenty. And me.'

Nick failed to hide his delight; the 'support' could have been Yamaguchi.

She laughed, flinging her bag onto the foot of the stairs. 'Lead me to it.'

He took her into the lounge and poured her a glass of red. She gulped it and riffled through her heavy mane of hair. Nick's tension started to ebb. The curve of her eyebrows, those laughter lines … desire for her flooded back.

'Well, my always surprising girl, at least you're open about who sent you this time.'

She held her glass out for a refill. 'We're to do the job tomorrow but without loss of life, which means waiting until the technicians have left the plant. Brief me on the plan – assuming you've got one. Though knowing you, I'm sure you've come up with an innovative solution.'

'Off the wall might be a better description, but it'll work. Remember Guy Fawkes Night? I've still got two rockets and have been sent a kilo of Semtex.'

'Homemade rockets? You're having me on. Is Q aware of this?'

'What do you think? Anyway, he's a results, not a details man. Those rockets will be more than powerful enough to set off the Semtex. No need for separate detonators, or for us to be anywhere near the building. Which means we can avoid detection and the subsequent inferno.'

'I never had you figured as an explosives expert.'

'There you go. Dynamite in all fields. Shall we get going?'

***

THEY SQUATTED ON HIS bedroom floor like two grown-up children playing with wooden bricks and plasticene. He'd already extracted the rockets from the shed and the blocks of Semtex from the cache under his bed. Now came the painstaking work – cutting and taping strips of the plastic explosive around the rockets.

Late afternoon the following day, Patricia drove them to Lousã. They scrambled up the hill and through the trees and took up position. In the valley below, plumes of steam from the stainless-steel chimney hung in the air over the gas facility.

Patricia peered through bracken. 'Looks more like a jam factory than anything. Entirely innocent.'

'Check out the windows at each end. The closest to us is production, the other end chemical storage. All we have to do is hit both. Once the temperature inside gets high enough, the canisters of liquid sarin will explode and the gas will be incinerated. Even if some of it escapes, convection from the blaze will carry it high into the atmosphere where it'll disperse.'

'So no risk to the good people of Lousã, or indeed ourselves?'

'None at all.'

'I believe you, darling, though thousands wouldn't. Could go spectacularly wrong.'

'Yes. But it won't.'

They waited, lying side by side, arms over each other's shoulders.

Patricia broke the tension. 'Look. Lights out down there.'

Nick pulled a black woollen balaclava from his pocket and passed it her. She pushed aside the bracken, knelt facing the rear window, and raised a pipe that Nick had repurposed from the old barn's chicken run to her shoulder.

There was a rustle as he inserted the stem of the rocket. He held her shoulders with both hands and twisted her a little to the right.

'Now don't budge a millimetre, my human rocket launching platform. We're all lined up.'

Patricia lowered her head and Nick struck a long match. It flashed and the rocket ignited, singeing the balaclava. The projectile smashed through the rear window and the sky lit up. They raced over to the next vantage point in line with the other end of the facility. The second rocket blasted through the front window. *Thud thud thud.* The building rocked and the windows shattered, belching flames and black smoke into the air.

They held each other for a moment, the explosion shuddering through their bodies – or was it triumph? – then slithered back down to the Fiat and departed the town at speed. A *Bombeiros Voluntários* fire engine passed them, heading into Lousã. An unmarked police car with blue flashing lights on its dashboard followed seconds later.

Nick stiffened, and Patricia glanced at him.

'*Calma e paciência.* Everything's going to be okay.'

She hit the brakes and swerved the Fiat onto a grass verge. Waited until the oncoming vehicle had passed them, then pulled out. The rest of the drive back to Coimbra was more sedate.

Nick sat twisted sideways in the front seat, arms crossed over his chest. Done. Over. Mission accomplished.

***

SHE'D DROPPED HIM OFF at home so he could make a transmission to London while she drove up to Mario's to brief him on the attack. He heard the Fiat pull up and opened the door for her.

'He wasn't there,' she said. 'But Augusta and I have agreed

to meet in the café in the Praça da República before I return to Funchal. Your favourite trysting place, she told me.'

'Hardly trysting. Just good friends.' No way was he rising to that bait.

That night, Nick tossed and turned to the rhythm of Patricia's gentle snoring, a demented anxiety overwhelming even his desire for her. Nothing at all about Lousã on the local radio and the TV news. No response from London. No phone calls. If he hadn't been shown around the building, he could almost have been persuaded that what he'd just blown up had indeed been a jam factory. Massive anti-climax.

He lay stiff on his back, arms by his sides, almost to attention. So what in the end was the point of it all – the sabotage, his role, his relationship with Patricia? Makeshift? Useful for the day and the job, but then what? He synchronised his breathing with hers and eventually drifted off.

***

NICK RANG IN SICK – it would be prudent to play truant from the laboratory for a day. Patricia drove them up to the Serra da Estrela, the highest range of mountains in Portugal. He dozed in the front passenger seat.

She nudged him as they cleared the tree line. 'Wake up and take in a timeless landscape. Do so hope you'll love it. For me, being up here puts my life into perspective. Which I think is just what you need at this particular juncture. Years ago, I came up in a creaky old minibus with a student hiking group. We stayed in a freezing, isolated farmhouse and lay fully clothed, huddled together between the loft rafters. Couldn't sleep a wink because of the scurrying rats.'

'Just my cup of tea then.'

'Enough of that, Mr Grumpy. Behave yourself. And for goodness' sake, relax. What's done is done. We're here to take our minds off all that.'

She parked by a low stone-and-slate building set just below a ridge in a desolate landscape. The sky had darkened and a sheepdog hunkered down by a large flock of tethered ewes in the biting wind.

Inside the restaurant, an ageing shepherd in a faded cloak and woollen hat with earflaps was mopping up the remains of an earthenware bowl of soup with a chunk of *broa de milho*, dark rye bread.

They sat on a bench at a corner table enclosed on two sides by roughly hewn stone walls and slurped from bowls of coarsely chopped cabbage soup dressed with pools of dark-green olive oil.

The shepherd polished off a massive portion of lamb stew and looked up. The cook replaced his plate with another bowl of steaming soup and wiped his hands down the front of a stained grey woollen jumper.

Patricia poked Nick. 'Don't stare. He'll be out all night in the cold with his flock.'

After lunch, they strolled hand in hand along a Roman road edged with dark-green moss, ash-grey lichen and vivid spring wildflowers. Intermittent sunshine splashed the well-trodden stones. But, despite Patricia's best efforts, Nick experienced no uplift from the scenery. Instead, rats scurried through his mind as he visualised himself adrift in the icy night like the shepherd. Cast out.

***

THE FOLLOWING MORNING, THE black depression hadn't lifted. He entered the laboratory and found that his mood matched the prevailing atmosphere. The foyer was deserted but for a pacing Laidlaw and Clara, who was polishing her glasses like her life depended on it.

The professor greeted him with a snarl. 'Where the hell were you yesterday? Absolute bleeding nightmare in Lousã. Whole bloody thing's been blown sky high. Sabotage. Mayhem.'

'What? What happened, sir? I mean I'm sorry I didn't show up yesterday – tummy bug – but is everyone okay? It wasn't on the radio or TV … obviously I'd have been straight in if it had.'

'Use your wits, Hellyer. We're hardly likely to broadcast the total destruction of a top-secret installation to the world, are we? The whole point was to be beneath the radar.'

Laidlaw flung himself into a creased black leather armchair. He crossed his legs, folded his arms, and launched into a graphic description of the damage. None of the staff had been injured, thank God, because the cunning evil bastards who'd carried it out had waited until evening – the only aspect he was grateful for. But if he ever got his hands on the perpetrators, their mothers would wish they'd never conceived them, never mind being unable to recognise them.

Nick glanced at Clara, but she wouldn't make eye contact. How much had the professor's blind ferocity shaken her?

'So what's our next step, sir?' Nick's squeaky voice echoed around the marble-floored lobby.

'I can see no point whatsoever in rebuilding the plant in situ. I'm already researching alternative locations, not necessarily in mainland Portugal. Probably in the overseas provinces. One of the remoter island groups like the Azores or Cabo Verde. Or, even better, somewhere in southern Africa itself, closer to the eventual theatre of use. Identifying the optimal site should be straightforward with enough governmental pressure. We can source much of the equipment from Portugal or South Africa, with specialist retorts coming from Quickfit and Quartz in Staffordshire. The flasks and vacuum pumps will have to come from West Germany.'

It made sense. The high-pressure flasks essential to the three-stage sarin production process had to be capable of containing temperatures over a hundred degrees Celsius. But this was an opportunity for Nick to dig a little deeper.

He held up his hand. 'Excuse me, sir. Could you possibly take it a little slower, making allowances for my lack of background?'

Laidlaw leaned back, hands clasped behind his neck, and sighed. 'It should be evident to anyone with a modicum of scientific sense that the hardware issue can be fixed. The problem is the stocks of base chemicals. The UK's recently enforced much stricter export restrictions on isopropanol, so we'll have to look elsewhere. Our supplies of hydrogen fluoride come from Belgium and this will continue.' He laughed. 'The Belgians are notoriously unscrupulous in these matters. But we'll have to source the other chemicals from a range of countries in Eastern Europe and Asia without leaving a paper trail.' The professor squinted and raised an eyebrow. 'Still following me? Not going too fast?'

Oh, yes, he most certainly was keeping up with the flood of gold dust. Now for the killer question.

'Most grateful, very clear. So, given these variables, how long do you think it'll take us to be up and running again?'

Laidlaw lumbered to his feet. 'Six months at best. That's how it is, I'm afraid. As for "us", let's face facts – not much need for you to hang about.'

'Today, or more permanently?'

'The latter. No immediate rush, you understand. We'll need to deal with contractual things, of course. Clara will take care of it all, won't you?'

No response.

'Come on girl, snap out of it. Not the end of the world. We'll bounce back.'

She stirred herself. 'Yes, sir. I'll attend to Nick's termination at once. And thank you for your reassurance that we can rebuild.'

The slow monotone of her voice matched the gentle brush of her hand on Nick's shoulder as she showed him out. Once in the fresh air, he wiped his sweating palms on his shirt and stared back up at the building. Clara raised a farewell hand and offered a half-smile. Nick returned the gesture and walked home. First job: transmit a verbatim account of the whole encounter to London.

***

LATE NEXT MORNING WHILE Patricia showered, Nick twiddled coffee spoons on the kitchen table, made little mounds of sugar and crushed them.

She came in wearing nothing but a towel around her head, and swept the sugar into her hand. 'Messy pup.'

As she swung around to the sink, a curl of dark hair escaped from the towel. Beads of glistening water trickled down her spine.

'Forgot to mention – yesterday, someone called Ella came by looking for you.'

'Oh yeah? Must be one of my many admirers.' His right foot started to jiggle. 'What did she look like?'

'Very attractive, and quite charming to boot. Mid-thirties, short, smart trouser suit.'

Sounded like Aisha.

'Laid it on a bit thick, though – said you were friends from way back. Some literary-criticism conference. Beirut or Jerusalem.'

He'd never visited Jerusalem and only passed through Beirut en route to his initial training in the Lebanese mountains.

He grasped his thigh, steadying his errant foot. 'Doesn't ring a bell, I'm afraid.'

'My best guess is a former lover inventing a professional connection for my benefit.' Patricia put her hand on his shoulder. 'No need to be embarrassed, my dear Nick. The past is the past, and we've both been around the block. In any event, I told her you were away on business. I'm sure she drew her own conclusions.'

He pulled her to him and leant his head against a soft damp cheek. 'Silly question, but do you think we'll ever see each other again?'

'*Vamos a ver.* Most likely in Funchal. Parting like this isn't exactly a pushover for either of us, is it? Too many complications by far. And your soppiness is messing with my mind.'

She pushed him away as if he were a slightly annoying child and retreated to the bedroom.

'Why can't you—'

His question lost itself in the ear-shattering blast of the hairdryer.

She returned, refreshed and composed, in crisp turquoise cotton blouse, long white pleated skirt and patent leather blue shoes. Her eyes sparkled.

'Enough of all that nonsense, darling. Being with you has been tremendous, but I've really got to go now. Try and learn to understand me better. Must rush – late for Augusta.'

She pecked him on the cheek, slung her bag over her shoulder and dashed down the stairs.

Nick stood by the window and watched her drive off. He'd deciphered her words: they'd meet again the next time Quinlevan moved his chess pieces around the board and her queen ended up adjacent to his king. When would that be? And would the major eventually deign to respond to the diamond-studded intelligence he'd just been sent?

Only one way to find out.

The damp outline of Patricia's buttocks remained imprinted on the sheets. He knelt before them and reached for the grooves in the floorboard. Instead, his fingertips found a small cardboard wallet. Her airline ticket.

Jacket flying, wallet in hand, he tore after her. A trailer laden with tiles blocked the pavement part way down Rua Alexandre Herculano, forcing him to swerve onto the cobbled incline. The *clang clang clang* of a bell made him lurch to the side as a tram roared past, blue sparks flying from its brake shoes. He stumbled, found his feet, and made out Augusta's distinctive black-and-white checked headscarf at a table outside the deserted café. She was sitting alone, head in hands. Two dark-suited men were dragging Patricia towards the green rental Fiat, their forearms high under her armpits. The toes of her shiny blue shoes scraped tramlines through the gravel.

He hurtled down to the square but arrived too late. The car sped off.

Chest cramping as he gulped in air, he struggled back to the café and rested his hands heavily on the back of Augusta's chair. She raised her head and looked over her shoulder. Her face was blotchy.

'DGS.'

Nick crashed down opposite her, stretched out his legs and folded his arms. 'Tell me.'

Augusta gripped the edges of the weather-beaten metal table and her knuckles whitened. 'Two men strolled up a moment ago and asked whom the Fiat belonged to. Patricia replied. They requested the keys. They were polite, quiet, almost respectful. "Come with us, please." That's all they said. Nothing more. Very matter of fact. And so quick. Over in a few seconds. The waiter didn't hang about. Straight back inside. And the other customers couldn't get away fast enough.'

Nick glanced at the surrounding tables – all littered with unfinished drinks.

'Why didn't anyone intervene? Why didn't you?'

'Shock, I guess. And for what purpose anyway? Keep your head down, don't get involved. That's how we Portuguese have historically accommodated to our situation. The curious thing is, the DGS men showed no interest in me whatsoever. Only her. Poor thing.'

Nick gave her a minute out of respect for her distress, but only a minute. Instinct drove him on. He stared into her teary eyes.

'Yes, that part's distinctly odd, don't you think? Everything you've told me indicates they conducted a carefully targeted lift, not just a chance sighting of her car. So why didn't they take you? You were a witness, could well have been an accomplice.'

'I don't—'

'We can't just brush this anomaly aside, Augusta. Don't you see? Something's not right.'

'I can't—'

'How do you know they were from the DGS? And how did they know you wouldn't make a scene?' He stood, forcing her to look up. He glanced around. The waiter dropped a curtain on the café window. 'Tell me the truth.'

'You can't possibly comprehend how terrifyingly complicated life is here. We live in a society where the DGS are everywhere, poking their noses into everything. And before them, the PIDE. That's why—'

'Spare me the historical analysis. You need to try harder. Much harder.'

'How dare you treat me like this? Perhaps they left me alone because they thought I'd lead them to Patricia's fellow conspirators.' She gasped, reached up and grabbed his forearm. 'I may have betrayed you – they could be watching us now.'

'Good try, but not quite good enough.' He detached himself from her. 'You obviously didn't pick up enough about convincing plot and dialogue from our play readings. For openers, if the DGS had been shadowing her, they must have already had information that she was staying with me.'

Behind her head, a rainbow arched high over the Mondego – a timeless, evanescent moment. How he longed to float away, avoid the inevitable conclusion of his inquisition …

Not an option.

He sat down again and leaned forward, took both her

hands in his.

'I suspect you're a double agent, my dear Augusta – a DGS informer.'

'That's crazy – I've told you how much I despise them. And you know better than anyone exactly where Mario and I stand. We've taken gigantic risks in extending our confidence to you.'

'As have I to you. The two goons who just hijacked Patricia looked more than a little familiar to me. Shouldn't be too difficult to persuade them that I'm willing to pass on a nugget or two about the MFA in exchange for Patricia's freedom. I'm sure they'd consider it an excellent bargain.'

'You couldn't. Wouldn't. Mustn't. Not after everything I've been through, all the humiliation I've been forced to endure.' She pulled at her scarf. 'I'm not proud of what I've done, but I won't hide it from you. I had to put the DGS off the scent … not just about what the MFA were planning, but also Mario's involvement in it. So, yes, I may have assisted them. Low-level information, I assure you – students, their beliefs and clandestine meetings.'

Multicoloured strands of wool fell from her scarf onto her thighs, scratched free by nervous nails.

'And? What else, Augusta?'

She took a deep breath. 'Sometimes information about members of the faculty and the office staff. My colleagues. But … once I'd started, it became harder and harder to stop because they threatened to reveal what I'd done.'

'The greater good has always been a comfortable friend to informers and traitors. Part of me is toying with the idea that you were the one who tipped off the DGS about this rendezvous with Patricia.'

'How can you possibly suggest that?' She clenched her fists.

'No, no, no. Insulting and hurtful. You must trust me. She has been and still is my best friend.'

'I accept what you say on that score, but I have no apology to make for my questions. Instead, since your acquaintance with them is so intimate, give me your best guess as to where the DGS could be holding her now.'

She winced as if he'd slapped her. 'Most likely their villa in Rua Tenente Valadim, just up from here. But you must understand that while I care deeply for her, we cannot jeopardise our great enterprise for the sake of one individual, however precious. You must give me your word that you won't use the MFA as a bargaining chip.'

'Patricia's not a pawn to be sacrificed in a power play, and I refuse to give her up. But I do take back what I suggested about the MFA – I suspect they wouldn't have fallen for it in any case if your security's as good as you say it is.'

'Thank you. Thank you so much. This betrayal's been gnawing away inside me. Mario's the only other person who knows what I've been forced to do to protect the revolution.'

The disappointment came like a gut-punch. 'Tosh. The whole DGS is in the know. So many well-meaning people … I think I'll wander down to that villa a bit later and exercise my charm. All friends together. Just a misunderstanding. All cleared up. And Patricia and I can walk hand in hand into the sunset. Good idea?'

Augusta's eyes widened. 'They'll eat you alive … I have to leave for Lisbon soon – events are picking up speed. I'll be staying at Casa de São Mamede, Rua da Escola Politécnica, 159. In the unlikely event of your escape, come and find me there.'

She walked stiffly away, scuffing the gravel. Nick stood to

follow her, but the ticket wallet he'd dropped on the table caught his eye. Patricia had to be his priority.

First, though, he'd need clearance.

***

HE LUGGED THE TRANSCEIVER out with low expectations of immediate contact, but received instructions to stand by. An hour later, he had Quinlevan's ear.

'So Patricia's in the bag with no further beam of suspicion on you,' the major said.

'Seems that way.'

'And the production facility's been neutralised. Useful data on Laidlaw's future equipment and chemical supply plans too. We'll see what we can do to disrupt them if it becomes necessary. Well done indeed, my boy. That's it then. We'll monitor events from this end and see what transpires.'

'But what about her?'

'Yes, well there's a thing. Portuguese citizen, you see. Difficult question for us, isn't it? Not much we can do while Caetano's still in power. Risk of the game, you follow? I'm sure she'll take it in good part. Kind of thing we all signed up for really.'

Though what Quinlevan himself had signed up for, Nick wasn't sure.

'We'll keep our options open on the vaccine laboratory. No need to move precipitately. As for the MFA, who can tell? Storm in a teacup, perhaps.'

'But what about Patricia?'

'Cheery pip, then.'

She'd been hung out to dry. Just as he'd been in Alexandria.

A major in British Intelligence had willingly sacrificed a pawn to preserve his king.

CHAPTER 7

Coimbra, Portugal, 24 April 1974

NICK DESCENDED RUA ALEXANDRE Herculano for the second time that day, passed the Teatro Gil Vicente and walked up to Rua Tenente Valadim. Ornate black railings set on a low stone wall with matching gates protected the anonymous two-storey villa with a portico and elegant stonework over the windows. A large olive tree lent shade to three parked cars, one a green Fiat.

Such a charming venue for torture.

The agent with the distinctive eyebrows opened the door and smiled. 'Good afternoon, *Senhor Doutor*. Most gratifying to see you again. And so soon. Perhaps you've recalled something you wish to share with us. We are always at your disposal so, please, tell us how we can be of assistance.'

Nick ignored the proffered hand. 'I'd rather not come in, if you don't mind. The fact is, I'm searching for a close friend of mine called Patricia. She's gone missing. It occurred to me that you might know of her whereabouts.'

'Forgive me, but kindly don't persist with this discourtesy. I politely invited you to enter, and you refused.'

Nick stood his ground. 'You did indeed ask me in, and I respectfully declined.'

The agent grasped Nick's lapels and jerked him through the door. Nick grabbed the doorjamb, exposing his abdomen. A sharp punch took the breath from his lungs. Eyebrows dragged him down some stairs and threw him onto the tiled floor of a windowless basement room. The cell door clanged shut and the light was extinguished from outside.

Augusta had been right of course. He hadn't needed to play the stupid foreigner – he was one, perhaps even the stupidest of all. Locked up again. A not unfamiliar situation, but this time he was prepared, mentally and physically. He closed his eyes and drifted off.

***

THE LIGHT SNAPPED ON. Had it been minutes or hours? Nick got to his feet and the agent pushed him away with the palm of his hand.

'I can categorically assure you that we're not holding your "friend" Patricia, the terrorist. High-category suspects like her go straight to Caxias prison in Lisbon. But we've got you to play with instead. Confess that you're also a terrorist or I'll squeeze you until you break.'

He jammed his right hand into Nick's groin and gripped his balls. Nick fell to his knees but held in the scream.

'Get it?'

Nick shook his head. A more forceful gonad squeeze. Nick let rip, exaggerated the scream even. Mind over matter. He'd win or pass out.

The agent left him gasping on the floor, but soon returned. Nick tensed his stomach muscles, anticipating an assault that didn't come.

'Nothing to say? Sure? Well, you're a tougher nut to crack than I'd have predicted, if you'll excuse my little joke. Shame, but in that case we have no alternative than to take you for a ride. Out of the kindness of our hearts, we're going to give you the opportunity to observe my esteemed colleagues "persuading" your girlfriend to confess. They're dedicated men and love their work, so she will break, however long it takes. Unless, that is, you can no longer bear to watch the proceedings and spill the beans first.'

***

NICK SAT HANDCUFFED IN the back of a nondescript blue DGS Toyota. As they crossed the Santa Clara Bridge over the shimmering Mondego, he bade farewell to Coimbra. His groin and abdominal muscles throbbed, but the drive would give him time to recover. He'd need to act soon, though – the closer they got to the capital, the quicker the agents could summon backup.

An hour passed. It was now or never. They passed Leiria and he let out a thunderous sulphurous fart, one of the few practical skills he'd acquired at his minor public school.

'What the hell's the matter with you?'

'I really need to take a shit. I can do it by the side of the road. I don't care.'

'I do. Can't have you running off into the forest, can I?'

'Honest to God, I can't hold it in any longer.'

'You're going to have to.'

They sailed past a brightly lit Shell petrol station, but a few kilometres further on pulled in to an abandoned-looking garage and came to a halt at the rear. As the driver reversed the Toyota, the headlights illuminated a dilapidated outside toilet.

Eyebrows dragged Nick out of the back seat, released the cuffs and pushed him into the blackness of the WC. He left the heavy door slightly ajar.

Nick stood on the balls of his feet, fists clenched, and grunted deeply.

The agent hammered on the door. 'Get on with it. Haven't got all evening.'

Silence. More grunts.

The agent yanked the door wide open and took a step forward. Nick slammed it back in his face, dragged him inside and against the wall, and smashed his right forearm into the side of the man's head. That would have done for most, but despite the blood pouring from a broken nose, the Portuguese man's gloved thumbs forced their way into Nick's eyes.

Nothing had prepared him for the pain. João's counsel to hold back in combat no longer applied. At any moment he could be blinded or dead. No more limits, then. He chopped the agent across the neck with the side of his right hand. Heard ribs crack as his left fist crashed into the man's chest. A heavy thump echoed against the tiled walls as the agent's head smashed against the toilet bowl.

In the darkness, Nick filled the hand basin, washed the blood from his face and dabbed his eyes. He traced his fingers across the agent's neck. A pulse still throbbed. Killing him now would be easy. But to what end? Far more important to secure his own means of escape.

He inched the WC door open. The Toyota faced the road. Cigarette smoke wafted from the half-open driver's-side window. Football commentary blaring from the radio masked Nick's approach.

He jerked the door open. The driver half-turned, and Nick grasped his neck, forced his head back and throttled him. Nick's arms trembled as the man thrashed. The driver's body slackened, and he passed out. Nick released him.

Twice in five minutes he'd come close to killing. And each time held back. Proudfoot and the Mossad agent might have died as a consequence of his actions but most definitely not his intention.

He dumped the driver against the wall in the toilet, passed the chain of the handcuffs behind the WC waste pipe, and assigned a cuff to each man's wrist. By the time he'd wrenched their trousers and underpants down to their shins, the toilet block looked like a sex game gone badly wrong. At least that's what their rescuers would think until the men's identities became apparent.

***

HE HEADED SOUTH, TOWARDS Lisbon. Passed a railway station and took his foot off the accelerator for a moment, then changed his mind and pressed on.

Billboards for the newly opened Pão de Açúcar supermarket signalled the outskirts of the capital. Nick sought out the darkest corner of its gigantic car park and used the car's jack to rip off the number plates, which along with the ignition keys were consigned to the nearest drain. He hopped on a packed tram bound for the city centre. The frequent jolts punctuating its easy rhythm mirrored his mood.

'Mrs Mendes is in room 37,' the severe receptionist at the Casa de São Mamede told him. 'You're in 38, and it's cash in advance for guests without luggage.'

Just before midnight, Nick climbed the marble staircase. He stopped halfway, leant his head against the cooling green-and-white tiled walls, looked at the stained-glass windows depicting the Discoveries but was too tired to appreciate them.

He slouched on Augusta's only chair and with a mixture of contrition and pride related his adventures. The jeans and coarse woollen sweater did nothing to hide the prowling tigress before him, tense, hands on hips.

'Patricia has been my closest friend for far longer than you've known her. But her rescue will have to wait. Your swashbuckling exploits, Captain Nick Errol Flynn, aren't going to secure her freedom. Nor is any last-minute cavalry despatched by your spymaster. But we *are* about to decide the fate of our country at last, and her release will inevitably follow.' She pulled a small transistor out of her bag and tuned to Radio Renascença. 'Have you ever listened to José Vasconcelos's show *Limite*?' She flung that night's edition of *República* at him. An item had been ringed in red biro: *The quality of its news items and its choice of music make* Limite *obligatory listening tonight.*

'I'm sorry, I don't quite follow you.'

'You should. You're the one who dwells in the dark espionage world of coded messages.'

Nick wallowed in confusion, barely absorbing Vasconcelos's engaging chatter. At 12.25 a.m. a book review came to an end and, with no introduction from the presenter, the soft tread of marching feet increased in volume until it filled the bedroom. A calm solo male voice emerged from the background and dominated.

Nick gave a cry of recognition. 'That's "Grândola, Vila Morena" by Zeca Afonso, from *Cantigas do Maio*. Land of brotherhood where it's the people who ordain. But *morena* – Moorish?'

'Sun-baked actually. Now, for Christ's sake, stop being so literal and listen. What you've just heard is the starting gun for our revolution. The most incredible moment – the one we've been striving for all these years. I cannot believe it.' She sat rigid on the side of the bed, dragging at her sweater. 'All over the country, MFA members have been waiting for that particular song to be played on this particular station at this particular moment. If everything goes to plan, we'll soon have closed the borders and airports, seized the media and overthrown the government.'

Bloody hell – this time they were really going for it. So much for Quinlevan's pessimism. He'd have loved to have been able to crow over the major at that moment, but it was a non-starter. Platinum-standard intelligence and no way of relaying it to London securely.

The singer's voice faded to the rhythmic tramp of boots, and Augusta flopped on her back.

'By three o'clock, the first columns will be near to Lisbon, blocking the entrance roads and bridges while Caetano and his cohorts are sleeping the sleep of the unjust. Mario should arrive at the Praça do Comércio by seven thirty. I'd love you to accompany me down there to greet him.'

A boyish, irresponsible delight at the possibility of being present at the event bubbled inside him.

'You mean I can get some shuteye and then witness regime change?'

Augusta patted him on the cheek. 'Deadly, deadly serious, once-in-a-lifetime stuff – no more jokes. But, yes, you can.'

***

Lisbon, Portugal, 25 April 1974

MIST HANGING OVER THE River Tejo obscured the vast open-ended Praça do Comércio. Completely rebuilt in 1755 following the earthquake and tsunami, the square was about to witness another earth-shattering moment.

By seven thirty, the intricate black-and-white mosaic-tiled surface was occupied by a group of M47 Patton tanks, AML-60 scout cars and Panhard armoured personnel carriers. Conscript soldiers with long sideburns smoked and lazed against the sides of their vehicles in the early-morning sun. To all outward appearances, a routine training exercise.

Augusta and Nick took up station in a deserted pavement café. A few minutes later, her transistor radio played the MFA's first communiqué: 'Our aim is to put an end to the regime which has oppressed the country for so long.'

An apprehensive, muttering crowd filtered to the edges of the great square. Elderly men in shabby dark suits and grey-haired women in once-colourful shawls mingled with sharply dressed business-people on their way to work. The complexion of the crowd soon altered. Now it was mainly pumped-up teenagers and students singing and linking arms. A primary-school outing of red-smocked children escorted by nuns became caught up in the gathering and took refuge from the clamour by sitting down and huddling in a tight circle.

Nick caught fragments of conversation from the adults: 'Did you hear the radio?' 'Communists ...' 'They say that ...' 'Now is the time.' 'Our time.' 'All these years.'

A column of eight government tanks rumbled into the square and surrounded the rebel forces. Silence fell.

Augusta and Nick jumped up as the doors of the Panhards clanged open and a group of soldiers led by Mario sprinted across to the newly arrived forces. The soldiers worked their way along the ring of tanks, debating with the crews through the driving slits. At the fifth one, Mario and two soldiers leapt up and rapped on the hatch. It opened, and a trembling lieutenant colonel crawled out. Faced with their pistols, he raised his hands in surrender. The other tank commanders fired up their engines, and tracks squealed on the mosaics as they moved to line up alongside the rebels.

'Yes, yes!' came the cries from the crowd. A fractured rendition of *Grândola* followed, each group pursuing its own tonal path. An F-86 Sabre jet fighter howled towards the square and pulled up at the last minute, almost drowning out the rejoicing.

'We've been assured that at least one air-force squadron is backing us.' Augusta sounded hesitant. The plane banked steeply and hurtled back towards them. 'But as for the other squadrons, we're not sure. That could have been an initial sighting run prior to strafing.'

People rushed into café and shop doorways as the approaching jet zoomed even lower, waggled its wings and climbed with a deafening roar.

'They're with us,' she said.

They rejoined the cheering crowd waving at the vanishing plane. Nick, shaken but relieved, pointed out across the murky Tejo. A naval frigate, the *Almirante Gago Coutinho*, emerged from the mist.

'The real trouble's more likely to come from that direction.'

Four 76mm guns pointed at the tanks in the Praça do Comércio. The rebel Pattons jerked their turrets towards it and a lengthy standoff ensued. The ship's siren bellowed, alarming the now greatly-enlarged crowd. Then its guns turned away from the square and pointed skywards.

Augusta was jubilant. 'The navy must have joined us. Or at least that vessel has.'

They pushed forward towards the centre of the square but came to an abrupt halt when the lead tank of two further advancing loyalist columns fired salvos into the air. Again, Mario and his men rushed to engage with the crews through the driving slits.

'Soldier against soldier? Army against army? Citizen against citizen? For what purpose?' Mario shouted. 'None of us wants civil war. The MFA are with the people, and the people are with the MFA.'

'Traitors! Saboteurs! Communists!' a well made-up and immaculately coiffured woman in her sixties screamed, shaking her walnut walking stick at the rebels. Tears of rage coursed down her heavily-powdered cheeks.

Augusta tapped her on the shoulder. 'No. They are not. Nor are they fascists, oppressors or torturers, unlike the bastards they're overthrowing.'

The woman spat in Augusta's face, then lost her balance and collapsed onto the mosaics. 'I'll lose everything. You've no idea what these revolutionaries are plotting,' she yelled.

'I do, actually – my husband is one of them.' Augusta helped the woman to her feet. 'We're setting out to right many, many wrongs. You may not feel as we do now, but I hope and believe you will, eventually.'

The woman pushed her away. 'Get off me, Satan. Scum. We know exactly what to do with your kind, and we will once this is all over. Just you wait and see.'

Shortly before midday, Augusta's radio broadcast a further communiqué announcing that the MFA now controlled the whole of mainland Portugal. Augusta waved her arms, and Mario pushed through the throng towards them. Lines of stress creased his camouflage-painted face.

'Caetano's taken refuge in the GNR barracks in the Largo do Carmo. We're going up there now to smoke him out.'

Augusta and Nick joined the determined but jittery crowd chasing the line of rebel tanks up the steep incline to the Carmo. Halfway up, the lead Patton's tracks skidded on the greasy cobbles, and the tank began to slide sideways towards them. The long gun barrel swept across the trees lining the street, showering the ground with blood-red oranges, and the roar of its engine reverberated in the narrow confines of the tall buildings.

They scrambled over to a group of demonstrators trying to push the Patton out of trouble. Heads down, slipping and sliding on the juice-covered surface, they persevered. Finally, equilibrium was restored, and with a huge plume of black exhaust smoke, the Patton clattered up to the Carmo to a resounding cheer.

Every fifty metres, youthful troops in jungle camouflage caps stood to attention, rifles at their side, disciplined gazes fixed straight ahead. Inhabitants of a parallel universe, oblivious to the cataclysmic change taking place in front of their very eyes.

Nick grinned warmly as he paused to catch his breath beside one of them, and waved the demonstrators behind him by.

'Move on,' the conscript said without breaking his forward stare.

'Why should I? Whose cause are you serving here, anyway?'

'Safeguarding the populace from the rebels.'

'But you are the rebels.'

The soldier's face softened, and he met Nick's gaze. 'So we are.' A slow smile crept over his lips.

An elated middle-aged woman across the street was holding out a huge armful of vivid-red carnations and calling out to soldiers and civilians alike as they passed. Nick swam to her through the crowd and grasped three blooms. He offered to pay, but she threw her head back in a gale of laughter.

'Today, all carnations are free!'

He kissed her on the cheek and returned to the soldier, who promptly stuffed a stem down the barrel of his G3 rifle.

With their own carnation buttonholes, Augusta and Nick continued up the slope towards the GNR barracks, once a monastery, which lay in the small square next to the Church of the Sacrament. The demonstrators had laid siege to it, chanting 'Power to the people' and waving green-and-red Portuguese flags.

By three o'clock, Augusta had had enough. 'Caetano must be hiding in there, but that old fox isn't going to give up easily. We're just massaging our own egos by hanging around. Come on – let's try to actually *do* something. Rescue Patricia.'

'In Coimbra, the DGS assured me they'd sent her to the political prison at Caxias.'

'And you believed them? Why on earth would they tell you the truth? Their main HQ's not far; they could well be holding her there.'

They walked the three blocks to the DGS offices, a four-storey nineteenth-century building in Rua António Maria Cardoso. The mood of the crowd became markedly less celebratory and more aggressive the closer they got.

'Out, out, out! Come and show us your faces! Disgraces!'

A demonstrator wearing a black scarf over the lower half of her face barged them out of the way and joined others digging up cobblestones that they then hurled at the building's shuttered windows. To little effect, from what Nick could see, apart from venting their justifiable desire for the two hundred secret police agents holed up inside to surrender to justice.

The demonstrators surged forward and pounded on the front doors. The shutters on one of the second-floor windows flew open and an automatic rifle barrel jutted out and sprayed bullets across the protestors.

Augusta gasped. A bullet had ripped through the right sleeve of her blouse.

A cry came from behind her. A teenage boy reeled backwards. A gaping wound in his thigh pumped blood through his torn jeans.

The firing ceased as abruptly as it had started, the rifle withdrew, and the shutters banged shut.

Nick wrapped his jacket around Augusta's arm; others rushed to help the wounded youth. Three demonstrators lay motionless, and others were being carried back to the Carmo. Augusta and Nick picked their way back through the pandemonium. She collapsed onto a battered metal chair outside a boarded-up café on the edge of the square.

'Well, no way of guessing if they actually had Patricia inside. Looked much more like a last stab at resistance in the face of certain defeat.'

'I agree. Now let me have a look at your arm.'

Augusta unbuttoned her blouse and jerked the sleeve off her shoulder, revealing an angry, bleeding groove. She pulled a yellow silk scarf from her bag.

'Tie that tight above around the bicep, such as it is. It's just a graze; it'll heal quickly – unlike the leg of that poor boy behind us. I suppose you could say I was asking for it. But he and the others weren't plotters, just ordinary people protesting against the regime.'

The echoes of gunfire had rendered the ten thousand-strong crowd in the Carmo subdued and tense. Some were still arguing and gesticulating; others had spread coats and shawls on the cobbles and sat cross-legged.

At 5.45 p.m., an olive-green Citroen DS, protected by lines of troops on each side, drove through, forcing the demonstrators to stand. It pulled up outside the gates.

General António de Spínola, monocle in place and horsewhip in hand, strode through the gates and accepted Caetano's surrender on behalf of the MFA. Fifteen minutes later, a captain climbed on to the roof of the Citroen and proclaimed the historic moment through a megaphone.

A deep sigh rippled through the throng. Then joyous cheers. The crowd started to drift away, leaving only a euphoric hard core in the square. At 7.30 p.m., their patience was rewarded – the prime minister was bundled into an armoured car and driven away. The celebratory mood darkened and chants of 'Assassin! Assassin!' reverberated.

Augusta grabbed Nick's arm. 'Come on, then – let's go to

Caxias. I know I said I don't trust those DGS bastards, but for once they might not have sold you a complete pack of lies.'

They headed for Rossio Station. Overwhelmed by the demonstrators, the station staff had long given up on checking tickets, and Nick and Augusta rode a much-delayed, jam-packed electric train out to Estoril for free. There, they joined the crowds marching up a low hill to a white complex of three buildings that looked down at the mouth of the Tejo.

Staccato horn beeps came from a line of cars parked beneath the high prison walls, and Augusta paused.

'How weird – doesn't sound joyful at all.'

'You're right – it's communication, not celebration. Morse code relaying news of the coup to the inmates.'

'How on earth can you make that out?'

'A long story, and none of your business. Morse in Portuguese differs a bit from the English version, but I can get the gist – Caetano's been overthrown, and political prisoners are about to be freed.'

'Let's hope that Patricia's one of the first.'

She flinched as Nick put a comforting arm around her.

Several hundred people waited impatiently outside the prison gates, exchanging cigarettes and passing around bottles of warming spirits. Spontaneous choruses of *Grândola* broke out. But desperation, anxiety and tension were etched on faces illuminated by candles and torches – faces of parents, sisters, brothers and friends of those who'd been held incommunicado for up to a decade, or even longer.

'Cowards, cowards!'

The chant broke out as evil-smelling clouds of dark smoke billowed out over the prison walls.

'Destroying the evidence, destroying the evidence!'

At midnight, six trucks arrived. Soldiers with fixed bayonets poured out and marched into the prison. At one thirty, amid jostling and screams of joy, the first small group of the seventy-seven prisoners held there emerged and were scooped up by their tearful friends and families.

A second followed. Then a third. Nick scanned the faces. And found her.

There, at the rear, was Patricia. Nick waved, and she raised a weak arm as they sprinted over.

He threw his arms around her. 'Darling.'

He tried to lift her and spin her around but failed. She shook her head, held his cheeks between her palms and brushed his forehead with her lips.

It was enough.

***

THEY CAUGHT THE LAST train back to Lisbon, then a taxi to the hotel. Throughout, the silence was prolonged and awkward. At the top of the stairs, Augusta broke it.

She put her arm around Patricia and stroked her hair. 'Thirty-seven or thirty-eight? Me or him?'

'Thirty-eight. But I need to get out of these revolting stinking clothes. I don't suppose you've got something you could you lend me …'

'Sure, come to mine first.'

Nick left them to it, and collapsed on the lumpy bed. Fifteen minutes later, Patricia crept into his outstretched arms and placed her head awkwardly on his chest.

'There, rest and tell me as much or as little as you want, whenever you want.'

A wave of relief washed over him as her body gradually relaxed and her breathing became more regular. Sleep took him.

In the early morning, he brought up coffee and warm bread rolls from the restaurant.

Patricia roused. Half-open eyes hunted around the room for a moment. She focussed, sat up, and blew the skin off the top of the thick milky drink.

'Heavenly.'

She smoothed the erect hairs on the back of his right hand, and the normality of her gesture drained away his remaining tension.

'Fill me in, Nick.'

A knock. Augusta's head snaked around the door as he was finishing his account of the previous day's events.

'Heard your voices. Are you feeling more yourself now? Would love to join you.'

Patricia sipped her coffee. 'Yes, please do. Incredible what you've been through.'

Augusta perched on the edge of the bed. 'But what about you? Is it still too raw or are you ready to share?'

'I'm slowly grounding. What happened to me? Well, basically the Coimbra DGS were just acting as messenger boys for Lisbon and shoved me straight into a van. We arrived at Caxias. The guards shoved me in a cell, took off the cuffs and pushed me down onto a bench. They never spoke directly to me. It was as if I didn't exist. Dehumanising – designed to make me feel like some worthless, dumb animal.'

'Did you resist?' Augusta said. 'Sorry, silly question.'

'How? I could hardly overpower them and escape, could I? I just hung on to the belief that I was stronger than them because I understood their tricks. There was one small thing … a guard ripped off the gold necklace my mother gave me. He grinned as he stuffed it in his pocket … that got to me. Then they left, and I lay down and just waited.'

Nick took her hand. 'For what? Did they …'

'Violate me? No, they didn't. Well, not my body. They raped my mind, my inner being, not my body. They came back and blindfolded me, forced me to stand with my nose against the cell wall, arms down by my sides. They jammed headphones over my ears … women and children screaming and sobbing, men being whipped and tortured, blasts of heavy metal. Then there'd be a blissful moment of silence, then machine guns and explosions. All deafeningly loud.' She put her hands over her ears as if blocking out the memory of the cacophony.

'How did you cope with it?' Nick asked.

'I just held on to a memory of João's calming voice. I can recite those words from our training sessions verbatim: "A disorientation tactic developed by the CIA for use in Vietnam on the VC and taught to the DGS. Much more effective than violence and leaves no bruises and broken bones. Recognise the aim and you can let the sounds wash past." Easier said than done, but I made it my mantra. I lost all sense of time, can't tell you how many guards were in the cell with me. All I know is, if I touched the headphones or moved away from the wall, someone would thrust me straight back against it.'

She took a deep breath and continued in a dull monotone, staring straight ahead.

'Eventually I became exhausted and thirsty. My legs buckled … and I begged for a drink. Big mistake. They forced glass upon glass of iced water into me. Swallow or drown.

And the temperature – it kept switching. Freezing one minute, tropical the next.'

Augusta moved closer to Patricia. 'I would have broken. Anyone would.'

'I did break. My bladder was bursting, but they wouldn't let me move. Finally the pressure became so excruciating that I just had to let go.' She chuckled but the sound was hollow. 'That hot pee running down my legs … for a moment it was bliss. Comforting. Affirming. I relaxed, confident I'd won. But I hadn't. I'd been humiliated.' She shuddered. 'The headphones and blindfold were ripped off and the interrogators swivelled me so my back was against the wall. They took turns dipping the toes of their shoes in the urine and flicking it towards my legs. And yet all the time they were reasonable. No shouting. No threats. Said they just wanted me to confirm a few things. Nothing more. Bit of goodwill from my side, then I could go. But I said nothing. Nothing. And then one of them picked up the headphones and blindfold, and told me to turn around …'

'Oh, my love.'

Patricia turned to Nick, tears in her eyes. 'I confessed to everything, Nick. All of our actions. The rockets and the explosives. Your role and mine. The base in Funchal. Even Q. Every word recorded, for sure. I betrayed you, my Nick, totally. I'm so, so sorry.'

He shook his head. 'Don't torture yourself – they've already done that.'

'I didn't see the interrogators again. Just heard car horns beeping. Then the door opened. Someone came in – a soldier, I guess – and I joined a line of other prisoners. And then there you were, like magic, both waiting for me outside the gates.'

'Nothing about the MFA?' Augusta's voice was brittle. 'I mean, did their questions reveal anything? Did you reveal anything?'

'No, they didn't go there. But I can't say what I'd have blurted out if they had.' She pulled her knees up and wrapped her arms around them.

Augusta relaxed. 'That's a relief, although it might not have mattered. The latest news is that Marcello Caetano, his wife and the president have just been flown to Madeira.'

Patricia's eyes sparkled. 'That's exactly where I want to go as well, Augusta. Back home.'

'I completely understand but it's quite out of the question – for today at least. Everything's been shut down – airports, banks, shops, offices, factories, the whole lot. Mainly because the MFA is quite rightly concerned that the band of corporate crooks who've been ruling us will attempt to flee with their stolen assets. I honestly think the best thing for you to do is stay with Nick and wait and see – the internal trains are still running.'

Patricia flexed her toes. 'But what about the DGS? They'll be able to track me down wherever I go. Listen, I held nothing back from them. And surely they'll have secured the tapes.'

'The cells you and all the other prisoners occupied at Caxias are now overflowing with their agents. The whole political situation's been turned on its head. Your destruction of the gas-production plant would be seen as exactly what the MFA desired, and indeed clandestinely requested. If these recordings ever come to light, which I very much doubt they will, you'll be regarded as a hero, not a traitor.'

'What are you going to do now?'

'I'll have a go at getting in touch with Mario, though he's

bound to have a million things on his plate. One way or the other, I'll aim to return home this evening, tomorrow morning at the latest.'

***

BACK IN COIMBRA, AT Patricia's suggestion, they chose a different route from the station, one that lead them past Penedo da Saudade. As the sun went down, they stood side by side, clasping stout metal railings, the city laid out far beneath them.

Patricia swept an arm across the vista. 'Haven't been up here since my student days, but I had a feeling that this place might call to you. People have always come here to reflect on what has been and what could have been. *Saudade* translates as nostalgia, but it's a much more powerful concept for us, a fundamental Portuguese sentiment.'

'And what about us in that context?' Nick said, his stomach cramping again.

'We've become so much closer recently, and I hoped we might find a way, our own unique way. But I truly fear I've done you very considerable harm with the DGS. Destroyed your whole career, never mind my own. Augusta views the world through an MFA lens, but experience tells me the DGS will have preserved my confession as an insurance policy … How about you?'

Nick clung tighter to the railings and stared into the fading light. 'I'm confused. There have been moments of longing, tenderness, passion, love. Then clouds of mystery. My darling, I was never sure where we were, but I think we could have sorted out the work/love issue … how much to reveal and how much to conceal. Perhaps I could have learnt to believe in you more deeply.'

'You don't want much, do you?'

He turned, pushed her hair aside and kissed her ear lobes. 'What I want is a way for us to be together. You're an incredibly strong woman who's survived a terrible ordeal. That's the important thing. We're both conflicted about our future because we're such different creatures. But that could also be our strength. So, let's have less talk about what could have been and more about what could still be.'

'You're very sweet, my romantic boy. Thank you.'

'I also appreciate your wanting to get back home. Who knows? By tomorrow, the airports may well have re-opened.'

Her hand shot to her mouth. 'My passport. It was in my bag, in the car … on the floor behind the driver's seat.'

'Why don't we walk over to Rua Tenente Valadim? The DGS are notorious for filing every scrap of evidence. It could still be there. Are you game?'

***

THE DGS VILLA WAS packed with men and women on their knees poking through charred and shredded files strewn over the floor like blackened confetti. The shutters of the ransacked villa banged to and fro, and the shiny brass nameplate had been ripped off. A group of students were jumping up and down on the roofs of overturned agents' cars under the olive tree. Patricia recognised her trashed rental and peered through the jagged edges of the broken rear window. No bag.

'Who are you, comrades? And what do you want here?' A grizzled man in grey roll-neck and black beret had approached them.

Patricia looked up. 'I could ask you the same question.'

'On the committee. We are the people and we control now. Kindly show me your ID.'

'*Filho da puta.* So, you unelected lot are taking up where the DGS left off, are you?' She turned her back, and joined those winnowing through the legacy of informers' reports, interrogations and investigations.

'Look what I've found!' A young woman with a red neck scarf held up a battered metal box. She waved it over her head, dousing herself in a cloud of ashes, then picked open the lock with a pocketknife. The lid sprung open, releasing a shower of ID cards and passports. Patricia dived in, extricated her blue passport from the detritus and brandished it at the man in the roll-neck.

'Don't think I'll be proffering this to you, Mr Pocket Commissar.'

***

THE EVENING CLOSED IN. Nick transmitted a lengthy message to London while Patricia rang the airport. At midnight, it re-opened. First thing the next morning, she tore down to the Agencia Abreu travel agency with money borrowed from Nick.

He took a cup of tea out onto the tiny balcony and peered down at weather-beaten red-tiled roofs and the River Mondego beyond. Smudges of smoke still hung in the air. Nothing in the vista before him had changed, and yet Portugal's political landscape had been completely reconfigured. The illusory timelessness momentarily calmed his anxiety.

The phone dragged him out of his trance and he scrambled back indoors. Clara's voice was laced with panic.

'You must come over to the laboratory at once – we're under attack.'

***

FIFTY DEMONSTRATORS STOOD OUTSIDE the lab building with raised clenched fists chanting: 'Out, out, out! DGS, DGS, DGS! Gas, gas, gas!' Leading the chorus through a loudhailer was the man in the roll-neck from Rua Tenente Valadim.

Clara's smile became a grimace as she greeted Nick on the fringes of the demonstration.

'May I introduce members of our university revolutionary student committee? As soon as the professor saw them arrive, he instructed us to barricade ourselves inside. Since Lousã, he's been very jumpy and, I'm afraid, increasingly paranoid. This demonstration only justifies his worst suspicions.'

'But you didn't follow his command.'

'No. I slipped out to wait for you. Yes, I'm concerned for my colleagues' safety, but decided I'd be of more use out here.'

'What about the security guards? Or the police?'

'The guards made off as soon as this lot turned up. No desire for confrontation at all. And as for the municipal police, you must be joking – holed up somewhere, scared they're the next targets. What infuriates me most though is that there's hardly anything left here to protest about. After the destruction of the production facility, the professor ordered the incineration of all our residual stocks of gas and the vaccine we'd started preparing.'

'Why did you call me? What did you hope I could possibly achieve?'

'Talk some sense into the demonstrators. Bizarrely, we Portuguese still have a residual historical respect for the English. They'd never listen to me but they might to you.'

She dragged him through to the front of the demonstration. He acquiesced, acutely aware of the irony – she wanted him to protect the very project he had set out to destroy.

At the top of the steps in front of the laboratory's locked glass doors, the roll-neck man roared: 'DGS, DGS, DGS! Gas, gas, gas!', and the crowd chanted back.

Clara climbed up beside the agitator and reached out for the loudhailer. 'Hand it over and let others have their say.'

The man swung it at her and struck her shoulder. The demonstrators fell silent, and Nick grabbed it and addressed the crowd.

'Yes, let others speak. I'm the professor's translator, not a scientist. I confess I have little understanding of the political ramifications of his research. But violence against the university staff in this building will achieve nothing. Instead, let's discuss the issues together.'

Renewed chants drowned his appeal. 'Out, out, out! DGS, DGS, DGS! Gas, gas, gas!'

New arrivals started hurling rocks at the upper windows.

Clara took the loudhailer and directed it towards the first floor, where an unbroken window hung open. 'Professor Laidlaw, do please think of your researchers' safety. Time to come out now.'

The window slammed shut. Minutes later, the entrance doors eased open and white-coated scientists streamed out. Some of the demonstrators attempted to embrace them as comrades, but the majority pushed them away and ran off.

Finally, Laidlaw himself towered in the doorway, clutching a substantial canvas holdall. He faced the crowd defiantly.

The chanting mass moved forwards as one, forcing the professor aside despite his bulk. He crashed to the floor and the demonstrators hurdled over his body and stormed up the stairs.

Clara and Nick rushed to Laidlaw's rescue through a shower of broken laboratory equipment being hurled from above. Clara slung the professor's heavy holdall over her shoulder, and they escorted him to safety.

***

LAIDLAW COLLAPSED ONTO THE sofa in Nick's flat, sweating and panting after the long trek. He rubbed his palms together.

'Brandy?' Nick said.

'Make it a double if you will, Nick. Ignorant bastards, scum, rabble.' The professor's voice trailed off, less blowhard, more hurt schoolboy. 'But they'll see. I'm far from finished yet.'

He swirled the amber liquid, stared into the glass and tossed the drink down in one go. 'May I use your phone?'

'Be my guest.'

'Confidential. Would you mind?'

'Not at all. I'll be in the kitchen if you need me.'

Clara remained seated, arms folded, silent.

Nick played out a brief charade of rattling cups and plates, then settled by the kitchen door, which was easily penetrated by Laidlaw's hectoring.

'Your lot got me into this mess – now you can get me out of it.' A pause. 'Far too much at stake? I couldn't agree more. But I've worked out a scheme to recreate the project if you'd just give me the chance to outline it … Here. Ten minutes? Fine.'

Nick counted to sixty and re-entered. Laidlaw's composure had swung back to stiff and cold. 'You'll be glad to hear that I'm not going to be imposing myself on you for much longer. Clara, I want you to return to the laboratory immediately, rescue whatever can be saved and await my instructions.'

Clara unfolded her arms. 'Take it easy, Professor. We Portuguese aren't used to change. This cataclysmic political upheaval will take considerable time to get used to. Didn't you say just now that you plan to rebuild the laboratory? Forgive me, I may well have misheard, but you must understand – that would be impossible. Times have changed.'

'Not here of course, woman. In Africa. And I'll require all your expertise – you're my anchor, completely indispensable. My friends will organise the necessary permissions for your absence with the university authorities.'

'I'm not quite sure how to put this, sir, but I've been having doubts about how "scientific" our research really is.'

Laidlaw's tone was glacial. 'It is totally scientific. And your name will be alongside mine when the results are published. Our collaboration will be the making of your academic career. The one thing I've been able to hang on to in life is scientific achievement. People can be malleable and weak; science, however, is forever dependable. Its strength lies in its austerity. Surely you appreciate that.'

The researcher fixed her gaze on the clouds scudding past the window.

Laidlaw continued. 'And now I'm going to meet those who share my position on this project and its implemen-tation. I'll soon be in touch about how we can pursue our joint enterprise. You can't jump ship now, my girl – I simply won't let you.' He turned to Nick. 'As for you, I'm afraid the game's over. Hard cheese and all that. Rely on Clara to sort you out.'

The professor bumped the heavy holdall down the stairs behind him. A uniformed driver closed the rear passenger door of a black Mercedes. Nick clocked the registration plate. The car passed Patricia as it rolled almost silently down the hill.

Minutes later, she bounded into the flat and planted a wet kiss on Nick's forehead. 'Success!'

'That's great, darling. Well done. I hate to spoil your ticket triumph, but events have moved on rather dramatically. Clara can fill you in. Shall we sit outside?'

Clara brought Patricia up to speed, though without revealing a scintilla of her personal views. His own career at the university had fallen off a cliff, so what harm could there be in digging deeper now?

'Clara, does a black Mercedes, UA-72-15, ring any bells?'

'UA's a Coimbra number. I saw that particular car at the lab frequently enough to check it out through a friend in vehicle registration. Registered to UCC, United Chemical Corporation – one of our military-industrial conglomerates with substantial interests in Angola and Mozambique. My best guess is that they were our major funders, hence their repeated visits. It wouldn't surprise me if it's with them that the professor's taken refuge.'

'Thank you. And yet it's blindingly obvious that this isn't fresh news to you. Where do you stand? You've been an active and positive supporter of the professor, but you've just revealed serious doubts to him. Is that because of ethics or because you think the whole enterprise is doomed?'

Patricia drew a sharp breath, drawing Clara's attention.

'I'm in a mess, Patricia. The experiment we conducted in Tete might well have been necessary. In any event, I went along with it, and the men we gassed were indeed captured guerrillas who would have come to a bad end anyway. But ethically, morally, I'm unwilling to continue. The professor is so insistent and, to be honest, I've become more than a little scared of him. Nick's seen what he can be like at close quarters. One moment a rational scientist, the next an erupting volcano.'

He'd got his answer, despite being excluded from the discourse. The two women were operating on a different plane.

Patricia reached over the teacups to Clara. 'I'm not necessarily the best one to advise you – you're older and much more experienced. But I'm leaving tomorrow for Funchal. If your present situation is as difficult as you say, why not come and stay with me for a bit? Far away from Laidlaw and sarin.'

'Thank you so much. I would love to, but how can I? Unlike the professor, I have no powerful connections. I'd have to apply for special leave from the university – in the current turmoil, that could take forever.'

'Your argument could work equally well the other way around.'

'Well, now that we no longer have a laboratory ...' Clara's face glowed for a moment. 'Yes, I'd love to come with you. And I'm in no hurry to sack Nick.'

Nick left them in the garden, finalising their plans to get Clara a ticket. Something nagged. He had a flashback to Golegã. And Patricia and Clara's casual ease with each other niggled. He almost slipped on the steep stairs, righted himself and thrust his doubts away.

His message to London detailing the destruction of the laboratory and Laidlaw's involvement with the UCC received only a standard acknowledgement. But an urgent request followed within the hour. He was to stand by at ten the next morning for voice contact with Quinlevan.

***

NICK SAT ON DAMP sheets redolent of his and Patricia's earlier lovemaking, before she'd left for Funchal with Clara.

Quinlevan's voice was his usual bright cheeriness. 'Dear boy, hope you don't mind, but could you possibly run the contents of your previous two messages by me again? Read them, of course, but would rather hear it from the horse's mouth. And spare me no detail.'

Nick obliged. Silence followed. He checked for technical problems but found none. Coughed a few times. Nothing in return, just the odd crackle.

'Major? Are you still there?'

'Cogitating – complex situation, isn't it? Great to have your eyewitness account. Real flesh-on-bones stuff and puts my briefings from the embassy into perspective, I can tell you. Don't think they dared stick their precious noses outside the front door.'

'But the coup's now a fact, sir. So whatever HMG's position is, what are my instructions from you?'

'Watch and wait. Counter-revolutionary forces are bound to become active, so far from a straightforward scenario yet. Contact me the moment you have something more tangible for us. You must understand, you're my only uncontaminated source of information. I rely on you completely.'

Quinlevan had clearly seated himself back on the fence or, at the very least, was trotting towards it.

'If you'll forgive me sir, "uncontaminated" is a most unfortunate choice of words. I'm only uncontaminated because I wore a protection suit in earlier experiments and didn't participate in the fatal one.'

'Your confirmation of UCC involvement in furthering gas development clearly puts a different complexion on the situation. Keep your eyes and ears open. I have full confidence in your ability to make the right judgement calls. Early days. And who can predict how things will pan out?'

'Sorry, that's all very well, but the production facility has been destroyed, the laboratory wrecked, and the professor has gone AWOL. He's made it clear I no longer have a role to play. I honestly can't see what would be achieved by my remaining here any longer. My gut instinct is to pull out.'

'Permission to withdraw not granted. Your instructions are to utilise your contacts and see what you can dig up. Root about, stimulate some action. Assumed you'd have grasped that much without my having to spell it out for you. Sit up and pay attention at the back of the class.'

'Instructions received, Major, if not fully understood. I no longer have any contacts to speak of. Captain Mendes is in Lisbon, at the heart of the MFA. I seriously doubt there's any way I can get near him. A dramatic political storm has blown up, and I'm not even a bit-player in it. Just a wind-swept spectator standing in the wings.'

'Very droll. Indeed, I recall that amateur theatricals featured in one of your previous postings. Update me as and when. Over and out.'

What on earth did the major expect him to do? His cover had been blown with the DGS. He no longer had a role in the university. Laidlaw had gone rogue. Yet Quinlevan persisted in this exaggerated faith in his ability to conjure a triumph from the jaws of failure. He lay back on the soiled sheets and slumbered, dreaming of shedding his coat of lies and half-truths and resuming his former academic career at Cambridge.

CHAPTER 8

Coimbra, Portugal, 28 April 1974

A RAP ON THE DOOR roused him from his fantasies. He showed Mario and Augusta into the lounge.

'What on earth are doing here? I've just informed the major that you were incommunicado in Lisbon, at the beating heart of the revolution.'

'Why do you think? We may well need your assistance again.'

'Grab a seat. I guess it's safe enough to talk indoors now.'

'Not sure. Not sure of anything anymore. Best we go outside.' Cobalt smeared the bags under Mario's eyes. 'The MFA has three problems. The first is we're out of our depth: successful plotters, yes, but not politicos. We're wasting endless hours in fruitless meetings attempting a political consensus.'

'I appreciate your frustration. But who invited the socialist Mario Soares and the communist Álvaro Cunhal back from exile? What did you expect? Harmony?'

'We needed political weight and legitimacy, and they both know how to pull those levers – slick as anything. Neither's in government yet, though the communists have considerably more clout through their long-standing cells in factories and universities.'

Mario pulled out a pack of small cigars, but a warning glance from Augusta made him put them away.

'Our second problem is counter-revolution. Although we're dismantling the DGS here, it's still active in the islands and the African provinces. The military-industrial complex remains an invisible power everywhere. Up till now, the people have been with us, but decades of authoritarian rule have seduced them into conservativism. The MFA's concern is that the populace will start longing for the security blanket the corporate state used to offer them.'

'Mario's right,' August said. 'Populist fears are fanned by extremist talk of seizures of land to create Stalinist collective state farms. No doubt a currently fashionable idea with the urban population who support us, but naturally much less acceptable to those who earn their living from agriculture in what remains to a large extent a quasi-medieval peasant society.'

'Yes, I can see that. And the third problem?'

'It's the most intractable and complicated one – General Spínola himself. The MFA rightly concluded that we had to select a leader to whom Caetano could surrender with dignity – someone with an international reputation. We were forced to make that decision in haste and are now repenting at leisure.'

Augusta leaned forward. 'My personal view is that Spínola only accepted the invitation because Caetano had publicly disgraced him upon publication of his book. I can imagine how the offer must have been such a sweet moment for Spínola. The MFA correctly judged that the general would be perceived as a positive, stabilising figurehead at home and abroad. And that proved to be the case, but then …' She glanced at her husband.

'He is, and always has been, old school,' Mario said. 'Autocratic and authoritarian – he knows his own mind and refuses to countenance contrary opinions. Okay, we knew who we were dealing with, true enough. Predictably, he's attempting to pack the government with cronies he trusts. We can deal with that. But he's also trying to spirit Caetano and Tomás out of our reach – to refuge in Brazil. We cannot and will not tolerate this. They must be held accountable here.'

'But you're the captains who made him president.'

'Yes, and if necessary we will unmake him. We desperately need international diplomatic support in this turbulent situation. The Yanks openly call us communists, and our European allies are equivocating – some because they rightly fear a pro-democratic military intervention in their own authoritarian regimes.'

Quinlevan must have been bloody prescient. The MFA had come to the Brits yet again, begging for assistance with international recognition.

'Therefore, I'm officially requesting you to use a separate line of communication with London. What I'm about to tell you must remain between ourselves for the moment. Tomorrow morning, the Co-ordinating Committee of the MFA is planning a showdown with Spínola. We'd like you to be present … so you can reassure your masters we're not just a bunch of communist hotheads.'

'"Present" in the past' – Nick smiled briefly – 'meant kicking my heels outside your discussion rooms. I very much regret I'm no longer up for that.'

'I'd expected as much, but this time I can guarantee your presence at a meeting of potentially greater significance than any of those from which you were previously excluded.

Without your government's strong backing, our achievement here could very well descend into anarchy. And you're the chosen instrument to obtain that support, my friend.'

'That's a tall order. I can only relay information – others make the decisions. But yes. Affirmative. The meeting will be in Lisbon presumably.'

'No, we're convening not far from here in fact, at the Buçaco Palace hotel. Spínola chose it. He loves a sense of drama and history, and your Duke of Wellington stayed in a Carmelite monastery at Buçaco during the Peninsular War in 1810.'

'Not sure that means I'll necessarily feel at ease. Aristocratic generals aren't exactly my bag either.'

'We supported his choice of venue because of its relative remoteness, deep in a pine forest. Much more secure than a well-worn location in the capital. And they've assured us we'll be the only guests.'

'Sounds like you're still concerned about a counter-coup.'

'We'd be fools not to be.'

***

AUGUSTA DROVE HIM TO the hotel in the evening, and they dined in solitary splendour in the chilly Neo-Manueline restaurant.

Nick wiped his lips with a monogrammed linen napkin. 'Don't mean to sound ungrateful for the delicious meal but I don't get it. Taking over this whole luxury hotel stinks of everything the MFA rejects. Or have you followed the path of other revolutionaries down the years and sold out already?'

Augusta put down her glass. 'No cause for concern. This particular setting encapsulates what tomorrow's all about – Spínola's delusions of grandeur. Even the wine we're enjoying is exclusive: the hotel's own vintage from vineyards close by. Meanwhile, our boys are in a meeting room upstairs with cheese sandwiches and a rough red, preparing for tomorrow's confrontation.'

***

AT NINE O'CLOCK THE next morning, Nick watched from the elaborately panelled first-floor meeting room as the Aéro-spatiale Alouette III helicopter touched down on the lawn. General Spínola ducked to avoid imaginary danger from the slowing blades, straightened, threw back his shoulders and marched across the gravel. The obligatory monocle and horsewhip were once more on display.

It was only the second time Nick had seen him in the flesh, but the general's ostentatious display of rigid self-belief struck him forcibly again.

Only after Nick had been body-searched in the lobby and relieved of his Walther – which had been placed on a tray on the side table alongside three standard issue NATO machine pistols – was he admitted to the meeting room by two clean-shaven, white-uniformed marines. They'd been meticulously efficient and scrupulously polite, ushering him through two sets of soundproofed doors. Nick had flicked his eyes around the assembled MFA, searching for any softening of the latent hostility to his presence. No dice.

A rap came at the door and the hotel manager announced: 'The president of the Republic'.

General Spínola scanned the gathering, stripped off his gloves and tossed them aside for a non-existent aide-de-camp to catch. He strode around the table, paused behind Nick, whose absence of uniform made him the sore thumb, and wordlessly jabbed him in the back of the neck with his whip.

Mario jumped up. 'General, may I present Dr Hellyer, the informal representative of our oldest ally. His presence has the unanimous endorsement of the MFA. I sincerely hope you'll both welcome and appreciate it, given the circumstances in which we find ourselves. Regrettably, our change of regime has not yet been widely accepted internationally – the Americans, in particular, are deeply suspicious of what they perceive as a communist takeover of a NATO member. Powerful British diplomatic support could make all the difference.'

Heads swung as two dull thuds and a crash of the double doors heralded the advent of a tall, thickset waiter. He backed into the room, dragging a trolley of coffee jugs, cups, and plates piled with sweet rolls. Nick shuddered, recognising the man's all too familiar gait and club-like arms.

'Most grateful, but we can serve ourselves, thank you very much. You may leave.' Mario turned back to the general.

The waiter slid Nick's Walther out from under the trolley cloth, raised his arm and fired a shot into the ceiling. 'Your attention, gentlemen.'

Spínola thwacked the table with his whip. 'Outrage! Who the hell are you?'

'Professor James Laidlaw of the University of Coimbra. I'm here to deliver a lecture. Please be kind enough to be seated. At once.'

Spínola remained erect and took a step away from the table.

Laidlaw looked around at the assembled officers, noticed Nick and frowned. 'Well, this is most fortuitous. I cannot fathom why you're here, but you may as well translate for me one last time.'

'Get out immediately, intruder. I command you.'

A second bullet raised dust from the carpet between the general's highly polished boots. Spínola ignored the shot and remained standing.

Laidlaw lowered the gun. 'General, your campaign in Guinea was most successful, and I congratulate you whole-heartedly on your achievements there. However, you and this ragtag MFA are now getting into bed with the very same people you defeated. My colleagues in the UCC could see where things were heading a while ago. The Portuguese could have defeated the guerrillas in the African provinces with the help of sarin gas and my vaccine. You'd have won the war, and the UCC's investments would have been secure. But as things stand now, your government is in danger of throwing everything away. We, that is the UCC leadership and myself, cannot and will not allow that to occur. Nick, close all the windows and draw the curtains.'

Nick finally got it. Laidlaw had vaccinated himself. He obeyed, jerked the embroidered net curtains together and edged towards the Walther.

Spínola stood motionless but for the whip in his right arm that thrashed his high-booted calves metronomically.

The professor pulled a small dark-grey cylinder out from under a cloth on the lower level of the trolley. 'General, you have spurned the opportunity for the total victory I offered you. As for the rest of those present, I consider you com-plicit in the destruction of my laboratory and gas-production facilities. And so the time has come for you to suffer the consequences of those most unwise decisions.'

Laidlaw began to release the valve at the top of the gas cylinder with his free hand.

Nick wasted no time. He tackled him side-on, grabbed the cylinder, and lobbed it hard through the nearest window.

Laidlaw regained his balance, jammed the Walther tight against Nick's neck and frogmarched him out of the meeting room. Behind them, the MFA officers rushed spluttering to open the remaining windows. Only General Spínola stood motionless by the table, whip at peace by his side.

Nick skidded on the anteroom's blood-spattered marble floor and fell. The two marines' unseeing eyes stared up at the elaborate stucco of the ceiling. He scrambled back to his feet and started towards Laidlaw, who was pulling on a jacket over the waiter's uniform. One sleeve of the coat dangled limply. From the pocket beneath, the Walther protruded. Nick backed off. Not yet. He wasn't a bloody hero, and at least he'd forestalled a mass gassing.

He thought about making another move as they crossed the deserted hotel reception. No, still too risky.

They scrunched across the gravel to the Alouette. Laidlaw slid in beside the pilot, who was engrossed in an automobile magazine, and jolted the man's temple with the Walther.

'Nick, tell this guy to take off at once. Complete radio silence. Order him to disconnect the transponder.'

Laidlaw ripped off the pilot's headphones and mic. Once airborne, he issued further instructions for their destination: The Algarve.

The pilot spoke. Nick translated.

'It's just been refuelled but has a limited range. He needs to know exactly where we're heading.'

Laidlaw threw his head back. 'I'm well aware of the Alouette's performance parameters, thank you. We have more than enough fuel.'

'The pilot will do whatever you demand, avoiding military air-traffic-control zones by flying low where necessary. But he needs to know the destination so he can plot his course accurately.'

'Aeródromo Municipal de Lagos – where I qualified for my own private pilot's licence a couple of years ago.'

Nick relayed the information to the pilot, who ran his long gloved fingers through his greying beard and nodded. Being hijacked by a gun-toting foreigner appeared to be all part of the job. Must have made a change from being the president's air taxi driver.

Nick turned back to Laidlaw, whose right hand was still cradling the pistol.

'You just attempted to gas the president of Portugal and members of the MFA committee. And now you're hijacking a helicopter. Radio contact has been broken and you've made the pilot turn the transponder off. But surely we're still visible on radar.'

'Only if they know where to look, and by the time they do it'll be too late.'

'But what's this all in aid of?'

'Weren't you listening to me in Buçaco? Can't you see the obvious staring you in the face, Hellyer? First the politicians and now the military have failed in their duty. So the time has come for scientists to direct affairs. And what must be done is blindingly clear to me.'

'But with the greatest of respect—'

'You don't get it, do you? In which case, shut up.'

Nick weighed his options. The Portuguese air force might blow them out of the sky at any moment, the pilot could fake engine failure and make an emergency landing, or Laidlaw might become distracted and give him an opportunity to grab the Walther.

How would Quinlevan want him to proceed? *No point in a mid-air shoot-out, dear boy. Get you all killed. Lie doggo and choose your moment. Play the long game and fall in with him. Discover his true objectives. And then act.* Fine words as always, but Nick could see little alternative.

Two and three-quarter hours later, the rotor pitch changed as they started their descent towards Lagos.

'Order the pilot to make a turn at Meia Praia and overfly the airfield.'

They changed direction above the four-kilometre-long beach, lost height and passed low over the empty runway. No aircraft visible and no parked cars.

'The flying school packed in the year I qualified, and all that's left now is a part-time weekend aero club.'

Laidlaw's expression cleared until, trance-like, he mirrored the helicopter as it banked and returned to hover over the airfield.

'Great shame – had a really inspirational instructor. Established star in the small-plane world, but always paid close attention to his pupils. A model, not a show-off. Except once when he did an inadvisably low loop and beat up the runway, scaring the hell out of us trainees. At the course farewell party, he explained: "Guys, that was just to show you how not to do it." Instilled a lot of self-confidence in me, he did.

I trusted and believed in him. Persuaded me I could achieve anything. And I can and will.'

Laidlaw stared down at the airfield and nodded rapidly to some inner command, then snapped back into command mode. 'Tell the pilot to put it down by the control tower.'

Nick watched spinning shadows of the slowing helicopter blades on the tarmac slicing through this complex man's personality. A moment ago, Laidlaw had appeared almost human. Three hours earlier, he'd been the callous murderer of two marines. As the blades ceased their chatter, Nick faced the chilling discovery of what Laidlaw had planned.

The professor's objectives became clearer as he marched Nick and the pilot over to the deserted three-storey control tower, fired at the lock and kicked open the door. He ripped a telephone out of its socket, bound the pilot's wrists with the wire and locked him in a windowless downstairs room.

Laidlaw motioned to Nick. 'You go ahead.'

They climbed the two flights to the control tower.

The professor trashed the radio equipment. 'Now let's get ourselves some fresh wings.'

He sounded almost upbeat, as if energy had replaced all his anger.

'You're actually enjoying the moment, aren't you?'

'Making things happen? Yes, that's what I do best. Without people like me, the modern world wouldn't exist. Consider Edison, the Wright Brothers, Marconi …'

'How about Marie Curie?'

'Yes, very good example, actually. Invented X-rays, saved humanity but unwittingly lost her own life in the process. That's something I'm prepared to do now. Wittingly.'

Laidlaw pushed Nick out of the control tower and strode over to the hangar. He dragged the heavy sliding doors open, revealing a cool semi-darkness in which light aircraft loomed like ghosts. Nick crouched against the cold metal door, a stranger in this aeronautical world of which Laidlaw's citizenship soon became apparent.

The professor patrolled the gloom, discounted some of the planes and clambered into others. He pointed at one that seemed to satisfy him.

'Here's a beauty, a real cracker. She'll do the business easily. Long legs and responsive to the slightest touch of the controls. Most importantly, fully tanked. Now give me a hand to shove her out.'

Remembering the long game, Nick put his shoulder under the front of the left wing and helped push the blue Cessna 172 backwards and out onto the runway.

Laidlaw completed his pre-flight checks and ran up the engine. 'Strap yourself in, sonny Jim. We're going somewhere you're well acquainted with, and this little beauty has just enough range to get us there.'

No conceivable point again in taking on Laidlaw in the air. If he succeeded, who'd fly the plane? Instead, Nick settled back in the right-hand seat and stared hypnotically at the ever-changing colours and forms of the Atlantic swells beneath. Images of the bull-like professor responding to his taunts and charging him as a lone forçado in the bullring flickered through his mind. The plane banked and circled a barren island, and Nick snapped out of his reverie.

Laidlaw greased the Cessna onto the 3,000-metre-long runway of a deserted but eerily familiar airfield. Terceira? Had to be but couldn't possibly be. Thousands of miles south.

'Welcome to Porto Santo Island, Madeira,' the professor announced, mimicking a plummy-voiced flight attendant, then reverted to his usual expository monotone. 'Had to come in here – we'd have been nabbed at once had we gone direct to Funchal Airport. But now we absolutely must get our skates on. Last ferry departs at six.'

Nick had glimpsed Porto Santo across the bay from Funchal but never visited. He couldn't conceive why an insignificant island should possess such an incredibly long runway.

'Officially, this is an unstaffed NATO diversion airfield. However, I've been given to understand that it also houses certain other underground facilities that would be extremely useful to the USA in a global emergency.'

Just like Terceira. Yes, of course. Same situation. Same layout. Same aim. So surely it would be well guarded, even if it were mothballed.

'They do get the occasional civil flight over from Funchal, so I'm hoping we've been mistaken for one.'

Laidlaw taxied the Cessna across the bumpy tarmac towards distant gates in the perimeter fence. A blaring siren from a military-police jeep with flashing blue lights broke through the roar of the engine. The jeep caught up with them and soon drew alongside.

'Seems we didn't get lucky. Here comes the welcome party.'

The vehicle stopped in front of the aircraft. The professor switched off the engine and opened the cockpit door. A furious barrage of questions came from one of the two military policemen.

Laidlaw shrugged. 'Sorry, don't have much Portuguese. En route from the UK. Headwinds. Low on fuel. Had to land where I could.' He grinned and waved his arms – a clumsy attempt to mime an emergency landing.

The unsmiling policeman replied at length and gestured to his companion. They trained their guns on the aircraft and indicated that both occupants should get out of the cockpit immediately.

Nick translated. 'You might not want to hear this, Professor, but he says you've landed at a military airport without permission, which you can hardly deny, and called you a lying son of a bitch, which you might find hard to contradict. He points out that not only does our Cessna have a Portuguese registration, not a British one, but also that it's recently been reported stolen from Lagos. End of story.'

Laidlaw, head down, shoulders defeated, clambered out of the cockpit and into the back of the jeep. Nick meekly joined him.

The jeep ground into gear. Laidlaw slipped out the Walther and shot both military policemen neatly through the backs of their high-peaked caps.

'Kind of them to provide us with transport, don't you think?'

Nick didn't move. The professor's action and his callous attempt to make light of it had stunned him.

Laidlaw lugged the policemen's bodies out of the blood-stained front seats and dumped them on the tarmac. He reversed the jeep violently and drove hard at the gates.

They held.

The collision threw Nick forward. He smashed into the front seat and slipped into the footwell. Heard Laidlaw reversing, revving the engine and ramming the gates again.

The result was the same. The professor abandoned the jeep, wedged up sideways against the fence, and dragged Nick out.

'Get up on the bonnet and give me your back. I'll catch you when you climb over. From then on, it's just a gentle stroll downhill to the ferry.'

Nick, now alert, pointed to the bodies of the military policemen.

'Done my research, laddie, don't you worry. Literally a skeleton base. Which, unfortunately for them, is exactly what they're well on their way to becoming. No other personnel expected until the evening shift, and by then we'll be well gone.'

Nick's mind split between outrage and passivity. The latter won the day and he clambered onto the jeep's bonnet and bent over against the windscreen. His back muscles screamed under Laidlaw's weight as the professor used him as a vaulting horse.

It took Nick three attempts to straddle the fence and cast himself into Laidlaw's arms.

They made their way down to the harbour, past children playing football in the street outside a straggle of red-roofed houses. Images of Laidlaw blowing the military policemen's brains out played over and over. He could have prevented it. Should have. But hadn't. Hadn't even foreseen it despite everything he'd already witnessed. Regardless of the bigger prize, his inaction felt unconscionable. *Lie doggo*, Quinlevan had instructed him in their imaginary helicopter conversation.

He had. And it had been oh so wrong.

∗∗∗

THE FERRY CRAWLED TOWARDS Funchal.

Nick and Laidlaw sat side by side on a flaking blue wooden deck bench, separated by a moral gulf.

What could he do with the next two and half hours? Tackle the prof and die a bleeding martyr? Go along with Laidlaw's game, however more complicit it made him? Or make his way to the bridge and inform the captain that one of his passengers was packing a gun and had just murdered two military policemen? Could be worth a try.

'Off for a slash.'

'Not on your own, you aren't.'

Laidlaw accompanied him down a narrow steep metal staircase. Stood beside him in the urinal while Nick addressed the green metal wall in front of him.

'What's the point, for Christ's sake?' Nick asked. 'Why are you dragging me along with you? Is this so you can rejoice in having an impotent witness to your murders? Why not just get rid of me? Throw me over the side? Most likely no one would hear the splash and your problem would be solved.'

Laidlaw shook his head, then his cock, spraying drops of urine. He zipped himself up and thoroughly washed dried blood from his hands at the sink. 'Because as you well know, I don't speak the fucking language.'

At the port, they joined the taxi queue.

'Tell him to go to Palácio de São Lourenço on Avenida Zarco.'

The taxi driver twisted his head and pushed his sunglasses back over a bronzed deeply lined forehead. 'What business do you have with the prisoners there? Times have changed. We, the people, rule now.'

***

Their business became apparent to Nick when they arrived at the seventeenth-century fort. Far from being incarcerated in a dungeon, Marcelo Caetano and his wife Ana Maria now sat sipping coffee in full public view behind shoulder-high glass panels on the lit-up terrace. Their demeanour was nothing short of denial. So much for a revolution; it was as if nothing of any significance had occurred. Américo Tomás had stationed himself at a considerable distance from the couple. He looked disconsolate.

Curious passers-by peered between the shoulders of a thin line of grey-uniformed municipal police, who stood facing out with their backs to the terrace. A father removed his beret and hoisted his son onto his shoulders, as he might have had they been visiting an aquarium. There were no murmurs of dissent or catcalling, just awe, residual respect and utter disbelief. As if the three captives were aliens, as if the seismic political shift had never actually taken place.

Nick baulked at the spectacle. Laidlaw interrupted him with an elbow. They pushed through the spectators and along the police line to the entrance. Two soldiers stepped forward, crossing their carbines. Nick tried to turn away, but Laidlaw gripped his arm tightly with one hand and rummaged in his inside pocket with the other. He produced a cream envelope with an embossed crest.

'Tell these guards that I have a *laissez-passer* from General Carlos Furtado. A vital message for His Excellency from the UCC.'

Nick translated, and one of the guards took the envelope through to the terrace. He returned, half-bowed, and swept his arm towards the ex-prime minister and his wife.

Nick had perceived the politicians as aliens from outside the terrace; now he'd become a guest on their planet. Must have been one hell of a letter.

'Your Excellency,' Laidlaw began, quite unfazed.

'One moment.' Caetano raised a finger. 'We may well be on display in our gilded cage but we can still, I hope, be hospitable to guests.'

Drinks were served. Caetano took a sip of water and scoured Laidlaw's face. 'I'm all too aware of the UCC's influence and ingenuity. But I quite fail to grasp on what conceivable grounds they would despatch a monolingual Englishman to me as their emissary.'

Laidlaw fished out a second envelope. Caetano read and re-read its contents. A minute's silence followed. He leant back, hands locked behind his neck. 'So, first there will be a counter-coup led by Furtado and others still loyal to me. Subsequently, your gas-vaccine discovery will enable us to defeat the insurrections and retain control of our African provinces.'

'Exactly correct, sir.'

'And, as a consequence of this victory, the UCC will continue to dominate the exploitation of Angola's diamond and oil wealth and Mozambique's agriculture.'

'Just so, Your Excellency.'

Caetano tossed the letter on to the table with a deep sigh. 'I became increasingly aware of the imminence of a military coup during nights spent reading and re-reading Spínola's inflammatory book. So far, thanks be to God, very few of our citizens have lost their lives in the face of this insurrection. However, I completely refuse to be party to the consignment of my beloved country to a bloody civil war like the one endured by our Lusitanian neighbours. Portugal will not suffer Spain's torment.'

'Your Excellency, I can assure you, all that's needed is your triumphant return to the capital. Once your people have come to their senses, they'll show no love for this communist takeover. Instead, they'll rise up to welcome their leader home. We'll take care of everything for you, I promise, and what we plan is all in your honour and service.'

'I haven't the faintest acquaintance with your standing as a scientist, but, evidently, you have minimal comprehension of Portuguese politics. Your communication is fundamentally concerned only with the UCC's commercial interests and the ambitions of the generals intertwined with them. I will not consent to becoming a mere puppet, and categorically refuse to return to Lisbon, even if it were possible, which I very much doubt. Contrary to outward appearances, my status here is that of a prisoner of the military junta that usurped me. Because my continued presence is an acute embarrassment, they have offered my wife and I safe passage to Brazil, and we intend to take up that invitation.'

Laidlaw rose leisurely from his wicker chair and strolled closer to the couple. 'We'll have to see about that, won't we?'

He thrust his right hand into his jacket pocket. To any other observer, the professor would have looked like a polite guest standing to take leave of his host, but Nick could make out the outline of the Walther through the fabric.

Now or never.

Second time today.

Nick launched himself at Laidlaw's thighs and both men crashed to the ground next to the Caetanos' table. The guards hurtled forward and pulled them to their feet. One guard covered them with his carbine; the other barked his intention to carry out a body search and passed in front of his colleague.

Laidlaw pulled out the Walther and pointed it at Caetano. Stalemate.

Both guards shifted their aim to Laidlaw. Nick inched away as Caetano stood and held his hands out to the professor, palms up.

'My friend, you have everything to lose and nothing to gain by continuing to threaten me. Kindly place your weapon on the table. Sit down and let us continue our conversation in a more civilised manner.'

Ana Maria positioned herself between Laidlaw's gun and her husband. 'Do please come and join us again, Professor. We have the whole evening in front of us. We're only just becoming acquainted.'

Nick glanced back over his shoulder as he slipped out of the terrace. Laidlaw was complying. He sat, flanked by the two armed guards, each with a hand on his shoulder. Outwitted by a veteran politician and his astute wife.

The municipal policemen, who were facing away from the palace towards the spectators, were unaware of the drama that had just unfolded behind them. They acceded to Nick's polite request and let him through. Once clear of the Palácio de São Lourenço, he quickened his pace and sought safe refuge.

***

NICK HOPPED FROM ONE foot to another for what seemed like an age. The security chain rattled, and the door opened.

'Darling, what on earth are you doing here? So good to see you, of course. Lovely surprise. But completely impossible at this moment, you must understand.'

'Patricia, my life is in danger.'

Her hand went to her mouth but failed to stifle a giggle. 'You do lay it on thick, you know.'

'No joke. I'm begging for your help. Now let me in.'

Clutching a shimmering green silk dressing gown across her bare chest, Patricia let him slide past.

'You absolutely can't sleep here tonight. I'm very sorry but that's not on the cards.'

'Why not? What's changed? We were fine together in Coimbra.'

'Clara's staying with me.'

'Yes, I know. So what? I'm hardly likely to come on to her, am I? Listen, I need to tell you what's been happening – you won't believe it.'

'Try me, but be quick.'

'Laidlaw tried and failed to gas Spínola and the MFA leaders in Buçaco, hijacked a military helicopter to the Algarve, stole a plane and flew here. He's murdered four servicemen, and I've just escaped from the Palácio de São Lourenço, where he's been holding a gun to Caetano's head.'

'Darling, you really don't sound yourself at all. Are you having some kind of breakdown? Not surprising in the circumstances. You've been through a lot, I know, but this is all a little hard to swallow. You clearly need help but, honestly, I'm not the one to get you through tonight. Come back in the morning and we'll work it out together.'

'You have to believe me. It's the truth. Hand on heart.'

'Why not look up João? I'm sure he'd be happy to provide you with a bed and a sympathetic ear.' She ran her forefinger down his cheek, kissed him gently and pushed him away. 'Now do go. Believe me, it's not you. But I've got more important things than politics on my mind just now.'

The bedroom door inched open and Clara's head, bare left forearm and shoulder came into view. Her features were softer, more vulnerable, without the forbidding glasses. 'Patricia, who's there?'

Patricia shrugged at Nick and inclined her head towards the front door.

He closed it behind him, slid down and lay back on the cold concrete top step. He hadn't seen this coming. Well, he had – just hadn't wanted to acknowledge his intuition. Fair enough. Her choice. Her life. But her decision had left him in a bad place. Literally.

***

THE RESTAURANTE LONDRES'S LAST customers walked out into the night. Tables were stripped and lights extinguished. Nick slipped up the side passageway and into the dark courtyard behind the restaurant. He squatted on the cobbles outside the entrance to João's dance studio.

No doubt Laidlaw would already be in custody and under interrogation. His inquisitors would want to know about the professor's motives certainly, but also the identity of his companion. It wouldn't take the police long to link Laidlaw to the hijacking of the Cessna and the killing of the military policemen at Porto Santo. And Laidlaw, coward that he was, would surely finger Nick as responsible for the events. Which was why he was initially reluctant to return to the brightly lit main streets in search of a public phone booth. However, when his joints started to stiffen from inaction, he ventured forth, found a booth and dialled João.

No reply. Shit. Must be out dancing. Or romancing. Leaving Nick with precious few options. If he wanted to stay below the police radar, hotels were out of the question. Cafés and bars stayed open late but he'd stick out a mile. He could sleep rough – that was an idea. He visualised a welcoming bench in the park that stretched up the slope behind him. Thank God for a temperate climate.

The whoop of a siren erupted from behind and a blue light strobed the street. By the time the police car had come to a halt, he'd already vaulted a low brick wall, and sprinted uphill past a water-lily-filled ornamental pond and across the dried grass of the park.

In a web of dark alleys, he tugged at doors until a rickety one gave. The workshop stank of paint but was a sanctuary of sorts. He stood with his back against the wall, shaking from fear, not the evening chill. He heard shouting and the pad of running feet. They receded, and he peered around the door. Darkness. No torches or pursuers. He ventured out, senses on alert, and returned to the only place of safety he could rely on.

At least he hoped it was.

***

'YOU AGAIN? I THOUGHT I'd made myself clear.'

'Police car spotted me. Gave them the slip, but the streets aren't safe. You're my only hope.'

'Followed?'

'No, I'm clean.'

'João?'

'Couldn't raise him.'

Patricia sighed. 'Come on in, then. The sofa's not the most comfortable in the world, but it'll have to do. You can tell me all about it properly in the morning. Good night, my sweet.'

She pecked him on the cheek and retreated to her bedroom.

For the moment, he was excluded. Fair enough. At least he was secure. He fell into a deep and grateful slumber.

***

SEVEN IN THE MORNING. Boots thumping up the concrete steps outside. Bugger. Had they found him? Nothing to do but brazen it out. Jumping from the terrace would mean a broken leg or ankle at the very least.

Nick inched open the door but kept the security chain on. Mario.

Nick let his friend in. The captain glanced at the half-open bedroom door. Two pairs of women's feet stuck out from under the duvet. Nick closed the door and motioned for Mario to follow him into the kitchen.

'You frightened the shit out of me just now – thought you were the DGS. How did you track me down?'

Mario grinned. 'Through my wife, naturally – she has Patricia's address, and I put two and two together. Although from what I've just seen, I may have made three.'

'Not at all amusing, and most certainly not the right moment to discuss that particular issue.'

'Your helicopter pilot managed to escape from the control tower in Lagos and reported the stolen Cessna, so we were able to follow your heading on radar. I've just flown in on a military jet, but apparently not in time to prevent two further murders at Porto Santo Airport.' Mario's voice deepened. 'Were you involved in those too?'

'Too? What are you insinuating? You yourself were present in Buçaco. You're perfectly well aware that I had nothing to do with the deaths of the marines. As for Porto Santo, I should have guessed I suppose, but Laidlaw completely wrong-footed me.'

'So much for Her Majesty's secret service. I can understand why you didn't tackle him in mid-air, but once you were on the ground—'

'One minute, Laidlaw was playing all meek, mild and submissive, but as soon as we got into the jeep he blew the backs of the soldiers' heads off. In cold blood. Just like that. And joked about it. I could have acted at that moment – perhaps I should have – but he had my gun, so I didn't.'

'You're in this up to your ears in the view of a number of my colleagues – far too many coincidences for them to credit, I'm afraid. But not in my book: for me, your story stands up.'

'Thank you, Mario. At least he's now under arrest and the killing spree's ceased.'

'Hang on a minute. Far too early to relax. The situation worsened considerably overnight. I flew here on behalf of the MFA to take Laidlaw back to face justice, only to discover that he's no longer in police custody. I've just come from the Palácio de São Lourenço, where the obsequious island authorities informed me that they've released the professor on the command of General Carlos Furtado, a Caetano loyalist. This island is a hotbed of counter-revolution – the authorities' actions reflect their inability to comprehend the reality of our revolution.'

'You haven't come to arrest me then. Despite plenty of circumstantial evidence.'

'No. But the DGS remain highly active and powerful on Madeira and are far from fully under our control. My information is that they've received orders to take you out on sight, in view of your escapade with their agents in Leiria. And the same goes for anyone unfortunate enough to be caught with you.'

Great. Not just Mossad. Now the DGS too. Flavour of the month assassination target. Shame he hadn't got around to writing a will. But then what did he have to leave? And to whom? He smiled. A good wallow in self-pity did no one any harm.

'Can't see what's amusing you, Nick.'

'Sorry.'

'Your life is in real danger. The only sensible course of action I can suggest would be to leave this address at once, because I might well not be your only early-morning surprise visitor. I hope you'll be gratified to hear that I've located a much safer haven for you. An out-of-season tourist hotel in the mountains, well away from Funchal. Eira do Serrado. Two rooms are booked in your name, but you'll have to make your own way there. I strongly suggest you use public transport – much more secure and far less traceable than a taxi.'

Mario left, and Patricia and Clara emerged bleary-eyed from the bedroom. Patricia took Nick's face in her hands and brushed kisses over his cheeks and lips.

Clara flopped on to the sofa and put her feet up. 'I'm completely lost. What's going on?'

'I guess Patricia's relayed the gist of what I shared with her last night. But this morning's news is that your professor is on the loose with a gun. And the DGS have put a price on my head and anyone caught with me.'

Patricia gave a bitter laugh. 'Oh, you do over-dramatise things sometimes, my dear.'

Clara sat up. 'Please don't think I'm complaining, but wasn't the whole idea of my coming to Madeira to get away from all this? Now you're saying that trouble's already tracked us down.'

'Tracked *me* down to be accurate, but unfortunately you two are involved by association. Mario has fixed a mountain hideaway for the three of us, and I strongly suggest we take up his offer. For a few days at least.'

Patricia tossed her head. 'I'm the only Madeiran in this room. Surely, I'm the best person to suggest somewhere untraceable, not Mario. He's not even an islander, and we could well be walking into a trap.'

'Good point,' Clara said. 'Where do you think we could bury ourselves?'

'Well, one option would be to hide in the open and stay in Funchal. I have friends who'd put us up, no questions asked.'

Nick shook his head. 'Though at some considerable risk to themselves. The police who chased me last night knew exactly who they were looking for. Stay with your friends if you want, but I'm poisonous. I plan to follow Mario's instructions.'

'Where's he suggesting we go?'

'Eira do Serrado.'

Patricia beamed and stuck her fist into the air. 'That changes things – I used to go there as a teenager. High up in the mountains with fantastic views down into the valley. Really remote. What do you think, Clara? Shall we?'

'I'm your guest; I'll be guided by you – anything to escape this hatefulness. But are you sure you're okay with me coming along, Nick? I'd quite understand if not.'

He smiled, relieved. 'Yes, it's absolutely fine. The warning related to all three of us, so we stand or fall together. I'd much rather we enjoyed your company than having to worry about the DGS squeezing our location out of you.'

***

AT TEN O'CLOCK, THEY boarded a small green-and-cream bus by the seafront and headed for the centre of the island. The half-full vehicle wound its way up along narrow ledges bordering precipitous drops. Nick, seated a couple of rows behind the two women, scanned their fellow passengers for followers. He swiftly discounted the three leathery-skinned old men in crumpled suits and caps whose shotguns proclaimed a hunting expedition, and the two women in dark-blue scarves clutching wicker baskets containing ducks. He paid rather more attention to a pair of younger sensibly clad German-speaking walkers. But they only had eyes for each other and, occasionally, the vista between the trees.

Mist descended and thickened, obscuring the landscape. The temperature plummeted the higher they drove through the dense pine forest. Now and then, they stopped to allow oncoming traffic to pass by. The bus finally rumbled into the foggy deserted car park of the Eira do Serrado Hotel. They were the only remaining passengers.

Mario had said he was sending them to a safer haven; this was more like the end of the world.

CHAPTER 9

Eira do Serrado, Madeira, 30 April 1974

IN THE CHILL OF the lobby café, the jolt of strong coffee and the sweetness of aromatic chestnut cake barely helped lift the sombre mood of the hotel's only guests. The initial euphoria of escape had evaporated; reality had wormed its way in. Patricia and Clara, who'd hardly spoken a word to each other on the journey up, sat deep in their own thoughts.

Nick broke the silence and read out a snippet from a tourist brochure he'd picked up at reception, his voice bright and cheerful. 'Listen to this. The valley below is called Curral das Freiras, so named because in the sixteenth century nuns from Funchal took refuge there to escape rape and murder at the hands of pirates.'

'Charming.' Clara pushed her half-eaten plate of cake away. 'Just like us then, I suppose. But I'm really not in favour of sitting around here expecting the worst. If they come for us, so be it. In the meantime, what can we do? Patricia, you're the one with the local knowledge.'

'Fair enough. As a fifteen-year-old, I used to bus up here with a couple of friends, and we'd hike down to the village for ice-creams. Why don't we do that? Bit of a struggle on the return I expect, but the exercise will do us the world of good.'

Clara bounced up from her deep armchair. 'Great idea. I'm all for it.'

Nick peered through the mist at the dank, slippery path snaking precipitously through chestnut and pine trees to the valley floor a thousand metres below. On balance, he'd take his chances in the hotel.

'Good for the calf muscles, I'm sure, but I think I'll get a spot of shuteye. Most grateful for a kip on your sofa last night but I'm more than slightly knackered.'

He gave them a cheery wave as they departed, made his way upstairs and crashed out.

***

CLARA'S TONGUE FLICKED OVER Patricia's salty thighs and slithered across her belly up to her freckled breasts. Her lips found a nipple and she began to suck. Then she pulled herself up, knelt with knees each side of Patricia's head and lowered her moistness onto her eager mouth ...

Nick jerked awake, his pillow sodden with sweat. Wild though the dream had been, something of this order had without doubt taken place during the night. Fact. So how did he feel? Spurned? Rejected?

Yes, naturally.

Jealous? Definitely.

Hypocritical? That too.

Aisha had by no means been the only lover in his life. Quite the opposite. He and Patricia had made each other no promises and told each other no ... Scratch that. They'd almost certainly told each other lies.

What did he want? Heavy question, that. Given the

demands of their lives, he could see no way in which their relationship could ever be exclusive. So why not accept the reality?

He lurched out of bed with the intention of meeting the women halfway on their return and asked at the front desk for directions to the path.

The portly receptionist shook his head. 'Not such a good idea, sir. You could easily miss your friends in this fog. Better if you climb to the viewpoint above the hotel and wait until you can pick them out.'

He handed over their passports. Nick thanked him for his advice, and he responded with a half-bow.

On the steep walk up to the mirador, Nick passed a couple of elderly Scandinavians in bright-yellow anoraks making their way down, but now he was alone on the path. The fog had descended abruptly, erasing his vision and muffling the forest sounds. It might have scared him under other circumstances, but right now the solitude of this magical place completed him, as if he were no longer part of the Earth, but elevated high into a swirl of cloud. A silent epiphany – the first he'd experienced.

A few minutes later, he'd become accustomed to his new environment and continued up, though cautiously. At the top of the narrow path, he felt his way forward step by step and made a right turn. The fog swirled, thinned and lifted slightly, revealing a platform that was cut into the rock and extended over the void. The floor was built from irregular planks of wood covered in damp green mould. They creaked as he walked across and steadied himself against a waist-high fence topped by roughly trimmed pine branches. Beyond, he caught a dizzying snatch of patchwork fields on the valley floor far below; farm dogs barked incessantly, but there was no sign of Clara or Patricia.

Thick cloud enveloped him again, restoring the silent harmony. Nick relaxed and rested his forearms on the fence. It groaned in protest against his weight.

A half-heard footfall prompted him to glance over his right shoulder towards the top of the path. Were they back already? He must have missed them.

A tall, heavily built figure emerged from the dense mist and lumbered towards him. A man. Dull green hiking gear. A scarf partially obscured his face, but Nick recognised the stranger.

Laidlaw, panting slightly, kept his distance and leant back against the rock wall.

He caught his breath and pulled out Nick's Walther. 'Just to put you out of your misery, I know your two lady friends are here. Reception informed me they'd been enquiring after your whereabouts. They went up to their room. Powdering their noses, apparently.'

Nick donned his best attempt at an engaging smile. Not that he had the faintest idea how to win over a homicidal maniac.

Took a step forward.

'No need for the hardware, Professor. Apologies for vamoosing during your conversation with the Caetanos. I'm sure it went swimmingly.'

Another step. Like the leader of the *forçados* challenging the bull, but with no supporting team behind him.

Another. Almost within reach of the Walther.

He hurled himself forward, grabbed the professor's body and brushed the gun arm aside. The stronger, heavier man broke his off-balance grip and pushed him away.

'Back against the fence.'

Nick obeyed. Laidlaw strode over, stood right in his face and Nick caught the rank odour of stale perspiration. The result of desperation? Or was it panic? No way would Laidlaw have sweated so heavily from a brief exertion in this chilly fog.

'No point trying to sweet talk me, sonny boy,' Laidlaw hissed in his ear.

But there was every point. His personal fate seemed settled, but he might buy a little time for the women. And flattery had worked with Laidlaw in the past. Why not suck up to him again?

'Sorry. Total misunderstanding. Look, I really am pleased to see you. Just got carried away. Been on tenterhooks what with everything that's been going on. Fantastic that you're a free agent. Must have pulled a few strings, I imagine. Man like you. And what a great job you did tracking us down.'

Laidlaw backed off slightly and smiled. 'You're quite right. Caetano's yesterday's man. Admit I made a mistake there, but he's no longer got any real power – I realise that now. Nothing really lost. My friends secured my release easily enough last night. As for locating you – piece of cake. The DGS still works hand in glove with the UCC on this island. You had to produce ID when you checked in at the hotel, didn't you? Figure out the rest for yourself.'

Women's voices echoed dully from the slope below, died away and became audible again. Nick's bridge-building began to unravel as Laidlaw tensed, pocketed the gun and retreated. The professor flattened himself against the rock wall.

Clara and Patricia emerged from the gloom hand in hand and skipped over to the fence.

Patricia embraced him. 'Here's where you've been hiding!'

Clara grinned. 'Much, much steeper than she promised. And halfway up, she confessed to always taking the bus in her youth. But we made it. How are you, all alone in the clouds? Brooding, I suppose. Not about me, I hope.'

'Not so. Skywalking in this mountain dreamworld while waiting for you two to show up. But I'm afraid someone else beat you to it.'

Laidlaw stepped forward.

'Professor! What on earth are you doing here?'

'Calm down, my dear. You'll find out soon enough. Only good as far as you're concerned, I promise. Stay right where you are.' He gestured towards the rock face. 'You two, get away from her. Over there.'

Nick started to move but Patricia stayed put. 'You can't order me about like that.'

'Oh, but he can, Patricia. He has an extremely powerful justification in his jacket pocket. Come on.'

'Good lad, Nick. You tell her. But you can be sure that's not going to change how I'm going to deal with both of you in a moment.'

Laidlaw's voice softened as he faced Clara by the fence. 'Now, my dear, I propose to make you an offer – the chance of a lifetime. But first I must make absolutely sure of your loyalty. The last time we spoke, you mentioned you were having some doubts about the scientific legitimacy of our research.'

She met his gaze. 'Yes, sir, that's correct. But I've had a chance to reflect on what I said, and I've changed my mind. I can assure you I fully support the project.'

Laidlaw's shoulders relaxed. 'And can you see that unless we suppress the mutinies in Africa soon, tens of thousands more will die needlessly?'

Patricia squeezed Nick's hand.

'Yes, Professor, I can. I'm at your service whenever and wherever you wish.'

'Excellent, my girl. Always believed I could rely on you. A UCC plane stocked with replacement laboratory kit and bound for Angola is standing by at Funchal Airport. Together, we can replicate the facilities and continue our great work. In time, our research will be seen as one of the century's grandest scientific breakthroughs – one for which you'll share the credit.'

'I can't thank you enough, sir. It really is the opportunity of a lifetime.'

Nick snatched a glance at Patricia. Had Clara over-egged it? Surely Laidlaw wouldn't buy such a sudden turnaround.

Clara patted the professor affectionately and brushed away imaginary specks of dust from the shoulders of his hiking jacket. 'And as for my friends, I suggest you let them go. There's no way they can damage our project – we'll be far away, out of harm's reach in Southern Africa.' Her hands rested gently on his chest.

'Not so simple or so fast, Clara. Not my friends. My enemies. You mustn't forget – they destroyed our production facility. I'm certain of it. Hellyer was the only person outside the team who knew about it. Undermined everything. And he's attacked me twice. Both guilty as hell. Time for a reckoning.'

It *was* time. Nick launched himself from the rock wall and rushed forward, but slipped on the mouldy planks. Laidlaw's hand dived into his jacket pocket and pulled out the Walther. He aimed at Nick's sprawling body. Clara's arm snaked around Laidlaw's neck and jerked his head back.

A shot ricocheted off the rock, and Patricia flinched as it missed her by centimetres.

The professor twisted out of Clara's neck hold, and grabbed at her face, ripping off her spectacles. She enveloped him in a powerful bear hug and crushed him tight to her, as if in passion. Laidlaw fought for breath and tried to wrestle out of her hold, but she held on, squeezing relentlessly.

Two shots, their sound muffled. Blood erupted from the professor's mouth and he crashed against the railing, dragging Clara with him. The fence groaned and splintered under their combined weight, then cracked.

Both vanished into the rolling mists towards the valley below.

Patricia hauled Nick to his feet, and they peered over the edge of the platform. Only twenty metres beneath them, the two bodies lay caught in pine branches. The back of Laidlaw's head had been smashed open, exposing a bloodied mass of brain tissue. Had Clara's neck not been at an unnatural angle, she might have been peacefully asleep.

Patricia's voice was thick with tears. 'My sweet, brave, brave girl.'

Nick put his arms around her. 'But a fitting end for a killer and potential mass murderer. The world's a better place.'

Patricia squatted and picked up Clara's spectacles, one lens smashed and both arms twisted. 'Not without her.'

Nick retrieved his besmirched gun. Whose blood? Laidlaw's and Clara's probably – there'd been two shots. He wiped it down and threw the tissue over the side. 'Probably best if you chuck the glasses over too.'

'No, I'm holding on to them.'

'Your choice. I doubt if anyone'll be able to identify exactly where the gunshots came from – the fog would have absorbed and distorted the sound. But once it lifts, the first people up here will notice the gap in the fence.'

Patricia looked up. 'How can you be so cold, so logical?'

'I cared about Clara as a fellow human. Your feelings are on a different level. I respect that. An exceptionally good woman. Agreed. But she's dead and we have to deal with the consequences. The next visitors to this platform will come across the scene of a tragic accident. Until the police recover the bodies and examine them ... then the deaths will almost certainly be pinned on us once the authorities have checked my gun.'

'Then throw it over as well.'

'No. I might need it. We'll have to put on a show of normality at the hotel until I can get hold of Mario. Are you up to returning there or do you want to stay and mourn here for a bit longer?'

Patricia looked down over the edge. 'Nick, there are times when you appear to be nothing short of a callous bastard.'

She set off for the hotel. Nick stayed a couple of paces behind. They made small talk in reception, as if nothing untoward had occurred, and went up to Nick's room.

He called the barracks in Funchal, listened, and hung up.

'Mario will be here as soon as he can with reinforcements.'

'I'm done for. Whacked.' Patricia, face drained of colour, crashed back onto the bed and raised her knees, clasping her arms around them. 'I need a drink, something strong.'

***

NICK RETURNED WITH A small bottle of Ginja, the local sour-cherry liqueur. Patricia poured herself a glass, drained it, and filled another. One for Nick too.

By the time the roar of revving engines had summoned them down to the foyer, the bottle was empty.

Mario stood beside a jeep. A camouflage patterned Berliet truck was parked behind. Six soldiers sat in the canvas-covered rear. Grim-faced, the captain met them halfway across the car park.

'Show me where it happened.'

***

Two of the soldiers abseiled down to the pine and secured the bodies. The others steadied the broken fence and hauled them up.

Mario walked over to the corpses. 'A tragic accident at first sight – a rickety fence that gave way. An open-and-shut case if it weren't for the bullet wounds and, of course, their identities. I shall introduce myself to the hotel staff and inform them that a foreigner and one of their Portuguese guests have died in a suicide pact. The foreigner is under investigation for an attempt on the life of the president, meaning the deaths are a matter for state security.'

Patricia's eyes followed the soldiers as they carried the bodies down to the truck.

'That's exactly what it is,' Nick said. 'This isn't just about us; it's a threat to the whole of your revolution. Clara saved our lives and prevented him destroying everything you've fought for.'

Mario nodded. 'True, but the real tragedy is that no one will ever know what she did. You won't spread it about for obvious reasons, and my men will keep their mouths shut. All the hotel staff need to know is that we're taking the bodies to the morgue. I'll hang around until the municipal police turn up. I don't want the local *bófias* interviewing either of you, so I suggest you both go back to town in the truck.'

'*Bófias?*'

'Finally, I've hit a chink in your linguistic armour, Nick. The plod. Isn't that what you call them? Though the *bófias* here aren't as reputedly stupid. They'd certainly have an abundance of questions for you, not only about your weapon, but also your line of work.'

***

PATRICIA AND NICK SAT opposite each other in the rear, clinging to the metal benches as the truck swerved around the hairpins and down the mountain. Between them, Laidlaw and Clara's corpses jumped and twitched as if alive.

Patricia stretched out a hand and patted Clara's arm. Nick's nostrils filled with the stench of bodily fluids that grew stronger with every bounce and bump. The whole business stank, and two more people had died as an indirect consequence of his actions. He didn't mourn Laidlaw, but Clara was a martyr who'd almost succeeded in deceiving a monster.

***

HOME. IT SHOULD HAVE been a relief, but Patricia pulled the sheets up to her neck and trembled. Nick lay on his back, eyes wide until her breathing calmed.

They woke late the next morning. She stroked his stubble with a forefinger and snuggled down to doze again.

Mario turned up during Nick's breakfast preparations. 'I hope you're on the road to recovery. A terrible thing – you were lucky to escape with your lives.'

'No luck involved. Clara sacrificed hers.'

'You might be interested to know that the episode in Eira do Serrado is done, dusted and swept right under the carpet. Clara's family has been informed, and her body will be shipped back to them for burial. How much do you know about Laidlaw's background?'

'Haven't a clue – he never mentioned relatives. I always took him for a loner.'

'So far less chance of any family snooping around after him. And I've made sure that the UCC got the message. Now, I have an urgent communication for your Major Quinlevan. Regardless of the apparent British assassination attempt on our president in Buçaco, the MFA still wish to continue a dialogue with your government.' Mario drew down his lower left eyelid with his forefinger.

It took a moment for Nick to work it out. 'Yes, I'll pass your message on in my report today.'

'I'm flying out later but will be back again quite soon if Spínola's madcap plan to deport our dictator to Brazil is allowed to go through. Must leave now – I can see myself out.'

***

NICK SET DOWN THE belated breakfast tray and filled Patricia in on Mario's news, and of his own intention to contact London through the consulate.

'You must be joking. Today's May Day. Everything's bound to be closed. This is the first time the municipal authorities have allowed political demonstrations to go unhindered on this occasion. Used to be totally forbidden.'

They ate and emerged from the flat into the glaring sunshine. The crowds sang, chanted and danced. Nick vividly recalled the euphoric atmosphere he'd witnessed in Lisbon on the day of the revolution: everything had become possible; the unthinkable a reality. While Mario had justifiable concerns about counter-revolution, Nick couldn't see how the lid could be forced back on this particular pot again.

Arm in arm, they pushed against the tide of the good-humoured procession on the Avenida do Mar and made their way to the British consulate. Nick had called ahead using the emergency out-of-hours number and given his code word.

Her Majesty's consul pulled up outside the shuttered building in a dust-stained brown Ford Consul. The man's woollen jacket – too heavy for the climate – strained over a less-than-crisp white shirt. And his suede Hush Puppies were stained. At least the crumpled pink bow tie matched his flushed face.

'Who the hell do you think you are? Pretty damned sure I haven't met you before. How dare you try to pull rank on me? That code is highest priority.'

'No, we haven't met, sir, but you were informed of my presence on the island a long time ago. London instructed you to make every facility available to me in an emergency. Every facility.'

'I'm familiar with that charming little Madeiran chappie from your lot who pops in from time to time to send messages. Always very respectful, I might say. But I don't know you from Adam. Can't it wait until tomorrow? You do realise this is a public holiday. We were about to have—'

'Lunch? Possibly. Sex? I doubt it.' Nick edged closer to the consul than strictly necessary or, indeed, polite. 'You don't have the faintest inkling of what's in play here. This isn't some piddly little diplomatic game. People's lives are at stake. So is the future of this state.'

'Sounds rather over the top if you ask me, but I'm obliged to take you at your word. What can I do for you?'

'Immediate access to the communications room.'

'All right, but your no-doubt-delightful friend stays outside.'

The consul made a prima-donna fuss of unlocking doors and turning off alarms en route to the sanctum.

Nick fired up the equipment. He was good to go.

He glanced back at the porcine figure hanging in the doorway.

'Leave this room at once. Actually, leave the building. Go and keep my "delightful friend" company – she could well be in considerable danger.'

'You can't speak to me like that in my own office. I'm—'

'I know exactly who and what you are. And I can assure you that it would not be at all in your personal interest to be privy to this call. Quite the opposite. Either leave me in peace or start packing your bags for an immediate and unaccompanied posting to Ulan Bator.'

Nick waited. Went through the protocols. A familiar voice greeted him.

'Nick, my son. Welcome.' Quinlevan's tone changed abruptly. 'Now tell me what in God's name you've been up to. You've not maintained regular contact as instructed. From where I'm sitting, you've gone AWOL. A deserter or worse, leaving a trail of bodies behind you.'

'Many thanks for your kind concern, sir.'

Nick delivered a full report.

The silence that followed lengthened and lengthened until he wondered whether the connection had been lost.

'Major? Are you still there?'

'Of course I am. Just running through a few permutations. On no account are you to return to the mainland. I'm sending Midnight Bike Rider to retrieve the transceiver. He'll airfreight the rest of your stuff to you, care of Joe. Understood?'

'Most considerate of you, sir. But what about the more substantive issue?'

'Yes, the good news is we've succeeded in a change of guard at the embassy in Lisbon. Should make a huge difference to our relations with the MFA. Couldn't ditch the ambassador because the FCO wouldn't wear it, more's the pity. But we now have our new man, Bending, in post with cover as commercial attaché.'

'And what about his predecessor?'

'Don't pretend to be dense, Hellyer. Doesn't deceive me one iota. He's dead: Proudfoot was one of ours. Before your arrival, we'd had our suspicions – subsequently confirmed – that he'd started batting for the opposition. The upper echelons have instructed me to pass on their deep gratitude for your actions, and their congratulations on not leaving any loose ends, if you get my drift. Now, give me the Lisbon contact details of your MFA captain, and Bending will pick up the baton, if you'll also excuse the pun.'

Nick obliged and Quinlevan continued.

'I do so hope the politicos in Westminster wake up and formally recognise the new regime pronto. Not really our role at all. I'll instruct Joe to fix you up with some suitable temporary billeting while we work out your next move. Until then, lie low and await further orders.'

The praise, while welcome, was unusual. A worm of disquiet wriggled in his mind.

***

PATRICIA AND THE CONSUL sat on a bench opposite the building, deep in conversation.

'Many thanks for the communications assistance, sir, and my sincerest apologies for the earlier abruptness. You can pull down the portcullis.'

'Your lady friend certainly is a fount of information about geraniums. Charming girl.' Her Majesty's consul waddled past his jalopy, and Patricia and Nick rejoined the celebrations on the Avenida del Mar.

***

NICK RECEIVED DETAILS OF his accommodation from João at the dance studio early the next day. For now, he'd remain where he was.

Patricia honoured her postponed client commitments, despite being due time off, and spent much of her time at work. Nick meanwhile filled his days with exercise and reflection, reliving and reimagining past horrors as he ran along the familiar levadas … his attacker sliding over the edge, Laidlaw and Clara crashing through the fence into the fog, the bloodied marines at Buçaco, the military policemen's caps at Porto Santo. But it was the faces of the Tete victims that most frequently haunted him.

And every day he heard nothing from London became a day to the good.

***

Funchal, Madeira, 19 May 1974, 4 p.m.

THE GROUP OF FRIENDS, one in uniform, stood in unison and raised frosted champagne cocktail glasses. The toast attracted gazes from the Sunday-afternoon customers lounging in wicker chairs outside the Golden Gate Café on Avenida Arriaga.

Nick raised his glass the highest. 'Augusta, Mario, what a splendid surprise to see you both again and so soon.'

'Given the price of the drinks,' Augusta said, 'I'm not sure it's a justifiable cause for such a celebration.'

Patricia patted her arm. 'Nick can afford it, my dear. Frankly, he's getting paid a fortune for taking endless long distance runs and sleeping with me, though the latter appears to offer him more satisfaction.'

Augusta grinned. 'You haven't changed a jot, Patricia. *Saúde!*'

They sat and Mario turned the conversation to more serious matters.

'The way I see it is this. Although I was initially opposed to the idea, I realise now that exiling Caetano and Tomás is the only viable solution. The MFA are so torn apart that any attempt to bring the pair of them to justice could be highly counterproductive. My role is to ensure they leave by air-force jet for Brazil tomorrow morning.'

Augusta reached across the table and took Patricia's and Nick's hands. 'I confess I hitched a ride here with Mario under totally false pretences. But I so much wanted to know how you both were. It's lovely to see how much more at ease you are with each other.'

Nick gave an embarrassed smile. 'That's kind of you. But you've caught us on a good day.' Patricia kicked him under the table. He turned back to Mario, massaging his ankle. 'I'm out of the game now, but I do hope you've been contacted by our new commercial attaché.'

'Yes, my friend. The wind has indeed changed, and the branches are bending in the right direction.'

Nick almost spilled his cocktail. 'And what follows tomorrow's deportation?'

'We can't be sure how long Spínola will last, and there are rumours of more strikes coming. It'll take time to organise elections – probably not until next year. As far as the wars go, Soares, now foreign minister, is starting with the easiest situation to resolve: Guinea. Then Angola and Mozambique. A staged handover to the rebels.'

'How does this play with the Yanks?'

'Badly, as you can imagine. But it's not just our overseas bases they need access to; it's the NATO control centre by the Tagus in Lisbon too. They're not going to rush. My best guess is they'll use the white regimes in Rhodesia and South Africa as proxies to subvert the liberation movements. But we'll still withdraw our involvement.'

Nick frowned. 'What about all the European Portuguese living in the overseas provinces?'

'It's more than likely they'll return to the mainland. We'll have to deal with that if and when it comes about. But I'm optimistic. We've achieved the unimaginable with little loss of life. We must hang on to the positives.'

Nick raised his glass again. 'I'll drink to that.'

***

NICK LAY ON HIS back, wide-awake in the dark.
  Patricia rolled towards him. 'Augusta ... did you ever?'
'No. Did you?'
'No.'
'Wanted to?'
'No. You?'
'No.'
'So she meant it when she held both our hands. Now come
to me, my darling.'

***

Funchal, Madeira, 20 May 1974, 9 a.m.

THE BATTERED LOCAL BUS rode up the steep hill to Monte.
Nick and Patricia hopped out at the botanical gardens just in
time for opening. She'd taken the morning off and suggested
the expedition – an opportunity to clear the air. 'You're holding something back from me,' she'd said.
  Nick berated himself as they walked through the gates.
He'd been distracted on the way up and failed to make his
usual routine checks on their fellow passengers. But Patricia
was right. There was something on his mind. She'd always
been open and loving towards him but had consistently withheld a kernel of her inner being. He wanted to believe they
had a future, but the cynical part of him worried that she
treated their relationship as work as much as love. Jealousy

gnawed too. The more he'd speculated, the wilder his imaginings had become.

They strolled hand in hand in the sunshine. A gravel path led them under the broad leaves of giant banana trees.

He stopped and pulled her to him. 'Tell me about my predecessor, Al. What kind of guy was he when you knew him? What attracted you ... still attracts you? You must care for him deeply – you've kept his sketch on the wall, and your desk drawer's full of his postcards. Highly insecure tradecraft by the way.'

Patricia paused. 'Al was certainly your predecessor, but as my first lover, not my first spy. Nothing whatsoever to do with your line of work. Now, is that enough personal information for you to be going on with?'

'Not in the slightest. How different from me? How special?'

'You just don't get it, my simple boy. You're a highly educated, most intelligent person, granted, but emotionally a complete dunce.' She cupped his hands in hers. 'Listen. Al is a she ... Alice. We were in the same class at secondary school, though she's a year older than me. We fell in love: brushing past each other in the corridor, exchanging glances, furtive handholding, a school camping trip. Plenty of complications, you can imagine, but such a momentous experience for both of us. Not just a teenage crush – the real thing. She dominated my being day and night, and I believed she felt the same way. But after her exams, her family moved to Lisbon. She'd shared nothing of the plan, and my fragile world collapsed. I knew her parents had concerns about our relationship, but never dreamed they'd go to that extreme. The bait, I later discovered, was a coveted place at the Tourism Academy, which they'd secured through influence. Anyway, she graduated and started a new life working on cruise ships in Asia … first as a steward, subsequently an entertainments manager. As far as I know, she's voyaged the world ever since.'

'Hence the postcards. How incredibly dim of me. You're right about my emotional blindness.' He paused but couldn't help himself. 'But it's strange that you didn't meet up … all those years you were studying at Coimbra. If your love had been that strong—'

'Stop. Right now. Do not attempt to interrogate me, Nick. Look, I felt hurt and betrayed, and wanted nothing further to do with her. Her family engineered a clean break and she went along with it. End of story.'

'Not really. She clearly wasn't of the same mind because she's kept in touch with you ever since.'

'My God, you really do know how to hurt me, don't you?'

Nick stared at the ground, avoiding her eyes, waves of inadequacy washing over him.

'Anyway, who are you to get on your high horse just because you've learnt something about my history? What's with the great shock and surprise? My bisexuality must surely have been obvious the minute you stumbled on me and Clara together. What did you think we were doing all night in my bed? Playing dominoes? And last night, you asked me if I'd slept with Augusta.'

'Yes, good point as always. And in some weird way, I don't feel as jealous now that I know Al's a woman.'

'You're a funny one. Not sure what that signals about your psyche. What difference does the gender make? Might it be that your relief comes from the certainty that I'll never see Al or Clara again?'

'I haven't considered it as baldly as that. But you could be right, I suppose.'

'And who's to say that our sexualities aren't so dissimilar, Nick?'

He poked at the gravel with the toe of his shoe. 'What on earth are you getting at? Who's interrogating who now?'

'Look me in the eyes. João let me in on a confidential briefing from Q about the circumstances of your admission to the service. No point in denying the unintended late-night gay encounter that triggered your recruitment.' She stroked his cheek with the back of her hand. 'That's who we are, so best to face it. But we can be incredibly strong together. I love you, and I will always tell you the truth. That's a promise.' She gave him a butterfly kiss on the forehead. 'And the current truth is I'm dying for a pee.'

Patricia headed over to a faded-green wooden café, leaving Nick dithering. On the one hand, he wanted this dreamlike existence in Madeira to continue forever. On the other, he longed for the handle of his soft leather bag and the hard edges of his passport.

The decision was made for him.

'Nick?'

The unsteady tone of Patricia's voice alarmed him. He turned. She stood arm in arm with a trouser-suited woman in high-heeled leather boots, a brown linen satchel slung across her chest. Al?

'Allow me to introduce Ella. She's the one I mentioned, remember? The surprise visit to the flat in Coimbra?'

'Vaguely, now you mention it.' Nick tried to keep his tone light, playing for time. 'Nice to meet you at last, Ella. So how—'

'Shut up, Hellyer. Start walking … into the plantation.'

Ella shoved Patricia forward and tightened her grip on her arm.

Nick went first. They pushed past a tall clump of bamboo and penetrated the grove. It was distinctly cooler and illuminated only by occasional pools of sunlight. The foliage grew denser, and branches whipped and slashed across his face.

He bent forward, right hand edging towards the ankle holster. 'Got to pause, I'm afraid. Old back injury.'

Ella gave him a vicious thrust that sent him face down into the rotting brown leaves. He rolled over. She shoved Patricia to one side and pulled a silenced Beretta 70 from the satchel.

'Fine. Your choice.'

Patricia lunged and made a grab for the gun. But Ella chopped her in the neck with the barrel of the Beretta and pushed her down beside Nick.

Patricia knelt in front of him and spread her arms. 'No. No. It's all a terrible mistake.'

'Out of the way, girl,' Ella barked. 'My orders are to kill him, and him alone. We Israelis have a code – an eye for an eye.'

Patricia wouldn't budge. Ella advanced slowly until she had a clear line of fire at Nick over Patricia's shoulder. Patricia tried to get up, but Ella head-butted her and she collapsed back on top of Nick.

'One bullet will do for both of you. Roll away from him at once if you value your life. I repeat: I have no quarrel with you.'

Nick squirmed underneath Patricia's weight. 'Do what she says and get off me, for Christ's sake.'

'Your last chance, woman. Move or die.'

Ella shot twice into the ground between Nick's legs. He screamed and bucked as if he'd been hit. Patricia bounced off, leaving him exposed to the Beretta.

'Farewell from Mossad, Dr Hellyer.'

Nick fired the Walther. It nailed the Beretta, which flew into the undergrowth. The impact unbalanced Ella and she fell backwards onto the rotting vegetation. He leapt to his feet, stood over her and trained the gun on her head.

'Simple dilemma, really. I could, and probably should, kill you now.'

Ella shook her head violently.

'But Mossad's vendetta against me has no basis in reality. If I shoot you, the revenge saga will continue. Or I can let you walk. You report to your commanders that I spared your life, as I hope they'll mine in the future. That way we can draw this pointless spiral of violence to a conclusion.'

Ella glared up at him and clambered to her feet. Nick retrieved the Beretta, unclipped the magazine and handed the empty pistol to her. She grasped it, spat in his face and pushed through the plantation.

Patricia brushed dirt off her clothes. 'Do you think that was wise?'

'Totally unwise, I'm sure. But I am not and will not become a killer.'

'She is. A professional assassin.'

'I've no intention of spending the rest of my life looking over my shoulder. And while Mossad must certainly have files on your identity and where you live, I think you can take comfort from her words – I'm the one she came to wipe out. Me alone.'

They scuffed the ground to erase traces of the incident and, hand in hand, like a slightly embarrassed couple post-clandestine encounter, emerged from a different part of the thicket and headed for the exit. She held his arm tight on the long walk down the steep slope.

***

AT THE DANCE STUDIO, João had shaken his head. 'Not again, my accident-prone friend. And you let her go? Unbelievable. I'll have to check with Q, but I'm sure you can guess what his response will be.'

They'd agreed he'd pick Nick up from Patricia's flat an hour later.

Nick sat hunched at the kitchen table and waited. The soft leather bag had been packed, and the passport in his jacket pocket dug into his ribs. He was ready – ready to put an end to this episode and move on. The weight of the deaths he'd witnessed sat heavily on his shoulders. Spying was one thing; killing another. Patricia had filled his loneliness for a time, and perhaps he'd alleviated hers. But. But. There was no way forward for them, whatever their relationship.

Patricia slid a hand over his shoulder. 'How can you be so calm? It's all in the balance. You know how much you to mean to me. I've shown you.'

Nick's hand shook as he lifted a glass of white port to his lips and drops fell like tears onto the red-checked tablecloth. His mouth remained dry.

'And you to me. But I can hardly say, "Come live with me and be my love". Just not feasible. We're both bound to the same wheel. And it keeps on turning, my sweet Patricia.'

She held him tight, but in the mirror he saw João grabbing his bag and beckoning. He stood, her lips brushed his hot brow, and they kissed … a long loving farewell.

She shook his shoulders hard, forcing him to respond to her gaze. 'Take care.'

'I'll send you a postcard.'

He hadn't meant it to sound flippant, but it had. She turned her back.

***

NICK CAUGHT THE AIRPORT bus from Heathrow and slumped in a seat on the top deck. Diagonal fingers of rain dragged across the filthy windows, mirroring his depression.

No prospect of some grand romantic adventure with Patricia.

Or was there?

Couldn't just throw the towel in on his job and endanger hers.

Or could he?

But what would they do and where could they go? Did it matter? And what did he even want, deep down?

He took a taxi for the final leg to the office. His heart thumped in time with the traffic lights dancing on the wet streets. Red. Amber. Green. Off. Maybe. On.

The darkened mews building was deserted but for security. He was sent straight up to Quinlevan.

'Well, you're looking yourself, my boy, despite recent events. Joe's filled me in. For reasons best known to yourself, you disarmed an Israeli agent this morning, only to let her go. And you insist you played no intentional part in the deaths of the first Mossad agent, the professor and his colleague, four members of the Portuguese armed forces, the British embassy's Lisbon military attaché and a group of guerrillas in Mozambique. Quite a tally.'

'That's correct, sir. This department trained and armed me, but I'm not directly responsible for any of those deaths.'

'I trust you mean we taught you how to defend yourself. Contrary to popular belief, our sole goal is to secure information vital to the nation's security, not to eliminate our enemies. You've been most successful on the information front, I grant you, but too many people in proximity to you have died recently. These are facts, laddie, not value judgements.'

'I cannot deny the part my action or inaction played, sir.'

'Well, whether you like it or not, you're turning into just the kind of agent my superiors—'

'I signed up, albeit under duress, to ferret out and supply you with information seven years ago. I've done that. I abandoned my former life; became an espionage gypsy. You've retrained me, reformed me. Even controlled my love life, what there is of it.'

Quinlevan raised an eyebrow and gave the slightest shake of his head. 'Listen—'

'No.' Nick leaned forward and slammed his fist on the desk. 'I'm here at your bidding, but for once try to understand how things are from my end. I've done bloody well to come through all of this in one piece, and that didn't happen through luck. My life was on the line this morning – Patricia's too – and I dealt with it as best I could. My judgement call. But if that's not sufficient for you, I'm more than happy to chuck it all in and return to academia.'

'If they'll have you. Not much of a life ahead as a remittance man in some godforsaken West African university, is there?' Quinlevan smiled thinly and leaned back. 'Surely you realise there's a slight technical problem too. We can hardly provide you with a reference, can we? An accurate transcript of your recent deadly track record would be most unlikely to endear you to any future employer. No, you're stuck with us, I'm afraid. Nor must we lose sight of your outstanding drug-dealing charge. A minor matter, of course, but weren't you facing seven years in the chokey until the service rescued you? Do correct me if I'm wrong.'

Nick stood, hands on hips. 'Blackmail, pure and simple. I could blow the whistle to the newspapers on your whole shadowy enterprise and take the lot of you down with me.'

'Rest assured, we've got the press covered, dear boy. D-notices – papers can't print a thing about us once one has been issued.' Quinlevan threw his arms open and gave him a disarmingly warm smile. 'Less haste, more speed, son. What I was trying to tell you before was that events have moved on apace. The powers that be, in other words the desk-bound warriors on the floor above me, wish to reiterate their deepest gratitude. Seems you're just the kind of agent they're looking for. I don't quite get it myself – bit like rewarding a tortoise for crossing a busy dual carriageway unscathed.'

What the hell? Blatant flattery and mockery. Maybe now was the time to chuck it all in and walk out. But he didn't. The weight of the rhetoric was too much, and Nick slumped back into his chair.

'That's better, laddie. Yes, seems they're firmly of the opinion that the sun shines out of your fundament. What my superiors regard as your Portuguese coup has given them, in my admittedly limited perspective, a vastly overinflated estimation of your capabilities. Hence, the new mission.'

'Which is?

'Frankly, an enterprise with such little chance of success that I wouldn't give it to a dog.'

BACKGROUND

T HE AUTHOR WORKED IN Coimbra, Portugal, for two years prior to the 1974 Carnation Revolution, and subsequently undertook government consultancy missions in Beira and Maputo, Mozambique, during the post-revolutionary civil-war period. More recent research visits to Portugal and Madeira, as well as contacts with former colleagues and friends, helped ensure the accuracy of the background to events fictionalised in this book.

In particular, he is grateful for feedback on earlier drafts from Carolyn Cemlyn-Jones, Ian Jones, Vic Prowse (his father, who achieved his PPL in Lagos at the age of eighty-one) and Grace Wilkins.

He is deeply indebted to Rhiannon Williams, who helped craft this project from its inception. She bears no responsibility whatsoever for what flaws remain but deserves his undying gratitude for the rectification of many others.

He is also most grateful to Rachel Rowlands (development editor) and Louise Harnby (line editor) for their matchless editorial skills, and to Andrew and Rebecca Brown for their design brilliance.

Readers interested in the, often conflicting, accounts of the historical settings of this work of fiction may find this brief bibliography useful.

Barker, C. (ed.), 1987, *Revolutionary Rehearsals*, London: Bookmarks.

Faye, J. P. (ed.), 1976, *Portugal: The Revolution in the Labyrinth*, Nottingham: Spokesman Books.

Kayman, M., 1987, *Revolution and Counter-Revolution in Portugal*, London: The Merlin Press Ltd.

Lind-Guimarães, G. (ed.), 2009, *Eyewitness Accounts of the Portuguese Revolution (1974–1976)*, Parede: British Historical Society.

Maher, P., 1977, *Portugal: The Impossible Revolution?*, London: Solidarity.

Porch, D., 1977, *The Portuguese Armed Forces and the Revolution*, London: Croom Helm.

Sobel, L. A. (ed.), 1976, *Portuguese Revolution 1974–76*, New York: Facts on File, Inc.

The Insight Team of the Sunday Times, 1975, *Insight on Portugal: The Year of the Captains*, London: Andre Deutsch.

Venter, A. J., 2013, *Portugal's Guerrilla Wars in Africa*, Solihull: Helson & Company Limited.

Online resources

Chemical-weapons research in Cornwall: the record of a Parliamentary debate in 2000 and two video excerpts from Graham Smith's 2001 Carlton TV report on Nancekuke (accessed 14 November 2019).

https://api.parliament.uk/historic-hansard/commons/2000/jan/18/nancekuke-base

https://www.youtube.com/watch?v=GP6aL43nYDw

https://www.youtube.com/watch?v=18ApUJJ8Hmc

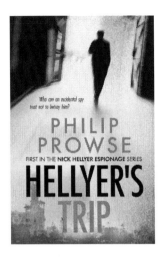

REVIEW OF HELLYER'S TRIP in the *Morning Star*, 14 May 2018

***

THE ACCIDENTAL SPY HAS always been a popular figure in espionage fiction, a reluctant agent's predicament being a good way of engaging readers' sympathies for an essentially unlovable trade.

Hellyer's Trip by Philip Prowse is the first in a series about Nick Hellyer, a literature student kicked out of Cambridge University in 1966 after a psychedelia-related indiscretion in sinful London.

He's given an opportunity to win redemption, and indeed avoid the magistrate's court, by taking up a post as a teacher in Alexandria. With, of course, a few other duties on the side, on behalf of Her Majesty's Government.

Nick enjoys his clandestine involvements with lonely diplomatic wives, but things become considerably more serious as the secret world counts down to the Six Days War.

This author knows and conveys his chosen period and place well, aided by a central character who displays exactly the right balance between naivety and foxiness.
Mat Coward

Hellyer's Trip, ISBN 9781527209350, is available on Amazon as a paperback, ebook and Audible audiobook.

HELLYER'S TRIP

AN ESPIONAGE NOVEL

Philip Prowse

Kernel Books

PROLOGUE

Alexandria, Egypt, 5 June 1967

A T MIDNIGHT ON THE first day of the Six Day War, Lieutenant Commander Abraham Dror eases the Israeli submarine *Tanin* through the defences of Alexandria's Western Harbour and brings it to rest on the seabed.

Six frogmen from the elite Shayetet 13 unit swim out of the torpedo tubes and head for their targets: two Egyptian Z-class destroyers, moored at buoys opposite the breakwater. The divers locate the vessels, attach limpet mines to the hulls and return to the underwater rendezvous point.

But the *Tanin* has slipped out to sea.

Oxygen cylinders running low, the frogmen head for shore. As they climb on to the jumble of rocks by Fort Quait Bey they hear the deep rumble of explosions from the mined vessels. The Israelis celebrate, unaware that the Egyptian Navy now rotates berths after dusk. Their achievement has been to sabotage a dredger and a supply barge.

Four are caught cowering in rock crevices at dawn and later the other two, walking jauntily along the Corniche in rumpled T-shirts and shorts, are spotted by an alert fifteen-year-old.

All are incarcerated in Ras-El-Tin naval prison. The thunder of boots and clang of cell doors heralding their arrival drags Nick Hellyer back into painful consciousness.

CHAPTER 1

London, 10 December 1966, 3 a.m.

'MY, THAT WAS A soft landing.'
She climbed off.

Slim figure hidden in an embroidered magenta fringed kaftan and tie-dyed jeans, eyes dark with mascara and mischief.

'Couple of tabs?'

'Why?'

'Say sorry I crashed on you.'

Multi-coloured worms on the great white drop sheet hanging from the hall balcony throbbed to the threatening organ-led rhythms of The Crazy World of Arthur Brown.

Until that coming-together, Nick had lain at peace with himself, cruciform, staring up at the mirror ball with its fractured images of people variously dancing, leaping and prancing, getting off on erotic movies, debating macrobiotics in cross-legged circles, snipping the clothes off a willing teenage girl under the instruction of a black-clad performance artist, smoking banana skins in the forlorn hope of a high, or dope with a more certain chance of success.

Peaceful, less from being stoned and more from not being there – Cambridge, that claustrophobic Fenland university populated by public-school boys, sailing on, blissfully unaware of the impending wave of change that would engulf it.

Here, he could will on unexpected eventualities. Here, in the haze of incense, the performance artist could really have been Yoko Ono, and it had actually been Andy Warhol cruising outside in the silver Rolls Royce. Here, a sky-borne dancer had just smothered him in long blonde hair as she crashed over his legs, mid-twirl.

'Acid? I've never—'

'You know – do or die. And you can call me Bex.'

'Nick.'

'Good boy, Nick. Tongue out now. Swallow.'

As the opening chords of Pink Floyd's 'See Emily Play' bounced off yellow brick walls, waves of strobe lights flowed over him and his legs slowly took on a life of their own, jigging restlessly.

'Babe, wanna dance?'

'Not yet. Know what I'm talking about. Come with me.'

Taking his hand, she led him to a dimmer corner where people lay on mattresses alone, or in couples or threes, some lost to the world, others exploring their own inner and outer worlds.

White-sleeved arms and denim-clad legs waved and glided through the incense-laden atmosphere. An intense awareness kicked in. Dancers came into focus, then blurred out again.

With a gentle half-smile, head tilted to one side, Bex unbuttoned the front of her kaftan and held it open with both hands. Firm flat breasts, outlined by target-like concentric blue rings, lurked behind the curtain of long blonde hair.

'Relax, lie flat and close your eyes. Feel the vibe with me, man.'

Straddling him, Bex stroked a sticky gel into his hair and beard, making him giggle. She rolled off and caught his hand.

'Let it dry.'

Expert fingers loosened his jeans, a warm mouth descended and silky hair brushed across his thighs as both kaleidoscope and cacophony faded away. Blurry eyes opened to a vision of Bex running her tongue around her lips before swallowing.

'Now, my turn.'

'Go on then.'

The Floyd pulsated through his head as he unzipped her Levi's to slip an eager exploring forefinger inside.

What the fuck?

A small, hard cock and balls.

A fully equipped guy who had just sucked him off. Now expecting him to return the compliment.

He ripped out his hand and lurched back against the wall, seeking support against the whirlwind.

'No. Can't. Sorry. Nothing personal. Got to get back to Cambridge now. Just not my scene.'

Bex slithered across the floor to recline forgivingly beside him.

'Sure, man, whatever turns you on. Cambridge, eh? Funnily enough, best mate of mine there's expecting something from me. Tell you what – you can take it. Save posting. Sort of make things up to me. Know what I mean? What train you going on?'

'Milk train. First one from Liverpool Street.'

They tramped in silence through ill-lit slippery streets to the station, where the dregs of Cambridge undergraduate society awaited. White-caped, dinner-jacketed party animals cheered as in succession they relieved themselves over the edge of the platform. Unconcerned, Bex sought out a payphone and, on his return, pulled a paperback-sized package from a deep pocket in his kaftan.

'Here. My mate Angel will be there when you get in – he'll know who you are.'

'How?'

'Don't worry, he will.'

***

A PROLONGED WHISTLE DROVE him hurtling half-awake towards the carriage door, only to dash back for the package before it was carried off to Ely. Dazed, he headed first in the wrong direction down Cambridge's endless single platform but, hearing his name called, turned back to see an arm waving.

'Hi, brother. I'm Angel. Got the stuff?'

'Here. From Bex.'

A firm tap on his right shoulder.

'Just a minute, sir.'

CID warrant card in his face. Another detective taking the package from Angel and leading him away.

'Why on earth?'

'Possession of marijuana with an intent to supply will do for a start, sir.'

'I haven't the faintest idea what you're talking about. Luke's College can vouch for me.'

'That's as may be, sir. But your college authorities could well change their minds when they see you in the flesh.'

'Sorry?'

'Well, you young gentlemen of the university might think it amusing to refer to us as the boys in blue. But this time I think we've caught Little Boy Blue.'

Turning his head, Nick caught sight of his reflection in a carriage window. His dark hair and beard were now a brilliant, startling blue.

Suppressing an overpowering urge to giggle, he allowed himself to be handcuffed and pushed into the back of a car for the short drive to the police station in Regent Street.

'Name and address? Empty your pockets. Shoelaces and belt.'

'Can I make a call, please?'

'Not now, sonny. Nine o'clock.'

The desk sergeant led him to a white-tiled cell and the mutterings of a malodorous vagrant, the snoring of a middle-aged man in a red-wine-stained business suit, and the grunts of two overly cocky arm-wrestling teenagers.

Head buzzing with shock, but irrationally secure in the certainty that it would all be sorted out soon, he lay back on a wooden bench.

'Let's be having you, Little Boy Blue. Telephone time.'

For once that day his luck was in, as he got straight through to Dr Fuller, the dean of Luke's College. Little consolation was to be had.

'This is most unfortunate, Hellyer, and no mistake. Doesn't look good at all, I'm afraid. But I'll see what we can do. If they do let you out, come straight here to see me.'

Two hours later the yawning desk sergeant obliged.

'Right, you can leave. You're on bail until a hearing at the next magistrates' court. And you can thank your lucky stars that your damned college has so much influence. Now get out.'

As he entered Luke's, Jackson, the famously discreet head porter, could not resist a raised eyebrow.

'Suits you, sir.'

He reddened, only to be confronted by James, with whom he shared a set of rooms in college.

'What's up with you?'

'Can't stop. Late. Summoned to see Sam.'

'Judging by your *dramatic* appearance, you're due for a bollocking.'

Dr Fuller, always addressed by surname and title but always referred to as Sam, nursed a legendary antipathy for university theatricals. Rumour had it he'd been a brigadier in Military Intelligence in the Second World War, and still retained active links to the secret world.

The inner door to Sam's set of rooms hung open, and Nick gave a polite cough as he entered. In a green leather swivel chair, sideways to a huge roll-top desk, sat a heavy figure in a capacious Prince of Wales check three-piece suit, the waistcoat dotted with fallen snuff. Sam removed his monocle and his frighteningly clear blue eyes fell upon Nick.

'Ah, Hellyer, you reported being in a spot of bother, and judging from your ghastly appearance that would most certainly seem to be the case. Not to beat about the bush, I may be able to help you, and you may be able to be of assistance to your country. Do I make my meaning clear?'

Although capable of processing the surface meaning of the words, Nick failed to detect any deeper significance. Sam had not offered him a chair, so he stood with his hands held stiffly by his sides.

'Not exactly, sir.'

The dean's jowls quivered.

'Must I spell it out? I'm offering you a way out of your predicament. As things stand you'll be tried and, when sentenced, receive a substantial prison term – I believe the tariff is at least seven years. Of course, the college would have nothing to do with you in that circumstance.'

'I—'

'Hear me out. I'd also imagine that, as a convicted drug dealer, you'd find it exceedingly difficult to continue your academic career elsewhere in these islands. Do you comprehend fully?'

'Yes, sir.'

'Now it so happens that I'm tasked by friends in high places to propose suitable young men. You're not unknown to me by any means – or indeed to my friends. Truth be told, they've had a very good look at you already, on my recommendation.'

'But—'

'In due course, you would have been approached and, I would hope, successfully recruited. What you've just related to me dramatically changes that scenario. If you wish, I can pass on news of your changed circumstances and immediate availability. However, I don't have the last word.'

'I'm sorry, Dr Fuller, I'm really not sure what you're suggesting. What does it involve doing?'

'Lying for your country, Hellyer.'

The shadow of a grin passed over Sam's features.

'Not as a diplomat – that takes years to perfect – but as someone undercover, someone who's not what they seem. You'll pursue your academic career overseas, while also undertaking certain other duties. If you agree, I'll make a telephone call. Depending on the result, you may leave for London at once where you'll be interviewed and vetted. What happens after that depends on operational needs, but I'd reckon on quite a long period overseas after training.'

'Training? For what, sir? I already have a doctorate.'

'Yes, but you'd surely admit that you're not exactly under-cover material yet.'

'But what about all the mess here?'

'Once your potential new role is explained at the appropriate level, the police will have no further immediate interest in you. The charge may remain on their books, but will not be actively pursued. Now, shall I make that call?'

'Yes, sir.'

'Very well, and do take a seat.'

The dean levered himself out of the swivel chair and lumbered across to his bedroom, pulling the heavy cream door to behind him. He reappeared ten minutes later.

'Hellyer, they'll see you.'

'Thank you, sir.'

'Now be off with you, young man. Clean out your rooms and leave your trunk at the porter's lodge. I don't advise trying to explain your departure to your girlfriend, or indeed any friends – we'll put about a rumour involving admission to Fulbourn Mental Hospital.'

Sam lowered his head for a moment, then raised it, his seemingly innocent blue eyes boring straight into Nick.

'In a way I envy you, my boy. Most people have one life in front of them, but you have two. For good, or for evil. Think about that.'

'Yes, Dr Fuller.'

'Right, now. Practicalities: this is where you're to present yourself tomorrow morning at eight a.m., and here is where you'll stay tonight.'

Nick accepted the two cards.

'Now, be gone. And, for God's sake, do something about that blasted hair of yours.'

***

BLUE DYE SWIRLED AROUND the plughole of his bedroom hand basin, disappearing as surely as his Cambridge career would. He chose those of his sketches he most liked and stowed them in his trunk with his clothes and academic papers. He packed a suit, shirt and tie into a soft brown leather bag and set off for the B&B in Sussex Gardens to which Sam had directed him.

Staring out into the darkness from the London train, he folded his arms tightly over his shoulders in search of comfort.

***

THE NEXT MORNING, FORMALLY dressed and rather more self-possessed, he presented himself at a mews building near King Charles Street. After he'd rung several times, a stiff-faced woman in a brown overall admitted him.

'May be a while – often is.'

As he perched in the cramped foyer, his confidence gradually drained into the shiny toecaps of his shoes. An hour and a flight of narrow stairs later, he entered an office whose uniformed occupant leapt to his feet and thrust a large sweaty palm over the file-cluttered desk.

'Patrick Quinlevan. Good to put a face to a name, Hellyer. Do apologise for keeping you waiting. We already know a considerable amount about you, but I'd better warn you that I'm going to put you through the wringer now – expect you've heard of positive vetting.'

Nick had not.

Major Quinlevan's oiled-down wiry black hair looked as if it might spring up at any moment and take on a life of its own. An air of guileless enthusiasm shone from his face.

For the next three hours, he grilled Nick about his life history: not only education and work, but also friends, family, foreign travel, cultural interests, political affiliation and opinions, sexual orientation, and career ambitions.

'Cross-referenced with others, of course – but they were mostly unaware of the purpose of our enquiries.'

After filling out detailed health and lifestyle questionnaires at his early-afternoon medical, his knees were tapped and his lungs listened to. He removed his shirt for three chest X-Rays, gave a urine sample and waited patiently to be interviewed.

The doctor, a kind, resigned woman with well-bitten finger-nails, took him through his questionnaires, then interrogated him about his sexual history. His answers omitted any reference to Bex.

Finally, he returned to Quinlevan.

'Capital! Should have all the results in the morning.'

***

CURIOUS AS TO WHAT lay ahead, and in the belief that the previous day had gone well, he entered the major's office with a purposeful stride, only to be brought up short.

Alone in the room stood a woman in her early sixties, with a helmet of close-cut white hair and the bearing of a Viking warrior. Her heavy grey-green tweed suit had a long flap at the back, beneath which she'd secreted her hands as if to keep them warm. She scrutinised him as he stepped forward, declining to accept his proffered hand, but clearly expecting him to say something.

He glanced at a tray on the desk.

'Milk and two sugars, please.'

The Viking tossed the tail of her skirt into the air and turned to Quinlevan, who'd just slipped into the room.

'Piffle!'

A mighty explosion of breath emphasised the P.

'You reported him as lightweight, Q, but really—'

Quinlevan gave a slight tilt of his head as he settled into his desk chair.

'I do apologise. Hellyer, before we can take things further, we need to allay some serious concerns about your suitability for the Service. That's the reason for my senior colleague's presence.'

The warrior in the tweed suit did not introduce herself.

'Sit down. As you know, we've been looking into your past, and in the process have uncovered disturbing anomalies that need to be clarified. Now.'

The Viking glared down at him and her tone sharpened.

'Yesterday, talking to Q here, you affirmed that, as far as politics went, you had little real interest. But when you did vote, you went Liberal. So what's this then?'

She lifted a folder from the desk and thrust an eight-by-ten black-and-white glossy print in front of his nose.

'Who's that then? At a Vietnam war demonstration in Cambridge last spring. And how about this one?'

She waved another photo at him.

'An anti-nuclear weapons rally in Trafalgar Square in the autumn.'

The images were both undoubtedly of him in black donkey jacket and washed-out Levi's. In the second, he was holding the pole at one end of a CND Ban the Bomb banner.

'So are we really a little commie, then?'

The Viking was relentless.

'Not some wishy-washy liberal?'

He recalled glancing up at a first-floor window of the National Portrait Gallery as they'd entered the square, and assuming that the cameramen there were all from the press.

'So, planning world revolution, are we? Don't lie to me, sonny. You've done enough lying already.'

Her gravelly voice ground on, before he could explain or protest his innocence.

'Drugs – now, come on! You admitted you'd experimented with grass years ago, when you were young and green. But that was then, you said, and this was now.'

'I don't—'

'Liar!'

'I'm not—'

'We found traces of hash and acid in yesterday's urine test – do you really think we were born yesterday?'

His head went down.

'So we have a dope fiend here trying to join the Service, have we? Liar!'

The Viking spat the last word out, and flipped her tail again with emphasis.

'If—'

'Shut up, you streak of dirt, you dirty little fibber.'

Her perfect vowels and clear enunciation contrasted with the vituperation.

'And then there's sex. Straight, you said you were, didn't you? Girlfriends – yes, we've looked into your past flames, even talked to a couple of them. Don't ask which ones. Though, come to think of it, you can probably guess as there haven't been too many, have there? But boyfriends – you never mentioned them.'

'No.'

'Liar! What's this?'

She rammed a picture in front of his eyes – of him and Bex holding hands.

So the flashes had come from police cameras as well as strobes.

'Short memory, have we? Or a selective one? Anything more to add? We've covered politics, drugs and sex. Any other vices? Cannibalism? Serial killing? Coprophilia? Come on, spit it out. Now's the time.'

She towered above him, filling his nostrils with powerful waves of lavender cologne.

'Nothing to say for yourself?'

The Viking spun around to Quinlevan.

'Will you tell him, or shall I?'

So, after all, it was to be the magistrates' court.

The Viking continued. 'Very well, I shall. You're a liar. Admit it.'

'Yes.'

'But not a very good one – you'll have to become a much better dissimulator. As for your demos, well, it would have been concerning for us if you hadn't been on a few. Acid and hard drugs, on the other hand, are something quite different, and I express the earnest hope that your recent *trip* has shown you as much. As long as you don't have delusions about being in control of it, I suppose there's no harm in a little dope now and again. But the crucial issue is that we know about your use, so no one can blackmail you. The same goes for your sexual orientation, of course. The fact that you're bisexual could make you a powerful asset indeed, depending on where you're posted.'

She paused and cast a quick glance at Quinlevan, who nodded slightly.

'So, as far as I'm concerned, that's it, Q.'

Her gaze returned to Nick and he raised his head.

'I hope we don't meet again, because if we do it will be in circumstances far less pleasant than these.'

Delivering a final flap of her tail, the Viking marched briskly out of the room, clutching her folder of photos. Quinlevan closed the door firmly behind her and began ordering the mess of papers in front of him. Nick's state of confusion paralleled that of the desk as he watched in silent wariness.

'Well!'

He jumped at Quinlevan's bark.

'Welcome to the Intelligence Service. Don't bother with acronyms like MI5 and MI6 here – all a bit blurred nowadays, don't you know? Just think of ourselves as Intelligence – diplomacy by another name.'

A weak grin.

'Doubts, eh? With a capital D, eh? Can see you're having them. Don't worry, everyone does. Bit late now anyway, what? Just a small formality before we can proceed. Signing the Official Secrets Act.'

'Sorry, Major Quinlevan, but I don't actually have the vaguest notion of what I'm letting myself in for.'

'All a bit hush-hush and up in the clouds, don't you know? But briefly, in summary, we're sending you on a crash course in Arabic and tradecraft at MECAS. Middle East Centre for Arab Studies – FO training place at Shemlan in the Lebanon. After that you'll take up your appointment as lecturer in English Literature at an Egyptian university.'

'But why tradecraft, whatever that is? Arabic, I can understand.'

'Because in addition to your cover job you'll be undertaking certain tasks for us.'

MOD Form 134, the unimpressive piece of paper that Quinlevan handed him, had already been completed with his full name, place and date of birth.

My attention has been drawn to the provisions of the Official Secrets Act, which are set out on the reverse of this document.

Nick flipped the paper over; the page was crammed with dense single-spaced text divided into numbered paragraphs.

'No need to bother with all that small print, old boy. Now, your signature here, and mine next to it as a witness.'

He signed at once, ready to be shunted on to the next stage of his re-imagining as a secret agent.

'Excellent, Nick, if I may call you that.'

Quinlevan carefully slipped the document into a crisp new buff cardboard folder, then dropped it into his desk drawer with a flourish of his right arm.

'There, that's done so off you go. I'll be popping out to MECAS to see how you're getting on in the not-too-distant future. We'll arrange for your effects in Cambridge to be collected and stored until you need them – best not to go back there now, just in case. Your flight's not until Monday, so you'll have plenty of time to kit yourself out for the Middle East.'

***

NICK RECEIVED AN ADVANCE on salary, a hot-weather clothing supplement, a return air ticket to Beirut and a travel allowance.

He headed straight for Carnaby Street.

'Shove over, granddad. You're not the only one that wants to get a look-in, you know.'

Reflected in the boutique window, a short-haired, side-boarded, sixteen-year-old was peering over his shoulder. Perhaps Quinlevan's advice to go to Selfridges had been sound after all.

The mod's face cracked into a laugh.

'No offence, mate. Just let the dog see the rabbit.'

He moved on, jostled by gaggles of mini-skirted, bouffant-haired girls and lean-faced, sharp-suited mods trawling for the latest trend. He had secret sympathy for passing beige-macintoshed middle-aged male office workers, out of place and time. The sounds of The Modern Jazz Quartet, Muddy Waters and The Who spilled out from open shop doorways. He'd never in his life been given someone else's money to spend on clothes and was determined to make an event of it.

In the end, he seized on unisex John Stephen, where the vibe was less frenzied although the terror of choice was equally strong. His vacillation was soon sensed by a purple micro-skirted assistant, who pointed him to racks of recent arrivals.

'Here we dress the mind, love, as well as the figure.'

In the changing room, swerving to avoid a collision with the raised bum of a teenager in paisley-patterned bra and panties who was bending over to pull on a pair of Levi's, he spilled his armful of tight-waisted jackets and wide-collared shirts.

'So sorry.'

He scooped up the scatter of clothes and retreated, only to come face-to-face with the micro-skirt, chin up, arms crossed over her chest.

'Problem?'

'Ladies.'

'No. Unisex. Back in.'

Nick soon worked out that no one in the changing room had the slightest interest in checking him out. The converse, however, could not be said to be true and he was unable to resist the occasional sneak peek while he spent his way through the afternoon under the tutelage of the micro-skirt.

On his return from the fashion frenzy, he consigned his sartorial past to history, sentimentally reserving only his linen suit.

In front of the full-length mirror in the wardrobe door, he paraded in extravagant lime green flares and tie-dyed T-shirts.

***

'HEAD FORWARD AND IMAGINE you're nauseous. Now make the *xh* sound as if you were about to gob out a ball of phlegm.'

His first lesson in Arabic.

The warmth of his greeting from Amina, his tutor, had contrasted with the chilly Lebanese mountain air.

'Welcome to MECAS, Dr Hellyer. And how does it feel to be here?'

'Bit disorientated. And cold, to be truthful.'

'Don't worry. That's normal for this time of the year. And the good news is that London has just cabled – your stay is now limited to two and a half months. Your studies are going to be intensive so you won't have too much time to worry about the temperature.'

Her positive attitude and sense of humour contrasted with an underlying brusqueness.

'You'll have Arabic every morning in my group and solo tradecraft with Scottie in the afternoon. Here you'll be known as Keith. The other trainees also only use first names, which may or may not be their own.'

Amina's methods were direct, which made her lessons exciting and challenging. Just as well, as he found the phonology of Arabic hard to master and the script terrifying in its apparent absence of vowels.

Tradecraft turned out to be a crash course in espionage for dummies. Scottie, a squat middle-aged Geordie, initially did not inspire trust. But the brilliance of the man's teaching technique became clear in the title of his first session: Never Trust Anyone.

Nevertheless, he did believe that Scottie had once been a radio operator on a North Sea trawler. Nick's induction into the world of Morse Code involved painstaking hours of transcribing dots and dashes into letters and words, followed by stumbling attempts to tap out messages on a key attached to a buzzer.

'Don't think of them as dots and dashes. Think of them as sounds. Dot is *dit* and dash is *dah*. So the letter A, dot dash, is *dit-dah*, the letter B, dash dot dot dot, is *dah-dit-dit-dit*, and so on.'

More demanding close-contact sessions featured strongly. At the first, Scottie stood opposite Nick on a judo mat, chopped his right leg out from under him and fell heavily on to his chest, painfully winding him.

'Now you do the same to me.'

He caught Scottie with a sneaky kick to the left knee, but the attempted chest-fall ended with Nick face down on the mat while his teacher rolled away laughing.

A month in, he caught a brief glimpse of Major Patrick Quinlevan climbing out of the embassy Land Rover in a sweat-stained tropical suit. While the mountain air was still cool, it had clearly been unseasonably hot by the sea in Beirut. Quinlevan spent part of the morning with Amina and Scottie, and then devoted himself to Nick, clapping him enthusiastically on the shoulder.

'Good to see you, dear boy. Let's go for a walk. Nothing like a bit of fresh air, eh? And in this place' – he lowered his voice mock-conspiratorially – 'you never know who's listening.'

The two men marched away from the centre along the dusty pine-lined road leading to the village of Shemlan.

'Something to take you to task about first, young man. Expect you know what.'

Nick did. Four weeks of vacuous conversations with pseudonymous fellow students, tussles with the new language, and romps with Scottie on the mat had left him restless and lonely.

One of the canteen staff, Fathiya, had appeared amused by his flirtatious remarks in halting Arabic and the previous weekend had accepted his invitation to ice cream in the village café. Pleasantries in Arabic soon exhausted, he'd switched to

English, rashly suggesting they move on to his room in order to get to know each other better. Not his greatest idea. She'd made a complaint.

'Hellyer, you're here as a student, and students don't screw the staff. Understood?'

'Yes, Major.'

'Good. Now to business. Amina's very pleased with your progress. Apparently, you have a gift for languages. Scottie reports your Morse transcription as still a little slow. But transmission's greatly improved. Second more important than the first. Tradecraft's coming on well. Scottie will be working more on your fitness. *Fit to Fight*. Name of the training manual, you know.'

Noticing Nick puffing, the major paused.

'Exactly. Now, pay attention. Here's the plan. In March you'll take up post as Senior Lecturer in English, University of Alexandria, Egypt. British Council has already submitted your CV to the Faculty of Arts. Approval expected shortly. Teaching duties to be discussed. Understand your predecessor taught mainly final-year literature.'

'Predecessor?'

'Yes, been there for four years. Built up quite a reputation. Had to leave abruptly last autumn.'

'Why?'

Quinlevan sighed and halted, patting him on the shoulder. 'You don't need to know.'

'Will I be teaching in Arabic? Because—'

'Good God, no! It would take at least four years to bring you up to speed. Wouldn't be welcomed at all. Department prides itself that all tuition is in English. Of course, you can sprinkle your social conversation with the odd *malish* or *shukran* to be polite. And ask the way in the street. But no more than that. The Arabic is for your other role. More on that once you're in post.'

'But what is my other role? Why can't I know more now?'

'Quite simply, dear boy, way too soon. Events moving quite fast in the region. Great start made here though. Those clothes. Been noticed, I can tell you. Good you're exploring that side of yourself. As Vera remarked in my office, could come in very handy.'

'Vera?'

'Boss lady in tweed suit, remember?'

'But I'm not—'

'Main thing is to give the impression you might be.'

They marched briskly on again in silence, hands deep in pockets and heads in their own thoughts. Nick had no doubt that the university post was right up his street; as for the *other* role, he'd make up his mind when he knew what it involved.

'Talking of clothes, I'll have a word with Scottie. Time to get you used to wearing Arab costume. Need to be able to swim like a fish in the sea, you know?'

'Forgive me, Major, but I've really no idea what you're on about. And, for God's sake, why am I spending so much time learning Morse Code? Surely that's yesterday's news.'

'There, there. No need to get agitated, dear boy. Hiding in the open, don't you see?'

***

AFTER QUINLEVAN'S DEPARTURE, HE was sent out after dark, decked in a galabeya to perform small tasks, like buying sweetmeats or asking the way. While he enjoyed these challenges, he soon came to suspect that he was far from the first to be sent on this particular path. The almost too helpful villagers seemed to know his lines as well as he did.

Scottie also initiated him into the technique of sending Morse in short bursts of high-speed transmission, U-boat style.

Six weeks later, he returned to London for a blur of briefings, jabs, visa collection and packing.

***

Marseilles, 5 March 1967, 10 a.m.

THROUGH HIS CABIN PORTHOLE on the *Esperia,* Nick followed the progress of stragglers scuttling from the steep steps of the Gare Maritime across the dank mist-shrouded quay to the Alexandria-bound vessel. A joy of irresponsibility at being among strangers who could only guess as to his real identity lifted his spirits.

The first to try had been the dapper third officer in the reception line of the first-class lounge.

'But why do you need to keep my passport?'

'Because Dr Nic-ho-las, because then we can give you landing card for wherever we enter port, and you can go ashore.'

'But perhaps I won't want to.'

'But you will, believe me. Napoli, Siracusa, Beirut – these are places you will desire to see. And it is excellent you are doctor. We have ship's doctor, but always good to have more doctors.'

'No, you see, I'm an academic doctor not a medical doctor.'

'Like professor, no? Is also good. Enjoy your time with us. Here is your restaurant reservation.'

As Nick joined the assigned table for lunch a tanned, muscular man with cropped greying hair rose formally.

'This is Aisha, my wife. And our daughter, Teresa.'

Introducing himself, he half-bowed to the confident woman in a well-cut lemon trouser suit and her shining daughter.

'Mertens, Colonel Mertens. On our way back to the Lebanon – we're with the UN there. And you?'

Nick, momentarily distracted by a half-glance from Aisha, was slow to respond.

'Me? Oh, on my way to Alexandria.'

Teresa was an entrancing ten-year-old polyglot. She spoke Arabic with her Lebanese mother, Flemish to her father, Italian to the waiters, French to both her parents, and English to him.

Her mother's calm self-assurance occasionally betrayed a hint of vulnerability when her eyes hunted to and fro before responding.

***

TWO DAYS LATER, SAILING from Naples for Siracusa in Sicily, he noticed through half-open cabin doors dresses and dinner jackets being laid out, and jewellery held up for approval. Preparation for the *Pranzo di Capitano*, the captain's dinner.

When the restaurant lights dimmed, a flotilla of white-coated waiters sailed out of the kitchen, bearing salvers with ice-carved swans candle-lit from within. Nestling between raised tail feathers were silver bowls of shiny black beluga caviar.

Aisha's eyes met his as she leaned towards him.

'Wait until you get to the Lebanon, Dr Hellyer – I know you'll love our cuisine. But perhaps you've already visited.'

'No, I'm afraid I haven't.'

After dinner, coffee and liqueurs were served in the salon. As the ship's band started to play a foxtrot, Teresa stamped her foot.

'I just don't believe it. This is 1967, not 1917.'

Feeling a light tap on his upper arm, he turned to Mertens, whose index finger indicated his right leg.

'An old injury, so I don't dance. But Aisha loves to – do please invite her.'

'Delighted, of course. Just a tad afraid she'll be disappointed in me. Not the world's greatest, you know?'

Aisha's firm hand on his back as they stepped on to the tablecloth-sized dance floor quelled his fears, and he soon understood how naturally gifted she was. With the slight movement of the ship beneath their feet, she guided them through the press of other couples without making it apparent that she was leading.

As he held her closer for a waltz, her perfume wafted over him, and her body, while always held at a correct distance, on occasion brushed his.

They scarcely exchanged words but, while glancing over her shoulder at Mertens laughing with his daughter, he caught the slightest of whispers in his ear.

'Dancing isn't the only thing he's no longer able to do, I'm afraid. I can come to you when they're asleep, if you wish.'

They swirled to a halt as the band announced a break. But when an Italian disc jockey followed his self-congratulatory welcome with Pink Floyd's 'See Emily Play', Aisha slipped gently out of his arms.

'Thank you so much, Nick. Not my kind of music at all. But I know Teresa would love to dance – if you're willing.'

'Of course.'

'Later tonight.'

Teresa bounded on to the floor, but light-headed after three energetic dances, he soon returned the flushed girl to her parents.

'Must be getting too old for this kind of thing! Going to get some fresh air.'

He forced open a heavy door on to the deck and hung over the rail, assailed by Floyd-induced memories, until a flash from the shore speared his peripheral vision. Great orange arcs of tracer were raking the sky, contrasting with thick deep-red worms of glowing lava wriggling inexorably down the side of Mount Etna.

Wouldn't come to him. Woman of her class. Harmless shipboard flirtation, that was all.

But he didn't lock his cabin door before drifting off to sleep.

Then, a finger on his shoulder.

Small and delicate, it moved to her pursed lips and then to the light switch. She turned her back. The gentlest whisper.

'Come, please help me.'

Hasty, clumsy fingers complied, but then he was left stranded hanging her dress over the back of a chair.

'Hurry up, my thoughtful boy – we haven't got all night. But you must understand I'm not like this at all, or hardly ever.'

He drank in the warmth of her skin as he stroked her cheeks, kissing her eyes and then her mouth.

Afterwards, eyes closed with his head on her chest, the pounding of her heart filled his consciousness.

'But what if he wakes and you're not there?'

'I'll say I couldn't sleep and went for a night stroll on deck. Don't worry, my sweet one. I can handle this. See you at breakfast.'

With a chaste peck on the cheek, Aisha slipped out of the cabin, leaving him between sheets redolent of their lovemaking.

***

IN SIRACUSA, HE ACCOMPANIED the Mertens family on a brief visit to the remarkably intact Greek theatre. No sign of awkwardness evinced itself, and at dinner they made the usual shipboard promises of keeping in touch.

In the night Aisha came to him again.

***

THE NEXT MORNING, HAVING skipped breakfast, he sipped a cappuccino in the stern bar as the *Esperia* docked in Beirut.

Aisha gave him a firm handshake and thanked him for his company before striding confidently down the gangway with Teresa. The colonel was next.

'I'm sure you'll have a great time in Alexandria. Our paths may well cross again as I'm summoned from time to time to Cairo for regional conferences.'

With the Mertens family gone, he was assigned to a fresh table at dinner.

'Hans.'

His tall, ascetic table companion rose, offering his right hand with an ironic formal half-bow while holding his left behind his back.

'I believe we will be working together soon, or at least in the same faculty.'

'Really?'

'I suggest you don't play poker any time soon, Dr Hellyer.'

Hans gave an expansive wave of his right arm.

'Or, at least, not with me. But for sure, I know who you are. They say there are no secrets in Alexandria and that is God's truth. The full name, Hans Fussmann, Dr Hans Fussmann, or to be more correct, Dr Dr Hans Fussmann. You are teaching in the English Department, yes? After Dr Bishop? Good. I am Cherman Cultural Institute, but I give some lectures at the Faculty of Arts. So, welcome to Alexandria. You know about the city history, no?'

'Well, yes, but not in any detail, I'm afraid.'

'So you need me to inform you, and I will. Take the Pharos, the hundred-and-twenty-metre high lighthouse that stood for a thousand years. One of the Seven Wonders of the World and a triumph of Egyptian engineering – the Chermans of their day, yes?'

'Fascinating, I'm sure. But if you'll excuse me, I'm going to turn in now. Need to be fresh in the morning.'

Printed in Great Britain
by Amazon